T0129562

NOEasy
Money

A novel by
J. E. HALL

authorHOUSE®

AuthorHouse™
1663 Liberty Drive
Bloomington, IN 47403
www.authorhouse.com
Phone: 833-262-8899

Published by AuthorHouse 10/15/2020

ISBN: 978-1-7283-6891-7 (sc)
ISBN: 978-1-7283-6893-1 (hc)
ISBN: 978-1-7283-6892-4 (e)

Library of Congress Control Number: 2020914146

Print information available on the last page.

Any people depicted in stock imagery provided by Getty Images are models, and such images are being used for illustrative purposes only.
Certain stock imagery © Getty Images.

This book is printed on acid-free paper.

Because of the dynamic nature of the Internet, any web addresses or links contained in this book may have changed since publication and may no longer be valid. The views expressed in this work are solely those of the author and do not necessarily reflect the views of the publisher, and the publisher hereby disclaims any responsibility for them.

CHAPTER

1

The prospective salesman sat in a relaxed posture, modestly elaborating on the accomplishments listed on his resume. With a personable demeanor, as his advisor at the personal agency had constantly reminded him to maintain, the applicant tried to impress the interviewer with his ability to master any situation that might arise. The man in the chair opposite him seemed to be enthused, and that was encouraging.

This job candidate, however, had already been eliminated. The enthusiasm displayed by Rick Gaines, Head of Human Resources at Affordable Electronics, was due to this being his last interview of the week, not because he was impressed by the applicant. He continued to question him out of a desire to be polite, listening patiently as the man answered some very pointed questions. Rick's attention, though, was focused on the two portraits that hung on the wall behind the individual. They were very old paintings, and no one in the office knew who the subjects were. The two men were very similar in appearance, and the employees referred to them as the mystery twins. Binny

Jenkins, one of the computer programmers, told all the new employees that they could earn an extra week's vacation by identifying the men.

"What do you think is the most important thing a salesman should keep in mind when dealing with a potential customer?" Rick asked.

"Always sell them more than they need," the man said with a smile.

The interviewer nodded. The President of Affordable would agree with that statement, though he insisted the salesman in his employ be low key and respectful of the people they were conning.

"Do you think there's anyone better at selling electronics than yourself?" asked Rick as he thought *I wonder what Karen will want for dinner tonight?*

The applicant hesitated. Answering in the affirmative would display a lack of confidence: doing so in the negative would indicate a very healthy, and perhaps an overly large, ego.

"I can do the job. You won't find anyone more determined, or reliable," he said, deciding to opt for the less modest approach.

"We'll be in touch," Rick said after he shook the man's hand and escorted him out the door.

Why do I always say that when I know I'll never call him? Rick thought on the way back to his office.

He found Colin Myers, the retiring salesman, waiting for him there.

"So, what do you think?" Colin, who was taking a keen interest in the search for his replacement, asked.

"I thought he might be a little too conventional for this company," Rick responded.

"He dresses too well. People don't want to buy their stuff from someone who looks too prosperous. It makes them think that the salesman has fleeced every person that ever walked into the store."

Rick smiled as he noted Colin's missing shirt buttons and haphazard hair style.

"Do you remember that time when you were trying to convince a couple to buy a home entertainment center? You pretended to receive a phone call from your sick daughter who was supposed to be in the ICU at the hospital," Rick said with a laugh.

"Well, I was trying to set the record for sales in a month. And I did it, too," Colin proudly replied. "There's nothing like getting a customer's sympathy when you're trying to make a sale."

"What are you going to do now?"

"I'm going to do a lot of fly fishing."

"I didn't know you were into that."

"I've never done it before. But that's why it intrigues me. I want to do something different after I leave here. Or what's the point of retiring."

"I hear you. And it sounds very challenging. You must have to use a very small hook to catch a fly."

"I'll have to remember that one, Rick. Have a good weekend."

"You too, Colin."

Bobby Holmes walked into his office just as the retiring salesman walked out. The long-time employee was in one of his agitated states, a condition that had appeared with greater frequency as the years went by.

"Bobby Holmes," Rick said in an upbeat tone. "What brings you to this end of the building?"

"I think I have a legitimate beef this time Ricky."

Like the last time, when you came here because one of your co-workers supposedly sabotaged the copy machine to make it malfunction every time you tried to use it. Then aloud he said, "Lay it on me."

"Wispy, who's been here for all of four years, has her own cabinet in the file room. On the other hand, I, who have been here for thirty years, don't even have my own drawer in the file room. Might you explain this inequity to me?"

"I might, and I will. Wispy is in accounts payable. She processes a lot of invoices, which means that she has a lot of paperwork to be filed. You, on the other hand, are an accountant, and keep most of your financial schedules on the computer. So there's never been a reason to give you space in the file room."

"Just give me a drawer. I'll keep my lunch in it."

"You're a busy guy, Bobby. You know there'll come a day when you skip lunch and forget that you put food in the drawer. Then it'll start to go bad and stink up the file room."

"I know it's going to sound childish, but it's all about perception. Without my own drawer, the other people in this company don't know I exist, because there's no visible evidence of the work I do here."

I wouldn't say childish. I'd go with infantile.

"And Wispy contributes to that perception among the other employees," Bobby continued. "When I brought the subject up she said *but it would be such a waste to give you space in the file room, Bobby. But if you ever produce enough paperwork to really need it, I'll make some space for you in one of my drawers.* Do you see what I mean?"

"I could see how the other employees might get the wrong impression," Rick responded while stifling a laugh. "I'll talk with Wispy and ask her to stop flaunting her drawers."

"Thanks Rick. And don't tell her I complained about it. It might make for a very tense working environment."

"She'll have to beat it out of me with a strand of wet spaghetti," Rick assured him.

Bobby stood up and walked towards the door. He suddenly turned around and laughed.

"I just got that. Flaunting her drawers! Like she was showing off her underwear."

"Don't tell anyone I said that," Rick told him. "These days, you can get in a lot of trouble over that kind of thing."

"They'll have to beat it out of me with a strand of wet spaghetti!" said Bobby.

Wispy Soul responded to Rick's request to see her, arriving at his office shortly after. She was a slight individual, appearing as though even the mildest of breezes could sweep her off the face of the earth. Wispy wore a white garment that reminded Rick of a toga. She sat in the chair in front of his desk, tucking her legs beneath her.

"So how goes it, Miss Soul?" Rick asked pleasantly.

"I'm getting it done for the man, carrot top," she replied with a reference to his neatly cut red hair. "You're looking good. You must be taking good care of the temple of your soul."

"I do what I can. The reason I called you down here is because it's come to my attention that you may have unintentionally suggested that Mr. Bobby Holmes isn't doing enough work for this company. At least not enough to warrant his own space in the file room."

Wispy looked at him with a puzzled expression on her narrow face. Then the light of recognition shone in her brown eyes.

"Oh, I know what this is about. You see, I've had an epiphany. I was thinking one day about how there are more and more people coming into this world, and realized that we're going to run out of water, food…"

"And file space?"

"Well, that subject didn't come up until a while later, when Bobby was complaining because I had my own filing cabinet. The point I was trying to make is that we, meaning the human race, can't afford to waste anything anymore. Or in a very short time we'll run out of everything. So when Bobby started going on and on about the filing situation, I just pointed out that giving him a drawer, or especially a whole filing cabinet, would be a waste of filing space. And we can't afford to do that. The human beings on this planet can't even squander the energy it takes to envy someone else. If we do, it will lead to our demise."

I'm talking with a woman who believes that giving Bobby Holmes a drawer in the file room will cause the extinction of the human race. And I went to college for this. Then he said aloud "I hear what you're saying, Wispy. But Bobby's at a very sensitive stage in his career. So maybe you could refrain from associating him with the word *waste*."

"Can do. You know what might make him feel better. I can compliment him on the fact that he produces very little paperwork. By having everything on the computer, he saves trees. We need more people like him."

"That's a good thought. But wait a while, so it doesn't look contrived."

"I hear you, Rick. You know, right after this waste thing occurred to me, I saw a guy on a cable access channel who was thinking the same thing. He even wants to start a movement called *Nada Prodigalidad.*"

"What does that mean?"

"No wastefulness."

He could have just said that. I wonder if I'm wasting my life.

"Anyway, it'll be icks nay on talking about the file ay for me. Isn't it amazing how I was thinking about eliminating waste when I just happened to come across that show on cable. It's karma. And speaking of which, karma made you ask me to come to your office. I have something to discuss with you."

"I'm all ears, Wispy."

"Those motion-activated light switches they put in the ladies' room are causing a bit of a problem for me. I know they're designed to eliminate wasted electricity, which is a good thing. But when I sit on the bowl, I'm motionless, except for bodily movements that the switch is incapable of detecting, if you know what I mean."

"I get your drift."

"So after a while the switch thinks there's no one in the bathroom..."

"And the lights go out."

"Exactly."

"That's a tough one."

"I could bring in my pom-poms."

"Your pom-poms?"

"Yeah. I used to be a cheerleader in high school, believe it or not. Talk about a waste. I used so much energy cheering for a bunch of guys who were beating the snot out of each other on the football field. I mean, what was the point? I could have been doing something constructive. But anyway, I could use them while I'm sitting on the bowl. I'll wave my pom-poms around while I'm doing my cheer. Here I sit doing shit, shit, shit!" Wispy said enthusiastically while waving a pair of imaginary decorative balls.

"What a great idea. You should have worked for NASA, Wispy."

"I'll bring my pom-poms with me on Monday. Let's do lunch next week. Are you into vegan?"

"Not really."

"I'll talk you into it. Have a great weekend."

Rick started to review his interview schedule for Monday when Dale Stephens, the company's Financial Vice President, and co-owner's son, came in.

"How goes it, Gaines?" he asked while finishing a mouthful of food, which Rick assumed was done to convince him that the gangly V.P. was so busy he had to eat on the run.

"Not, bad, Dale. How are things in finance?"

"Just humming along. I wanted to talk to you about Tammy. It seems to me, and I might be talking out of turn here, that she's spending an inordinate amount of time on the phone."

"Tammy's the receptionist. That's part of her job."

"I know that. But she spends too much time on each call. I think we'd do a lot better with one of those automated systems."

"A lot of people think they're too impersonal."

"This is a business. The bottom line is all that matters. I think we should look into it. It would allow us to get more work out of Tammy."

"What else do you want her to do?"

"She could do some filing. Or even keep the kitchen clean, so the cleaning people who come in at night won't be able to charge as much."

Rick knew this conversation would last for at least an hour, which was more than he was willing to spend on the subject.

After years of dealing with Dale he knew how to end it quickly, however.

"Chris was the one who put the kibosh on the automated phone system. You could take it up with him," Rick suggested, referring to the company's president.

"Ah...maybe I will. I also had another thought. It has nothing to do with this company. But I'd like to run it by you."

"Shoot."

"You know how annoying the sirens on the fire trucks are when they go past this building, or any place else for that matter."

Almost as annoying as you. "I know. But they have to be so that people pay attention to them."

"There has to be a better way. At first I was thinking about something like a dog whistle for people. It would only be heard by the drivers in the immediate vicinity of the emergency vehicle."

When they pull over to let the fire truck go by you could reward them with a doggie treat Rick mused as Dale continued.

"But the whole dog whistle thing is based on it making a sound that only dogs can hear," he said. "If you make a whistle that the people you want to warn can hear, then everyone else in the area will be able to hear it as well, which is the same thing as a siren. So I gave up on that idea."

The people who drive ambulances, fire trucks and police cars will be forever grateful, thought Rick.

"Then I was thinking, what if someone came up with a device that could be installed in everyone's car. It would alert the drivers in the immediate vicinity to an approaching emergency vehicle. The device would have a display that showed the location of the emergency vehicle and what action the driver should take. I'll make a fortune. And people wouldn't have to hear those ear-splitting sirens anymore. I'll call it the Targeted Alert."

"What about the pedestrians?"

"Well, if an ambulance hits one, they can just throw the

person in the back and take him or her to the hospital. I mean, they're going there anyway."

Dale continued after he failed to receive the expected laugh from Rick.

"The system could alert the pedestrian's cell phone. Then they'd know not to cross the street until the emergency vehicle passes."

"I guess it sounds plausible, in theory," Rick responded as if he were giving the idea serious consideration. "But as a practical matter, it would be difficult to implement. You'd just need one or two people who didn't have the device to create a horrific accident."

"But if it's mandatory..."

"Who follows the rules all the time?" Rick pointed out. "They can't even get everyone to use seatbelts."

"The glass is always half empty with you, Gaines."

"That's because I drink too fast. See you later, Dale."

"I'm always thinking about new products," he said before leaving.

And your trust fund.

Rick returned to his schedule, only to become aware of someone looking at him. He turned around and found Chris Conners, the graying President of Affordable, behind him. Rick was constantly amazed by this man's ability to enter a room without anyone being aware of him. He began to believe that the president had the ability to materialize out of thin air. Rick referred to him as Ches, which was short for the Cheshire Cat, though never to his face, of course.

"If that man's father didn't own half of this company, I do believe he'd starve," Chris observed. "But when you have a partner in a business, you have to tolerate certain things, and nepotism is one of them."

"That was a pretty unrealistic idea. But I guess he was just spit balling, as they say."

"You're a very diplomatic man. Which is why you're so good at what you do. You can deal with people like Wispy, Bobby and

Dale without offending them, despite their idiosyncrasies. And since that's the kind of person I like to employ, you're perfect for your job. I like people who don't choose the beaten path. Give me someone who's a little off beat every time. They have an enthusiasm for most everything they do, including the most mundane job you can think of. You're the anchor, Rick. You hold this group of misfits together."

Chris leaned over and wrote something on Rick's memo pad. He then solemnly pointed to it as if the pad had now become sacred.

"That's my personal cell phone number. I've given it to very few employees over the years. You have arrived, my good man."

"Thanks, Chris. I hardly know what to say." *You should give it to Dale so he can talk to you about the automated phone system and his people whistle.*

"Don't give it to anyone. Enjoy your weekend, Rick."

"You too, Chris."

■　■　■

Dale Stephens arrived at the entrance to the gated community where he lived. The security guard in the booth smiled after ascertaining that the person driving the Mercedes Benz belonged there. Dale took in the fall colors on the way to his home. This relatively small patch of land had a magical quality to it. The rest of the world and its problems were kept out of sight, and mind, here.

Dale walked through the door of the house he shared with his wife Lauren. He rarely came home for lunch, but on this day her husband had decided to surprise her. Dale had a selfish motive for doing so. Lauren would listen intently to his plan for a silent alarm, just as she had listened to all his other fanciful ideas over the years.

"Honey, do I..."

He stopped in mid-sentence, being taken aback by the individual who now stood before him. Lauren glared at him, with a venomous expression on her pretty face. She held an iphone in one hand, and a machete in the other. The petite brunette looked physically incapable of wielding the blade, yet in her agitated state, Dale realized that his wife was capable of anything.

"You bastard! You and Jennifer!"

"What? Honey what's the matter."

"She told me!"

"Told you what?"

Lauren swung the machete, missing her husband but slicing the end off a sofa cushion.

"Hey! Put that thing down!" Dale tried to take control of the situation.

. "You slime ball!"

Lauren lunged at him, and Dale quickly decided to abandon his efforts to communicate with her. He ran out the back door, with his wife in hot pursuit.

"When did you get so damn fast?" Dale exclaimed as she closed in on him. "And where did you get that machete!"

He knew she would catch him. Dale Stephens would become another victim whose demise was heralded on the front page of the Daily News. Then he saw a tree in front of him and climbed it. He had not done this since his youth, but Dale's intense fear enabled his muscles to recapture their youthful strength.

"Come down here!" Lauren screamed at him.

She was too short to reach even the lowest branches of the tree. Out of frustration Lauren threw her iPhone at Dale, who made an amazing one-handed catch. He looked at it, and suddenly understood the reason for her behavior.

"This isn't true. I'd never do that to you," Dale told her with all the sincerity he could muster. "I'm calling Jennifer right now."

■　■　■

Two hours later Rick Gaines' phone rang. Tim Shelby, the company's general manager, was on the line.

"We've got a real problem. Get down here right away."

Rick walked through the corridor at a quickened pace. He entered Tim's office, and was instructed to close the door.

"Have a seat. Binny Jenkins sent this email to Lauren Stephens. Read it."

Rick obliged him.

I'm actually quite ill. I don't believe I'll last much longer, so I'd like to get something off my chest. I've been sleeping with your husband. Please forgive me.

Rick looked at his superior with a perplexed expression on his face.

"Are Binny and Dale gay?" he asked him.

"Not that I know of," Tim responded.

"Why would he send this email to Dale Stephen's wife? Why would he send any email to Dale Stephen's wife?"

"Read the email she sent him. He was responding to it."

Rick looked further down the page and read the message from Lauren to Binny.

Is this you Jennifer? How are you feeling?

"Now I'm totally confused. Why did Lauren email Binny?"

"Apparently she found his email address in her directory. Jenkins' personal email is JEN106 at AOL.com. Lauren thought it was her friend Jennifer."

"How do you know Binny's personal email address?"

"Because Dale contacted someone at AOL and found out whose email address it was. And it's also in my address book, too, and I'd like to find out why. You can get the answer from Binny just before you throw his ass out the door. Our VP of Finance is furious. Lauren chased Dale around the house with a machete!"

"Where did she get a machete? I mean, it seems like an unusual thing to have around the house."

"That's not the point. I don't give a shit about where the machete came from. This is an outrageous thing to do. She chased Dale up a tree, like a hound dog hunting a bear," Tim said dramatically.

"I didn't know they used hound dogs to hunt bears."

"Again, not the point. Dale could have been hurt. This is serious," the middle-aged man with graying hair said in a stern voice.

"I agree. But we both know Binny is prone to pulling practical jokes, which I'm sure this is. You remember when he put a whoopee cushion on your seat."

"Yes, I do. I didn't even know they still made them. I was meeting with the distributor from Sony Electronics at the time. We both got a laugh out of it. But this is very different, Rick. It involved the personal life of not just an employee, but the Vice President of Finance. His wife treed him, for God's sake!"

"Treed him?"

"When the hounds chase a bear up the tree, they say it's been treed. Anyway, that's not the salient point here. Whatever his reason for sending that email, the man is finished at Affordable. So tell Binny to gather up the Star Wars action figures on his desk..."

"They're actually from *Dungeon and Dragons*."

The middle-aged man behind the desk gave him a stern look that said *not the point*.

"He's done a lot of good work for the company," Rick reminded him in a final effort to save Binny's job. "The inventory system he designed is twice as efficient as the old one. I understand the gravity of the situation, believe me, but maybe an apology with a suspension would be enough."

"Stephens wants him gone. If Jenkins is here on Monday we'll both be canned and he'll probably be dead."

Rick reluctantly realized that the die had been cast. He left the GM's office and returned to his own. Binny arrived shortly after, at his request. Rick closed the door and motioned him towards a seat in front of his desk. He then occupied the one behind it.

"You look stressed, my liege," Binny observed.

"Did you send this?" he asked while handing the email to him.

"Oh, yeah," Binny responded with a laugh.

At any other time, Rick would have laughed with him, not because of the prank, but at the way the rotund computer programmer's body shook with mirth.

"How could you do this!? Do you know how much trouble it caused? Dale's wife was chasing him around with a machete."

"Where did she get a machete?" Binny, now made somber by Rick's response, asked him.

"That's not the point, or so I've been told. How the hell did she get your personal email?"

"Remember about two years ago when we started having trouble with the company email. I used my own AOL account in the office until we were able to fix it. Dale asked me to send the web address of a travel agency I had used to his wife because they were planning a vacation. That's how it got in her address book."

Rick looked at the computer geek, and despite his anger at his recklessness, felt remorse for what he was required to do.

"I'll apologize, Rick. I mean, I was just kidding around," Binny said in a contrite tone.

"I know. But that won't be enough. I have to let you go."

The now former employee was speechless.

"But Mario needs me to get the server upgraded, or everything is going to start crashing around here. It was just a joke," Binny finally responded while nervously running his fingers through the black curly mat on his head.

"Look, you do great work. Your supervisor has nothing but good things to say about you. But there isn't anything I, or Mario can do. Stephens is really pissed off. And while I wouldn't fire you over it if it was my call...well, you should learn from this, Binny. You can't just go off half cocked all the time. You have to think about what you're doing."

"Two days from now, I bet they'll be laughing about it," Binny predicted.

Sure, as soon as Dale gets out of the tree, Rick thought as he shook his head.

"The demon usually comes out on Monday," Binny said in a perplexed tone.

"What?"

"The demon, that thing that sneaks up on you and knocks you on your ass. It usually comes after me on Mondays. That's when most of the bad things have happened to me. By Friday afternoon I'm usually home free."

"Look, you'll catch on somewhere. Use me as a reference. I'll tell them that you were laid off. Let me know if there's anything else I can do for you."

"I'll be okay. I have a few ideas I was thinking of trying anyway. I can do better"

"Good. Keep in touch, Binny," he said as they shook hands.

"It's been a pleasure, my liege."

Rick decided to beat the traffic. Karen Fields was waiting for him at his apartment, having also left her job before five. The perfunctory kiss Rick offered his girlfriend in greeting told her that something was wrong. She waited until he had poured himself a glass of beer before requesting an explanation.

"What's the matter, babe?" she asked as they sat on the sofa.

"I had to fire someone today. One of the people from the data processing department named Binny Jenkins. He was the best they had."

"Binny? What kind of a name is Binny?"

"His real name is Vinny. Binny is a nick name his family gave him as a child."

"He must have a cruel family. What did he do?"

"He sent a prank email to the wife of the Financial Vice President."

"Why would he do that?"

Rick explained the circumstances that had led to Binny's dismissal. Karen looked at him in disbelief.

"And you feel sorry for this guy? I could understand feeling that way because of his nick name, but sending that email was a really stupid thing to do. The woman must have flipped."

"She chased her husband around with a machete. Don't ask me where she got it though, because it's not important."

"No wonder you had to fire him."

"But he's a good guy, and a really talented programmer. And I have to admit that I'd probably laugh my ass off if I heard about someone sending that email in another office."

"You admire irresponsible behavior?"

"Don't look at me like I'm in league with the devil, or Binny, for that matter. I just think it's funny, though inappropriate. Every once in a while I get the urge to do something crazy like that."

"But think of what that woman went through. It's not funny when someone gets hurt, emotionally or physically. I think the creep got what he deserved."

"He did a lot for the company. And everyone enjoyed working with him. It's depressing to think that all the good things a person does can be wiped out with one indiscretion."

"That's how the world is. It's called being accountable."

"So how are you going to cheer me up?"

"You're taking me to dinner," Karen replied while taking a brush from her pocketbook and attending to her long, curly blonde hair.

"I ask again, how are *you* going to cheer *me* up?"

"I'm letting you take me to dinner. What more could you want?"

"I can't think of a thing."

Rick walked into his office on Monday morning. A small object had been placed on his desk by Binny before his departure from Affordable. This was Bowmarc, the good crusader from the *Dungeon and Dragons* game. Rick at first felt a sense of melancholy when he thought about Binny, and then a sense of dread after remembering his description of the Monday demon. Fortunately for Rick the white armored action figure on his desk, with a shield depicting a fierce lion in one hand and an axe in the other, looked like it was capable of vanquishing such a dangerous entity.

Rick met with Mario. The Computer Department Head was depressed, wondering how he would find someone with Binny Jenkins' ability. Rick showed him the ad he planned to run, and then returned to his office, closing the door behind him. The phone rang. Tim Shelby wanted to see Rick immediately.

He opened the door without typing his password into the keypad on the wall next to it. This resulted in the alarm going off, the clangor created by its kazoo-like siren now filling the building. Rick thought of Binny. That sound had reminded him of the noise created by a million-dollar slot machine in Las Vegas after a player won. Binny would yell *we have a winner folks* every time the Affordable alarm went off.

"Why do I have to use the password when I leave my office? I feel like a criminal escaping from his cell," Rick thought aloud.

He looked at Bowmarc while calling security to have the alarm shut off. Rick experienced an ominous feeling and slipped Binny's departing gift into his pocket.

"You'll protect me, Bowmarc."

Rick walked down to the General Manager's office. After greeting his superior and shutting the door behind him as instructed he felt very vulnerable. The demon seemed to be in the room.

"Rick, I really don't know how to say this, so I'll just come right to the point."

For a moment Rick feared that Binny had done something drastic. That would explain the sense of dread he was feeling.

"I met with Dale over the weekend. He's decided that you can no longer work for this company."

Rick's concern was now of a more personal nature.

"What!" he exclaimed.

"You hired Binny, and Dale feels that you're responsible for his conduct."

"I've hired just about everyone here, at least technically. And when someone's gotten canned, which has happened before, I've never been held accountable for their failures. I also consulted with both Mario and you before making the decision to hire Binny. We all knew that he was fired from his last job for putting a caricature of that company's president on their intranet. He made him look like the Green Goblin and depicted him flying around the office terminating employees. And I do mean *terminating*."

"Was the Green Goblin from Batman?"

"No, he was from Spiderman, but that's not the point!" Rick responded angrily. "My point is we all believed that Binny would clean up his act if given another chance."

Tim looked down at his desk, unconsciously grooming his beard with a pen. Rick struggled to maintain his self-control.

"Look, I like you Rick," the GM said after finally raising his head. "So I'm going to level with you. Jenkins isn't the real reason that Dale wants you out of here."

"Illuminate me," Rick responded.

"Do you remember a couple of years ago, when someone broke into the office and stole several computers."

"Yes. I was just thinking about it, because I accidentally set off the alarm. That's when Chris had everyone's office door connected to the security system. It was also the longest night of my life. I was on the list of people the police were given to contact in case of an emergency. You and Dale were the other two on it, but they couldn't get in touch with either of you. So I got the call at twelve thirty in the morning. I had to come here and stay all night, because the thieves broke the big window in the back of the building, and until it was fixed the office was wide open."

"Dale thinks you stole something on that particular occasion."

"He thinks I was in on it?! Why would I steal computers from this place?!"

"Not computers. A slice of pizza."

"What the hell are you talking about?!"

"Dale always buys pizza for the finance department on the first day of the month. He saves one slice and puts it in the refrigerator in the employee's lounge, so he can have it for breakfast the next morning. You ate his pizza while you were watching the building that night."

Rick looked at him incredulously.

"Do you mean to tell me that I'm being fired because of a slice of pizza that I ate two years ago?!"

"He's always held a grudge against you for taking his breakfast."

"That stupid bastard didn't even put his name on it!"

"I know how you feel. But in his mind, you took something that didn't belong to you."

"You don't know how I feel! I've been working here for almost ten years. And that wasn't the first or last late night I spent in this office! I can't believe you're going along with this, Tim. Talk to Ches. The president of a company can override a vice president. He just told me that I'm the anchor holding this whole operation together."

"You might be the anchor, but Dale's father owns half the ship. And that makes Dale a very powerful person in this company. He calls the shots. That's the way the game is played. You know that."

"Chris even gave me his personal cell phone number," Rick added while ignoring the GM's response.

"He gives just about everyone his personal cell phone number at one point or another."

"I know. He gave it to Phil in the stockroom a couple of weeks ago."

"He also changes it every week."

"Chris will listen to you."

"Maybe, but then I'll be screwed. Stephens would never forget that I went over his head. I have a wife and kids, Rick."

"That's bullshit!"

"Try to keep your voice down."

"The hell with that! There are some things that are just too wrong to go along with, Tim!"

"You can use me as a reference. You're still young, and I'm sure you'll find something soon. I'm really sorry about this."

Rick turned and was about to punch the wall when he realized that having a broken hand would do nothing to improve his current situation.

"If I knew it was his slice of pizza, I would have gone out that morning and bought him another one," Rick calmly stated after turning around once more.

"The pizzerias are closed in the morning, Rick. And the frozen kind in the grocery store just doesn't make it," Tim responded with a weak smile.

"I'm going to have a talk with that ass."

"He's not in the office this week. And please don't come back here next week looking for trouble. You've got enough to deal with right now."

"I guess this is it, Tim."

"I'm sorry, Rick," he replied before looking away. The GM stood up and disarmed the alarm.

The terminated employee walked out the door and found Mike Stenson, one of the security guards, standing there.

"I'm sorry Rick," he said. "They told me to escort you out of the building."

Now I really feel like a criminal Rick thought. Then aloud "I guess there must be more pizza in the refrigerator," he said bitterly while glaring at Tim. "You're afraid I might steal another slice."

Rick mechanically cleaned out his desk before saying goodbye to his stunned co-workers.

"This is the biggest waste of talent I've ever seen!" Wispy said as she hugged him. "They don't know about *Nada Prodigalidad!*"

"I'll find something else," Rick said with more optimism than he felt at that moment.

"Do you want me to slash his tires," Colin offered. "They can't do anything to me now."

"I appreciate it, but what would be the point. Take care, guys."

Rick walked out of the building humming *Anchors Away*. He turned around and looked back at it after reaching his car.

"We've got a winner! A never-ending vacation without pay for Rick Gaines!"

He came close to causing three accidents on the way home. After arriving at his apartment several glasses of strong liquor provided the desired numbness which now slowly permeated his shell-shocked mind. Rick stared at the figure of Bowmarc, which he had placed on the coffee table in front of him.

"It's just you and me, pal," Rick thought aloud.

Karen arrived shortly after and received a look that made her feel like a stranger.

"What's that all about?" she asked him. "And who's your little friend?"

"Binny gave him to me."

"Don't tell me you're still depressed about him being fired."

"I'm depressed, but the cause isn't sympathy for someone else. It's caused by an event that hit just a little bit closer to home. I got fired!"

"What! Why!"

"Officially it was because I hired Binny. It was really because I ate a slice of pizza two years ago that belonged to the Financial Vice President. I mean, I could understand it if I took it out of his hand just as he was about to eat it. But this slice was in the refrigerator with no one's name on it."

"You can't be fired for eating a piece of pizza!"

"New York State believes in employment at will. You can be fired for anything, short of race and age. And those two exclusions are circumvented more often than a politician lies."

Karen walked over and hugged him. She observed how every hair on his head remained in place, despite Rick's agitated state.

"That's the most ridiculous thing I've ever heard of," she told him. "I'll have a drink with you."

He poured himself a refill and then filled a glass for her.

"Ten friggen years, and this is how it ends. I was escorted

out of the building by a security guard, like I was a common criminal!"

"Don't be so dramatic."

"I should go back and torch the place."

"I know how you feel, but that won't do any good. You've got to come up with a plan."

"I just did. I'm going to torch the place!"

"Bad plan."

"Well, I could put my resume together and look for another job."

"A much better plan. You're still in your forties. And you look like you're in your thirties. You'll have no trouble getting another job."

"This could ruin our vacation if I find something right away. I wouldn't be able to take any time off for a while."

"I really didn't want to see Vermont anyway. What's so exciting about watching a bunch of trees standing around."

"I just hate the thought of getting another job so someone else can screw me."

"My mother always said that when God closes a door a window opens."

"I hope it's a window on the tenth floor. Because after I jump out of it my troubles will be over."

"That's a defeatist attitude," said Karen.

"And that's completely appropriate for me, because I'm defeated."

"No you're not. Things will look better in the morning."

Only if I win the lottery, Rick thought as he finished his scotch.

A month later Rick Gaines found himself in a very familiar setting, though he was not sitting in his customary position. Now in the role of job applicant, Rick sat in the office of Ken Miles, in front of a desk, rather than behind it. The President of Action Sporting Goods was interviewing him for the position of Human Resources Manager. Rick had anguished over this being a Friday afternoon, but found solace because of the position Miles held. Someone at his level would be likely to remain focused despite the approaching weekend.

At least he hoped so.

"So you had quite a run at Affordable, Rick. What did you learn there that would help you succeed here?"

Never hire a computer programmer that sends outrageous emails to the V.P.'s wife Rick thought before saying aloud "It's all about teamwork. I've learned that a company's success depends on the ability of its employees to pull together. I can create an atmosphere here that will encourage them to do that."

"I think we're on the same page."

Rick left the interview feeling confident, if not certain. Tim's reference could very well be the deciding factor, and he anticipated no negatives from his former boss. Still, one could never be completely sure what a person was thinking, especially someone who had been a stranger before today. Rick vowed to put the subject aside for the weekend. There was nothing to be done now, except wait for Miles' decision, which would not come for at least a week.

He took his car in to be serviced the next morning. Karen picked him up at the dealership.

"They must have nuclear physicists working here," Rick said after he got in her car. "They're charging me three hundred and sixty dollars for labor, and it's only a two-hour job."

"I don't think nuclear physicists make that much," Karen pointed out with a grin.

"I better get a job fast or start taking the bus. My 401k took a beating last week because production in Malaysia was down. I guess they all called in sick or went on vacation. Who knows with Malaysians."

"You'll be back to work in a week," Karen encouraged him. "I have to do some shopping. I'll drop you off at your place and come back in a couple of hours."

"Sounds good. Maybe I should become an auto mechanic."

"You couldn't stand the grease, babe," Karen responded.

After she drove away Rick went up to his apartment and found Binny waiting outside his door.

"Hey Rick," he said sheepishly. "I heard what happened. I'm really sorry."

"Oh, it's all bullshit," Rick told his unexpected guest. "Come inside."

He opened the door and Binny followed him into the apartment.

"Can I get you something to drink?" Rick asked him.

"No thanks. I really can't stay long."

"So...have a seat. Tell me what you've been doing."

"I've been working on a few ideas," Binny said as he sat on the sofa. "Do you have anything lined up?"

"I just interviewed with Action Sporting Goods. It went very well."

"Good. I have a friend that works there. He likes it a lot."

"Oh, really." *You'll have to give me your friends name so I can watch out for him.* "Tell me about your ideas."

A wide grin appeared on the programmer's corpulent face.

"I'd be glad to. That's why I came to see you, actually. I've got a plan that will make me a multi-millionaire."

"Really? How are you going to do that?"

"I'm going to rob a bank."

Rick looked at his former coworker carefully. Knowing his penchant for jokes, he assumed that Binny wasn't being serious. Yet there was a gleam in his eye.

"And I'm the King of England."

"A pleasure to meet you, my liege," Binny said with a laugh. "I haven't called you that for a while. But I'm serious, Rick."

"You could get yourself killed, not to mention a very long prison sentence."

"That would be true if I did it the old-fashioned way. But I have a fool proof plan. It's all going to be done with computers."

"They're still going to miss the money, no matter how you do it."

"But the bank will never be able to find the money."

"Look, Binny, don't do something foolish. There are plenty of jobs out there for someone like you."

"I know, Rick. But they're really all very ordinary when you get right down to it. I want to do something interesting with my life. Getting another nine to five job just doesn't do it for me. Have you ever heard of Rosa's Café?"

"Yes, it's over on Bleeker Street."

"I'm meeting my partner there on Monday. We're going to watch a little football while we go over the plan. Stop by, even if you don't want to do it."

"Won't your partner object to discussing the idea with an outsider?"

"He trusts my judgment."

Then the guy can't be too swift.

"It was good to see you, Rick," said Binny while shaking his hand.

"Keep in touch."

Rick spent Monday morning trying to mentally will the phone to ring. After a while he recognized the futility of his efforts and found something to take his mind off his employment situation. There was an old apple juice bottle filled with pennies in one of the cabinets. Rick had been intending to deposit them for years. Now he had the time to insert the cooper-plated coins into the paper wrappers provided by his financial institution.

After returning from the bank, some forty dollars richer, the unemployed personal director checked his answering machine for messages. The display on the device indicated that a total of zero calls had been received. Rick found another task to occupy his mind. He cleaned out the bedroom closet. There was a pirate's costume hanging there that Rick had worn to a Halloween party years before. He put on the triangular hat and eye patch.

"Maybe I could be a man of adventure," Rick said aloud as he stood in front of the mirror. "A person who takes what they want, instead of relying on someone else to grant it to them."

There was also a shark skin suit he had not worn in twenty years.

"I really miss the eighties," he mused while putting it in the pile of garments to be discarded.

He looked at the suits that comprised his current wardrobe. For just a moment, Rick felt the urge to put all of them in the pile. The positive feeling he had about the Action interview was rapidly waning.

"I'm just on edge," he told himself. "I'll have a job by the end of this week. I need some fresh air."

He granted the rest of the items in the closet a reprieve

and walked to a park five blocks away. Several swans leisurely drifted across in the pond there, perhaps aware that the pleasant October day would be one of the last of its kind for several months. He sat down on a bench and basked in the warm autumnal sun. Rick suddenly appreciated the fact that he was here, instead of in an office.

"There is nothing like the freedom to do nothing," he thought aloud. "I just hope I haven't lost my ambition at the ripe old age of forty-four."

There was a message on the answering machine when Rick returned home. The excitement it generated quickly dissipated after he hit the playback button.

"Rick, it's me, I have to work late tonight. Give me a call."

Karen's voice had never left him with such an empty feeling before.

"Hi. How late are you going to be?" he asked when she picked up the phone.

"I'll probably be here till nine. Did you hear anything about the job?"

"No." Rick replied in a dejected tone.

"It's only Monday."

"That's the scary part. I could have four more days like this to look forward to."

"Stay positive. Isn't that what you always tell people?"

"Of course. But I never really expect anyone to do it. If ever there was a time in my life to be negative, this is it, baby."

"What are you going to do tonight?"

"I guess I'll just watch the football game..."

Those words brought Binny's invitation to mind. He had not thought about going to Rosa's until now. Suddenly the chance to see the game on a big screen television, and have his curiosity about the programmer's plan satisfied, had become his best option for the evening.

"Are you still there," Karen asked him.

"Yes, I was just swatting a fly. I'm going to watch it with an old friend of mine."

"Should I be jealous?" she teasingly questioned him.

"Only if I discover that I'm gay."

After eating a fast food dinner Rick walked into Rosa's. His eyes struggled for a moment before adjusting to the dark environment, as the owner of this establishment was not one to waste energy on lighting. Binny's voice suddenly rang out from across the bar.

"Rick! Have a seat."

Binny was sitting in a booth with an excellent view of the television. A much older man was sitting next to him. He was currently engaged in a conversation on his cell phone. Binny poured a beer for Rick from the pitcher on the table.

"I'm glad you came," he said as they tapped their glasses together.

"This seemed like a good place to watch the game," Rick responded.

"My plan is coming to fruition. I've worked out all the details."

"The Kansas City quarterback's dog died this week," the man said into the phone. "He had that animal for ten years. The guy won't play for shit. Okay, I've got you down for a deuce. Speak to you later."

"This is my uncle, Oscar Anastas," Binny introduced him. "This is Rick Gaines."

"I take it you follow football," Rick said as he shook his hand.

"Uncle Oscar is a bookie," Binny informed him.

"I like to think of myself as a wager enabler," Oscar corrected him.

"How did you know about the quarterback's dog?" Rick asked.

"A little birdie told me," he said coyly. "I have contacts all over the country. You name a team and I'll tell you something you don't know about them."

"Seattle Seahawks," Rick responded.

"The offensive coordinator not only thinks the head coach is a jackass, but he wants his job. So you can expect their offense to tank this week."

"Wouldn't that make the offensive coach look bad, too," Rick questioned him.

Oscar ran his hand over his balding head. He then looked at Rick with a perplexed expression on his face.

"You know my wife said the same thing. I never listen to her, but Binny tells me you're a sharp guy, so I'll have to rethink that game. Are you coming in on my nephew's brilliant scheme?"

"I'm curious about it. I'm also concerned. I'd hate to see you get into a jam, Binny."

"Not to worry, my liege. It's fool proof."

"What do you have in mind?" Rick asked him.

"Well, since it's my idea, you know it involves a computer," Binny began after looking around to be sure no one else in the bar was listening to their conversation. Fortunately for him the game had started, and the other patrons, including Oscar, were transfixed by it. "I'm going to have the Federal Reserve loan a large sum of money to a certain bank. Then I'm going to move the money to an offshore account that we're setting up."

"What's to stop the bank from finding the money?" Rick questioned him.

"The transactions won't be done in the usual way. I'm going to copy the banks software to a different place on their computer's hard drive and initiate the transfers from there. Then I'll erase all the information after the money's in our offshore account. They'll never be able to find out where the money went."

"Catch the damn ball!" Oscar suddenly blurted out.

"That's interesting," Rick conceded. "How much do you intend to take?"

"Let's just say enough to make it worth our while."

Oscar suddenly slammed the table when his team was penalized.

"But no plan is ever foolproof," Rick warned him while using a napkin to clean up the beer that had spilled from his glass. "And how are you going to explain where this money came from?"

"Uncle Oscar took care of that," Binny said with a smile. "We're going to launder it. So are you in?"

"This kid has a lot on the ball," Oscar told Rick, his attention off the screen now that half time had arrived. "He's as smart as...."

His cell phone rang, and the bookie became engrossed in a conversation with a client.

"This isn't for me," Rick said.

"But think about it. Affordable screwed you. And again, I'm really sorry that I gave them an excuse to do it."

"It wasn't you, it was the pizza," Rick corrected him.

"But I did give them a bogus reason to fire you. So I'd like to make it up to you. And you're due for something really great to happen to you. Your good karma has to be really strong right now."

"I always thought karma was something you got from your own actions. And I didn't fire myself."

"Taylor's wife is screwing the team trainer," Oscar spoke loudly into his phone. "The guy has to be an emotional wreck."

"Isn't that the quarterback who just threw for two hundred yards in the first half?" Rick asked Binny.

"I wasn't watching. Karma is fate, and it will even the score for you. I really believe that. Having you in on this would be like Oscar and I having a rabbit's foot. We can't miss."

"When did you get so philosophical?"

"Wispy turned me on to a whole new way of thinking. I really miss having those existential discussions with her."

Now I believe it's a sure thing. Then he said aloud "I appreciate your confidence in me, but in my experience, life just doesn't work that way. If you get screwed, you get screwed. Fate won't make it up to you. It's up to the individual to straighten things out on their own. Besides, if fate is going to compensate me for losing my job, I should just take my life savings to a casino. I could win a lot of money without doing anything illegal."

"I know you, Arnie. You're thinking Green Bay over Minnesota," Oscar answered another call. "Good choice. McHenry has the flu. He won't do anything! I'll put you down for a c note."

"Isn't that the guy that Minnesota traded to Oakland last week?" Rick asked the bookie after his call ended.

"Oh, *really*?" Oscar responded, with a smile and a wink. "I needed more action on Green Bay."

"We're going operational on this next week, so you still have time to think about it."

"Listen to the kid, Rick," Oscar urged him. "He's got a lot on the ball. You could be a rich man."

"I could also wind up in jail," he replied. "But thanks for the offer, guys."

There was no phone call from Ken Miles by the time Thursday evening fell. Rick was almost frantic and tried to divert his mind by doing a crossword puzzle. The first clue read *something to make or steal.*

"Money," Rick decided, but discovered that there weren't enough spaces for it. "Something to make or steal."

"The answer is scene," Karen, who had entered the apartment while Rick was engrossed in the puzzle, told him.

"I can't do this thing!" Rick, who was startled by her sudden appearance, said. "I'm too preoccupied with the job."

Karen responded by engaging him in a long session of escapist lovemaking. Rick lost his concern about the phone call that never came in his desire for her shapely, warm body. After they finished he lay in bed staring at the ceiling.

"What are you thinking about?" she asked while putting her arm around his waist.

"Robbing a bank."

"What? Oh, be serious."

"I am. Those guys I met at the bar on Monday are going to rob a bank."

"Who are they?"

"You don't know them. But their plan seems to make sense to me now."

"They'll be caught, and at the very least, go to prison. They could also be shot, and possibly lose their lives."

You always look at the negatives, my love.

Rick stood up, put on his robe and walked over to the window. The traffic on the street below made him think of all the people in the world who were going somewhere. He, at that moment in his life, was not.

"No, it's a white-collar operation. There'll be no way to trace the money," Rick finally responded to her assessment of the thieves' chances for success.

"They'd still be taking a big risk. There's no such thing as a perfect crime."

"Really? How about the banks ripping off the government, and the consumers? Not to mention what the outstanding citizens on Wall Street have done. They all seem to be getting away with it."

"That's different. What they're doing is legal, even though it shouldn't be."

"Taking money from the government should be legal. They're going to lose it anyway. Nine billion dollars disappeared in Iraq without a trace. And nobody batted an eye. The people I talked to aren't taking anywhere near as much. So what harm could it do?"

"Please tell me you aren't really considering doing this."

Rick looked out the window for a while longer. The stress the job seeker had been feeling seemed to suddenly vanish when he thought about Binny's plan. Yet he did not lose sight of the consequences if it should fail. Rick walked over to the bed and ran his fingers through Karen's blond locks.

"No, not really," he said with a grin. "But it is intriguing to think about being a rich man."

"I'll grant you that," Karen conceded.

Friday morning came and went with no word about the job.

There were no more pennies to wrap or closets to clean, so Rick spent some time browsing at the mall. When he came home the light on his answering machine was blinking. He nervously pushed the play button and listened to the message that he believed would determine his fate.

This is Verizon, and we have good news for you! Now your internet access will only cost....

Rick hit the delete button. He called Tim Shelby at Affordable Electronics.

"Rick! How are things going?" the GM asked.

"I'm doing pretty well. I had an interview at Action Sporting Goods...."

"Yes, I know. Miles called me about you on Tuesday, I believe. We had a very interesting discussion."

"What did you tell him?"

"I told him about the work you did here. I mentioned how reliable you were, and how you excelled at relating to the employees. Then we started talking about his company, and how conventional its hiring practices are. I couldn't help but point out how that differed from your approach. You hired people who brought their toys to work when you were here," he finished with a chuckle.

"You said that to him?" Rick asked while squeezing the phone.

There was silence at the other end of the line.

"Tell me you really didn't say that to him!" Rick exclaimed.

"Well, it did come up in the conversation. As one professional to another, I felt obligated to give him the full picture. But I also pointed out that it was our company policy to look for quirky people." Tim paused once more before continuing. "I think I said that. Yes, I'm sure I said that."

"You fucked me!"

"Now hold on a minute, Rick. I said a lot of positive things, too. It's not my fault if you don't get the job. Besides, there are plenty of other opportunities out there. You're still a young man."

"Thirty is young. Forty-four is someone with significant miles on him."

"I have another call."

"You're a professional asshole, Tim!" Rick screamed at him before the phone went silent.

Karen came by two hours later, expecting to hear good news. She walked into the apartment and discovered that the phone had been shattered into a countless number of pieces. Rick was sitting on the couch wearing the pirate hat and holding a glass of scotch in his hand. His brief case had been pulverized, and the want ads from the newspaper were now reduced to ashes in the wastebasket.

"I see you had a little phone trouble today," she asked, trying to sound flippant.

"Shelby fucked me! That son of a bitch screwed up the reference. I'm not getting the job."

"Why would he do that?"

"Because," Rick paused for dramatic effect. "He's a damn asshole!"

"Don't shout. The neighbors will hear you."

"They should be warned! That idiot is a menace to society!"

"Calm down. I know this hurts, but these things happen for a reason."

"Yeah, and the reason is life sucks!"

"You have to keep things in perspective."

"I can't afford any perspective! I'm going to be broke pretty soon," Rick replied while pouring another glass of scotch. "And I lost my reference when I called that asshole a professional asshole. I'll never get another job now. If I was sober I'd drive down to his office and throw him out the damn window. My only concern would be how much damage he'd do to the pavement. They'd probably make me pay to repair it, and I can't afford that right now."

"Is that the same window you were going to jump out of after the door closes?" Karen asked with a grin. When that failed to lighten his mood she said "I'll help you out."

Rick's anger dissipated for a moment.

"You're the best, sweetheart. But there's only one thing for me to do now. I'm going to torch his office!"

"That won't accomplish anything."

"It'll make me feel better."

Rick staggered towards the door, but then changed his mind.

"I should wait until tomorrow," he said before collapsing on the couch. "But I'm going to get those bastards!"

"That's just the liquor talking."

Rick looked at the glass in his hand and exclaimed "Shut up!"

"You need something to eat. I'll go out and get dinner."

"Bring back another bottle of scotch, too."

Karen returned with a pizza. Rick looked at her as if she had stuck a knife in his heart.

"How could you bring that in here!?"

"I'm sorry, I wasn't thinking. But have a slice. You need something to eat."

Rick refused, pouring another drink instead.

"Where did you get the hat?"

"I was cleaning out the closet and found the pirate costume I wore to a Halloween party years ago. And it's a good thing I did. This is what I am now. A pirate. A pirate on the Cyber Sea. With Bowmarc as the first mate."

Rick raised his glass to the toy crusader on the coffee table.

"You're not going to start that again," said Karen in a dismissive tone.

"Why not? I could be rich overnight. And there's a lot of money in being rich."

"I'm sure there is," Karen agreed. "But you have to earn the money. You'll see things clearer in the morning. Right now you're talking crazy."

"Why shouldn't I rob a bank? They rob everyone else. My last bank statement had a column that showed the *year to date lack of interest*. And everyone's stealing everything anyway. They even stole the police crime scene van from in front of the office when it was broken into. That's probably why the cops were never able to bust me for taking the slice of pizza." Rick then told her in a serious tone. "The door closed and something better than a window opened. It's a bank vault! I could do this. And then I'll have enough money for the rest of my life."

"But you wouldn't have earned it."

"Did Dale Stephens earn his money? If his father didn't own half the company he'd never be able to support himself. Besides, I would be earning the money. As you pointed out, I'd be taking a hell of a chance. I could wind up in a prison cell with some guy named Bubba who starts singing *Sweet Home Alabama* every time he looks at my ass."

"You're flattering yourself, darling. Your ass isn't that great," Karen said with a grin.

"That's not what you said the last time we were together."

"That was in the heat of the moment."

"Where is it written that I have to be a regular working stiff for the rest of my life? Do I have to spend the majority of my time on this planet being at the mercy of pricks like Dale Stephens and idiots like Tim Shelby? Why can't I be among the elite? Am I excluded from that group in the grand scheme of things? Is Rick Gaines precluded from being rich because of the universal plan?"

"Of course not. But you have to get what you want legally. Start a business, invent the next pet rock. That would be fine."

"I could sell Panda poop. Do you know that people pay thirty-six thousand dollars a pound for it? Pandas have a poor digestive system. It doesn't absorb most of the nutrients, so their droppings are very nutritious."

"Is that true?"

"How do I know? I'm drunk."

"Stealing money, that's not who you are. You and I weren't raised that way. What would your parents say if they were still with us?"

"My old man would say *could you get me a Cadillac?* He always wanted one."

"He would not."

"How do you know? You never even met him. I can do this!"

"You're too self-conscious to be a criminal. You couldn't look someone in the eye while you're scamming them out of their money."

"I used to wear a shark skin suit. How self-conscious can I possibly be!"

Karen finished her pizza in silence. She then put on her coat and walked over to Rick with a slice.

"I know you had a bad day. But these things happen. A friend of mine got fired once for wearing one of those buttons with a happy face that said *have a nice day*. Everyone in the office started wearing one after she did. Management apparently interpreted it as a symbol of unity and feared that the employees were about to rise up against them. They terminated Alice and twenty other people. But she got through it. So will you. Do me a favor and eat this. And then get some sleep. You'll feel better in the morning."

Rick said nothing until she walked out the door, when he shouted "They should have been fired! Those have a nice day buttons are obnoxious!" He then looked at Bowmarc and said "Aye, matey. The wench thinks me rum is to blame. But it's that bilge sucking Stephens that's really the problem. He'll be feeding the fish when we get through with him. Aye."

Rick grinned at his plastic companion before standing up and throwing the slice of pizza at the wall behind the couch, where it stuck.

"I'll get that tomorrow," he said while flopping on the couch.

Several moments later the pizza came off the wall, hitting him squarely in the face.

CHAPTER

3

The next day Rick called Binny and set up a meeting. He suggested that they come over to his apartment, but Oscar wanted to have it somewhere where the three of them were not likely to be seen by anyone else. Rick was to meet his former fellow employee at a supermarket, and from there they would rendezvous with the bookie. Three cups of coffee after twelve hours sleep was enough to at least partially eliminate the effects of yesterday's drinking binge. What he was now about to become involved in was the most radical, and dangerous, undertaking of his life. Still Rick's current state of mind made his decision to participate in the scheme nearly inevitable, despite the risks.

"This is just so right," Binny said with a huge grin as they walked inside the store. "This is why we were both working at Affordable. The forces that control our destiny want this for you and me."

"I think we determine our own fate."

"I'm going to pick up some sandwiches. What would you like?"

"A roast beef hero with mayo and salt would be fine."

"You can pick up the beer."

"Will do. But I'm also getting soda for me."

Binny got the food and met Rick at the self-checkout line. They watched as a heavy-set woman scanned her groceries. Binny took a key chain out of his pocket and spoke softly into a small round device on the end of it. His words came out of the station currently being used by the woman to purchase her half gallon of ice cream.

"Do you really need that, ma'am?"

"What?" she responded while looking at the machine with a perplexed expression on her face.

"I mean, I don't want to get personal, but you could stand to lose a few pounds," the electronic cashier told her.

"Help! Someone help me!" she screamed while Binny and Rick tried to hide their laughter.

"What's the problem?" the store manager asked after responding to her shouts.

"This machine told me I was fat!"

"That isn't possible. It's only capable of saying things like *thanks for shopping at our store* and *don't forget your change*," she politely pointed out.

"The voice coming from your machine said I should lose a few pounds."

The manager looked at Binny and Rick for an affirmation. They just shrugged their shoulders, feigning to know nothing about it. She tried to find a diplomatic way to dismiss the customer's complaint, though experience told her that it was going to be an impossible task.

"You may have just imagined it. I know sometimes the thoughts going through my mind sound like they're coming from somewhere else."

"I don't think I'm fat! I'm not buying anything here!! And I'm going to write a letter to your superiors! What's your name?!"

The woman in charge of the establishment pointed to the name tag on her shirt and then used the keypad on the machine to cancel the order. She breathed a sigh of relief after the disgruntled customer left the store. Binny paid for their lunch, managing to control his laughter until they were outside.

"How did you do that?" Rick asked him.

"A friend of mine fixes the self-checkout machines in that store. The last time they called him in he put a receiver in one of them that picks up the signal from the transmitter on my key chain. I can make it say anything. One time I asked a heavyset guy if he really needed a twelve pack of beer when he already looked as though he was carrying around a keg in his gut. He got really pissed off. The guy wouldn't leave until the manager threatened to call the cops. Last week I had a ten-minute political argument with a man who got mad enough to punch out the monitor on the machine. The people who run the store didn't appreciate it, but I thought it was great."

"You're a dangerous man, Binny. So where are we going?"

"There's an abandoned mental hospital about ten miles from here. They're supposed to turn it into a park eventually, but for now it's not being used."

"Why are we meeting there again?"

"Oscar doesn't want anyone to see the three of us together. Follow me."

They drove for about thirty minutes before Binny turned onto an obscure side road. At the end of it was a fence with a sign reading *no trespassing*. The two of them parked their cars on the roadside. Binny went up to the chain link fence and pushed in the bottom of it. The fasteners attaching it to the frame had been broken off long ago. They crawled through the opening, a particularly arduous task for the ungainly programmer. After following a path through the trees for fifteen minutes they came to a clearing where Oscar was waiting for them.

"Rick. Good to see you again. Did you get the food Binny?"

"Sure did."

"We'll have to sit on this log. It's the only seat around. You want a beer, Rick?"

"I'll stick to soda for the moment."

"You had a rough night?" Oscar asked him with a grin.

"A rough night that was preceded by an even rougher day."

"I'm glad you decided to do this with us."

"I'm still sitting on the fence, so to speak. I mean this is really out of character for me. But I'm willing to listen."

"Good."

They sat down and ate their sandwiches. The mild autumn day provided a pleasant atmosphere for their meeting. Rick's mind was clear now. The thought of exchanging his job search for a life of leisure had numbed his conscience.

"So Binny tells me you're pretty good at handling people," Oscar said between bites of his provolone hero.

"I can hold my own. So tell me more about your plan."

Binny put down his beer and took a small plastic object from his pocket. He showed it to Rick.

"You know what that is?"

"Yeah, it's a zip file. It's used to copy information from computers."

"Right. All you have to do is leave this on someone's desk at the bank. Then we're in business."

"How so?"

"If you found this on your desk at work, what would you do with it?"

"I'd put it in my computer to find out what was on it."

"Exactly. And that, by the way, is what the people in my profession are always telling computer users *not* to do. But like you, they do it anyway. The person at the bank that finds it on his or her desk will be no exception, I'm sure. After he or she puts it in their computer a pretty racy message will pop up on their computer screen, supposedly from a secret admirer. What the person won't see is the program on the zip file that will record every keystroke on their keyboard. Then it will email the log that was created to me."

"What will that do for you?"

"I'm going to access the Elmendorf Bank's computer from a p.c. But I need the username and password of someone that works at the bank. The keystroke log my program creates will give me that. Then I'll be able to get into the bank's operating system. I'll borrow fifty million from the Federal Reserve Bank. As far as the feds are concerned, Elmendorf bank will have borrowed the money from them. I'll wire the money, using the Elmendorf computer, to another bank, where we've opened an account. After that's done I'll erase everything I did on the Elmendorf computer. We'll have fifty-million-dollars in our account. The feds and Elmendorf bank will just have a fifty-million-dollar mystery."

Rick looked at him skeptically. The plan sounded too easy. He could not believe that so much money could disappear without a trace. Then the prospective thief remembered the missing money in Iraq. Rick also took note of the fact that Binny was an absolute wizard when it came to computers.

"We're going to need about eleven million to grease some palms, so things go smoothly for us," Oscar told him. "But we'll each wind up with thirteen-million-dollars. Isn't this kid great!"

"He's the best," Rick replied as Binny received a hug from his uncle. "But isn't the Federal Reserve going to expect the loan to be repaid?"

"Of course," Binny said in a matter of fact tone. "And they'll go to the people at Elmendorf, who will have no record of ever borrowing the money. They'll spend a long time trying to sort it out. And by the time they do, if they ever do, our money will be somewhere else."

"So all I have to do is leave this on someone's desk." Rick said.

"We thought you'd be the ideal guy for the job," Oscar explained. "Binny says you can think on your feet. Not that I don't know how to put things over on people. When too many of my clients bet on the favorite, I start spreading around some dirt about the players on that team to get some action for the underdog. That way the odds stay within reason, and I make out. But dealing with a bank official, well that's in a different league. You just have to go into the bank and pretend you want to open an account."

"Banks have surveillance cameras all over the place, including under the desks," Rick pointed out.

"Under the desks?" Oscar looked at him quizzically.

"I was being facetious."

The bookie gave him another puzzled look.

"I was kidding," Rick clarified "I just mean that I'd be exposing myself. And after the Fed comes looking for the money, the Elmendorf people might look at the tapes, to see if anyone did anything of a suspicious nature before the fifty-million-dollars was spirited away."

"Good point. And we thought of a way around it," Binny told him.

He stood up and picked up a bag resting on the log. Inside was a blonde wig along with a false mustache and mutton chop sideburns. There was also a body suit with enough padding to make someone of average girth appear to be a much heavier individual. Rick imagined himself walking down the street in this disguise and laughed.

"I'll look ridiculous," he told them.

"That doesn't matter," Oscar told him. "Just talk to the banker until he or she looks away for a minute. Then you put the zip file on the desk and get out of there."

"We thought you should go a branch in the city," Binny added. "That way there'll be less of a chance of you bumping into someone you know."

"If I bump into anyone with this on I'll probably knock the person on their ass."

Binny and Rick laughed uproariously, while Oscar grinned.

Rick looked at the contents of the bag and suddenly felt eager to partake in this absurd charade. He had no plans for tomorrow, or the next day, or any day after that. The idea of becoming someone else in order to make off with millions of dollars was the most exciting thing he was likely to do for the foreseeable future, perhaps even for the rest of his life.

"I'll do it, guys," Rick told them.

"Good," Oscar said. "The branch is on West Fifty Third Street. The address is twenty-five thirty-five. Don't forget to use the dye on your eyebrows so they're the same color as the wig. I also had some fake id made up in case you need it. You'll be Ken Close. Your wife is Ann Close."

"Come over to my house the day after you go to the bank," Binny told him. "I'm at twenty-five Cedar Lane. Be there after five o'clock."

"I'm going to hang back until you guys have driven away," Oscar said. "Good luck."

"I'll get it done," Rick assured his partners.

The next morning he stood in front of a mirror, wearing a shirt and slacks that were many sizes too large for his slender body, that attire being made necessary by the suit worn underneath them. With the wig, sideburns and mustache Rick looked preposterous, and it occurred to him that the description of his appearance might also turn out to be appropriate for his actions on this day.

"Better not buy ice cream at the self-checkout today, or it'll rip me to pieces," he said with a laugh. "Oh, well, I wasn't doing anything else anyway."

He walked out of his apartment and was relieved to see no other tenants in the corridor. Rick used the stairs instead of the elevator to increase his chances of avoiding any encounters. He reached the first floor and was just about to open the door when his neighbor used it to enter the building.

"Good morning," she said as they passed each other.

"Hi Betty," Rick replied.

She turned and looked at him, his voice having triggered a recognizant response. Yet his physical appearance produced nothing in her mind.

"Do I know you?" she asked him.

Rick felt perspiration under the padding as his mind scrambled to find a response.

"Why, yes," he replied in a deeper than normal voice. "I used to deliver the mail."

"Are you Jesse Gleason?"

"Yes. I retired several years back."

"Good for you. What brings you here?"

"Oh, I've been feeling nostalgic lately, so I decided to visit my old route."

"Would you like a cup of coffee?"

"Thanks, but I have to be going. My grandchildren are waiting for me."

"That's great. Enjoy yourself, Jesse."

"Take care."

"That man should get more exercise," the neighbor thought aloud after he left.

Rick walked to the train station, all the while congratulating himself on his virtuoso performance. Riding the Long Island Railroad into Manhattan, he nearly slid out of his seat three times before mastering the art of sitting on the moving train in his cumbersome disguise. Next there was a short trip on the subway, where a young boy accidentally stuck him in the ribcage with the tip of the umbrella that he carried for his mother. The padding prevented Rick from feeling it, and his assailant, having expected a reprimand, was now curious as to why none came. The boy repeatedly poked the large individual sitting next to him, until Rick finally became aware of his activity. He good naturedly asked him to cease and desist: the scolding anticipated by the child finally came from his mother immediately after.

Rick hailed a cab at Penn Station, and shortly after struggled to get out of it in front of the Elmendorf Bank. His heart skipped a few beats as he peered through the window at the people inside. There was no turning back if the unemployed human resource director delivered the zip file. His life would consist of two very distinctive parts. There would be the period before the robbery, during which Rick, for all practical purposes, followed the rules and had a very moderate lifestyle. Then there would be this day and its aftermath, when he could find himself financially well off, but never really secure.

Why am I doing this? Rick thought as he walked into the bank. *Oh, I remember, to get millions of dollars.*

Rick went into the store next to the bank and purchased a bottle of water, in anticipation of the dry mouth that would result from the tension building within him.

"We can do this," he whispered to Bowmarc, who was in his pants pocket. "Besides, I've already been branded a pizza thief, so my reputation is already ruined. I've got nothing to lose."

He then waddled into the bank and approached the desk of an account executive named Roger Knapp.

"I'd like to open…. a savings account."

"You came to the right place, Mr….?"

Rick forgot the alias Oscar had provided for him.

"Eh…Gleason. Jesse Gleason." Then to himself *I hope he doesn't ask for id.*

"Have a seat."

Rick carefully sat down as the banker began to fill out an application. The first-time thief slowly took the zip file out of his pocket, holding it discretely in his hand while waiting for the right time to place the key to their fortune on the desk in front of him. Rick took a sip of water as he struggled to maintain his composure. Everyone in the building seemed to be looking in his direction.

"So what's your occupation, Jesse? Do you mind if I call you Jesse?" the man asked him.

Who's that? Rick thought to himself. Then he remembered it was his alias.

"Oh sure, go right ahead."

"Call me Roger. What's your occupation, Jesse?"

Rick had not anticipated that question. He remembered his false address and his fictitious wife Ann, but no occupation. Then he saw a picture of a young girl on Knapp's desk, which he assumed was his daughter. She was on the gymnastics team and had posed on a balance beam.

"I'm a gymnast," he said.

The banker was taken aback by his response, given the applicant's physique. Rick quickly came up with an explanation for him.

"I'm not in very good shape at the moment. I cut my foot on a piece of grass and had to stop working out for a while."

"Grass?" Roger questioned him.

"No, I don't use any drugs," Rick assured him.

"You said you cut your foot on a piece of grass."

"Did I? I meant glass. You know, ever since I stopped working out my mind has turned to mush. I need to get more exercise."

He stretched out his arms for emphasis. The water bottle accidentally slipped out of his hand and flew over the head of Roger. When he turned around to pick it up, Rick placed the zip file on his desk.

That worked out well he thought to himself. *I'm good at this. And more importantly, I'm lucky.* Then aloud "This is going to be a joint account. *And I don't mean the grass kind of joint.* I forgot my wife's information, so I'll have to come back tomorrow."

"Take the application with you," the banker said as he handed it to him with the water bottle. "The next time we can have a nice chat about gymnastics. I'd like to learn as much as I can about it, to impress my daughter."

Roger pointed to the picture on his desk and then shook Rick's hand. The novice con man walked out of the bank as quickly as his outfit would allow. Though the suit was slightly lighter now, by the weight of one zip file, it was just as cumbersome. Rick took a cab back to Penn Station and went to the men's room. He went into a stall and removed the camouflage. He had worn his own pants and shirt underneath it. After peeling off the fake facial hair and washing the dye from his eyebrows Rick looked like himself again. He discarded the items used to create Jesse

Gleason, almost throwing out Bowmarc in the process. Rick then got on a train bound for home.

Relieved that it was over, he took a long swig of the scotch and soda purchased in the station. Rick looked around the train and suddenly felt as though everyone in the car was aware of his charade at the bank. Shutting his eyes to escape their phantom stares, he leaned his head back. A short time later someone tapped him on the shoulder, startling the bank robber. The paranoid passenger crushed the plastic glass in his hand, spraying its contents all over himself. Rick opened his eyes, and found the conductor standing before him.

"I need to see your ticket."

"Oh, right," Rick responded in an unsteady voice. He produced it, and then asked the man "I'm sorry I spilled my drink all over your train."

"It's not really *my* train," he responded with a grin.

"Do you have a towel I can borrow?"

"I'll see about that, sir."

I've got to get a grip he thought to himself.

The conductor never returned, so Rick used the newspaper lying on the empty seat next to him to clean up. He did not sleep well that night, the enormity of the consequences that would result from being caught weighing heavily on his mind. He drove over to Binny's house the next evening. A pleasant woman answered the door and introduced herself.

"I'm Binny's mom. You must be Rick."

"That's right."

"Come in. He's expecting you. I'm sorry to hear about your being fired. The people at that company are just a little too high and mighty for my tastes."

"They do leave something to be desired."

Rick walked down the stairs to the basement where Binny resided. There he saw the familiar *Dungeon and Dragons* action figures on the television, absent their leader, who now resided in his pocket. A poster of Einstein adorned the wall over his bed. His partner was surfing the web on his computer.

"Rick! How did it go?"

"I left the zip drive on Roger Knapp's desk."

"I'm aware of that, my liege. The program on the zip file emailed me his username and password. I knew you'd get it done. You know how to handle people."

"Well, actually, I was more than a little nervous. I'm amazed that the bank officer didn't call security, or a psychiatrist, after some of the things I said."

"It's done, that's all that matters. Now for phase two. I'm going to try to access the bank's system."

Binny terminated the web connection and then turned off his computer.

"Don't you have to use the machine?" Rick asked him.

"Oh, I'm not going to use *my* computer. I'll use someone else's."

After saying goodbye to his mother they drove to an Internet Café. Binny bought a latte, while Rick purchased a traditional cup of coffee. The establishment was not crowded, so they were able to find an unoccupied section that afforded them privacy. Binny sat down at one of the computers and began to type in commands.

"I'm going to use a computer in Pittsburgh. It belongs to John Moore."

"Who's he?"

"I saw Mr. Moore's name on a high school reunion web site. It had his email, and I used it to gain access to his machine, which I discovered, is always on. I also found out that he works for Elmendorf Bank as a consultant. He accesses their computer all the time. Only his user id and password gives him very limited access. That's why I needed you to get me someone else's information. From reading his emails I learned that John is taking a trip. By now he should be on a boat traveling down the Amazon River. I sent him an email about a month ago that was supposedly from the travel agency that booked his Amazon excursions. It contained a program that will enslave his computer. It's under my command now."

I never realized you were this diabolical Rick thought as he observed the expression on Binny's face, which reminded him of one he had observed on a master criminal's face in a Batman movie.

"I'm going to use his p.c. to copy the bank software onto the partitioned part of the Elmendorf computer's hard drive. Then I'll do our transactions."

"Partitioned part?" Rick questioned him.

"The head IT guy at Elmendorf set aside five percent of their hard drive to use for testing software. He wanted to make sure that there were no bugs in it before the employees starting using it."

"How do you know that?"

"I used to work at Elmendorf Bank."

"That wasn't on your resume."

"I left it off. I got canned because I sent around an email saying that the employees who showed up on Halloween dressed as their favorite gorilla would be eligible for a twenty-five-hundred-dollar bonus. Most of them went bananas when they found out it was a joke. Get it? Gorillas and bananas?"

"Very funny."

"Anyway, management took a dim view of the episode. Especially the human resource director, since I signed his name to the bogus email."

"I'll say this for you, you're consistent," Rick said with a grin.

"So anyway, I can copy the software used to communicate with the Fed and other banks onto the partitioned area. I'll make sure there aren't any tests scheduled first."

"What if Moore accesses his computer? Won't he know something's going on?"

"I don't think he'll be able to do that from the Amazon. But even if John could get on his computer it won't run any differently. The bank's computer is doing the work. Moore's computer is just giving it instructions. I'm going to set it up so it's done after I log off his computer. There'll be no way to trace the activity back to this internet café. Make sure no one comes over here while I do this."

"How can I stop them?"

"Tell them I'm writing a very personal letter to the woman I love."

Rick complied with his request. Fortunately, no one ventured near them, so there was no need for an explanation. He watched Binny while contemplating what the ramifications would be of the success, or failure, of the techie's scheme.

Hey, it's just the rest of my life that's hanging in the balance.

"Yahtzee!" Binny suddenly exclaimed.

"What?" Rick asked him.

"Most people would say bingo, but I've never played bingo. Moore's computer has started my program, and it's telling the bank's computer to copy the software."

Rick was silent for a moment. He was really participating in a bank robbery.

"How long will it take?" he finally asked.

"Probably a half hour. It's a complicated program. Then the software will setup the wires to be done tomorrow, since it's now after banking hours."

"Why didn't we do this during the day so the wires would go right out?"

"Because I went into the system using Knapp's credentials. He also uses them during the day. The system will only allow one R. Knapp at a time to log into it. Let's go."

They got into Rick's car and drove away.

"Now you get to do phase three, which is the fun part. Have you ever been to the Cayman Islands?"

"No."

"That's where you'll be tomorrow. You're supposed to meet Oscar at this hotel." Binny handed him a piece of paper. "Oscar's already on his way there. He didn't think you should fly together, since you only know each other because of the job we're pulling. I always wanted to talk like that. *The job we're pulling.*"

"You sound just like Edward G. Robinson."

"Who's he?"

"A movie star from before your time. And mine. But I like old movies. Why are we going there?"

"You guys have to make the arrangements to launder the money."

"I don't know anything about that."

"But Oscar does. You'll be there to watch his back. And to have a good time."

"So what will you be doing while we're sunbathing?"

"After Oscar verifies that the money was sent to the Caymans, I'll erase the information on the bank's computer, and John Moore's machine. We're going to be rich, my liege!"

Rick stopped the car in front of Binny's house.

"Do you think Oscar would mind if I took someone with me?" he asked as his partner in crime got out of the car.

"I don't think so. As long as it's someone you can trust."

"The next time you see me, I'll have a tan."

"The next time you see me, we'll have a ton of money. Have a great trip."

Rick went home and sat on the couch. He closed his eyes and began envisioning a life of leisure. His thoughts were interrupted by a knock on the door.

"Open up, Gaines!" the voice of Roger Knapp echoed through the building. "Do you think I'm stupid!? Do you really think I believed you're a gymnast!? We're going to put your ass in the stir!"

"This is detective Barns. You have the right...." another voice began. The rest of his sentence was lost to the din created by the sound of the alarm from Affordable's office going off.

"Who's the asshole now, Gaines?" Tim Shelby said with satisfaction in his voice after it stopped.

"How the hell did he get here?" Rick asked in a perplexed tone.

"We have the zip file, Mr. Gaines," the detective informed him.

"I never saw it before!" Rick insisted.

"Rick!" Karen exclaimed in a concerned tone.

"You were right, baby! I'm going to Bubba!"

Rick opened his eyes and realized that it was a dream. Only Karen's words were real, as she was the one who was knocking at the door. He let her in.

"What's the matter with you!" she asked him.

"I was having a crazy dream. I dreamt that a slice of pizza was eating me. So how was your day?"

"Very ordinary. How about yours?"

"Anything but. How would you like to go to the Grand Cayman Islands with me?"

"I'd love to. But can you afford it? Did you find a job?"

Rick suddenly displayed the mischievous naughty little boy expression that Karen found to be both charming and at this moment, disconcerting.

"What did you do?" she asked him.

"Well, I didn't find a job. But I'm in the middle of pulling a job."

"What are you talking about?"

"I'm robbing a bank."

"Stop bullshitting me!"

"I'm not kidding. Even as we speak, the plan is going forward."

"I'm going to have you committed! What's the matter with you!?"

"It's foolproof. I'm going to have millions of dollars. I'll never have to work again."

"Who put you up to this?"

"I'd rather not say."

"You mean you're so sure of this plan that you're afraid to tell me who else is in on it. It sounds like you have some doubts."

"Binny Jenkins."

"As in Binny who sent the stupid email that got you fired! He'll probably send one to the FBI and get you arrested. How you could you get involved with that jackass!"

Because no one else I know was planning to rob a bank.

Then he said aloud "It wasn't Binny that got me fired; it was the slice of pizza."

"He gave the VP a legitimate reason to fire you!"

"So you think I should have been fired!"

"No, of course not."

"You said it was a legitimate reason."

"I meant it was a reason that he could give the others in the company, without sounding like a petty fool. But you can still get another job."

"How? I lost Tim the asshole as a reference. And I belonged at Affordable. I was the anchor there. I won't fit in anywhere else."

"That's bullshit."

"Even if it is, I don't want another job where I'm at the mercy of some idiot like Dale Stephens and working with a bunch of other people who are only there because they weren't exciting enough to make it as a librarian. And what am I really working for, anyway? Not my retirement. The social security system will probably be bankrupt by the time I'm old enough to retire. My 401k savings will be worth nothing. Given the aging population in this country stock prices are going to become depressed because there will be so many retirees selling their stock. I'll probably have to work forever."

"The money doesn't belong to you. Have you lost your sense of right and wrong?"

"Oh, come on, don't be naïve. The banks are ripping off people all the time."

"You made that argument before, and it wasn't convincing." Karen said coolly.

"Maybe I'll be remembered in songs, like Bonnie and Clyde. People still know who they are, and they've been dead longer than they were alive."

"That's a hell of a thing to be famous for!" Karen exclaimed in a loud voice.

She regained her composure and sat down next to him on the couch.

"How do you think this is going to turn out?" Karen asked in a more moderate tone. "They're going to catch you, and you'll spend the best years of your life in jail. People lose their jobs everyday Rick. They pick themselves up, and brush themselves off, and find another one."

"I was doing my job, and then suddenly I'm out the door."

"So start your own business. Invent the next pet rock. Earn your fortune."

"I've heard that somewhere," Rick said with a grin. "There's too many rules and regulations to deal with when you run a business. I want to control my own destiny. I'm adapting to my current circumstances, Karen. I want to live by my wits. It makes me feel so fecund."

"Fecund? That must mean crazy. And you want to live by your wits? You told me that you couldn't even convince the guy at the unemployment office that you'd been laid off instead of being fired. It doesn't sound like you'll live too long."

"That didn't matter, because they go by whatever the company tells them. Tim didn't fuck that up for me, at least. And for your information I had a conversation with Betty this morning while pretending to be someone else. She never suspected it was me."

"You mean Betty who lives next door. The woman who once failed to recognize her husband because he walked into their apartment wearing a new pair of eyeglasses for the first time."

"I think she knew it was Ray. Betty was just joking about not knowing who he was."

"Joking? She called the cops. That sounds serious to me. I think you're the one who's joking."

"Betty didn't call the cops." *Because her husband took the phone away from her before she could.* "Anyway, I'm talking about living on the edge, not knowing what may happen day to day. I've spent years hiding out in my daily routine, taking comfort in the sameness of each day. I want to have some adventure in my life before I get old and turn into a human pill receptacle. The people at Affordable took away my livelihood on a whim, but they also gave me the means to be free for the rest of my life. Because that's where I met Binny."

"You don't really believe that you're going to pull this off," Karen said, while squeezing a pillow to relieve her frustration. "And no matter what happens, someone always gets hurt when you do the wrong thing. It's inevitable. There's no easy money. Not unless you win the lottery."

"I think my odds are better with Binny. It's a great plan. He's...."

"No! Don't tell me. I don't want to know anything about it. That way when the authorities come to question me I can deny having any knowledge of what you've done."

Karen stood up and looked down at Rick.

"Who do you think you are? John Dillinger? Do you remember how he wound up? I only hope that you come to your senses before this goes any further. You're throwing your life away. And what about us? You're ending our relationship. I can't be with you if you're running from the law. They might accuse me of being your accomplice. I'm not cut out for that kind of life."

"All you have to do, if I'm caught, is to say that I never told you anything about it. How hard is that."

"Someone always gets hurt when you do something wrong, Rick," Karen repeated. "And I'm going to be the first one. Because I care about you. And I'm really going to miss you."

"You won't have to. It's...."

"I don't want to know anything about it. There are a lot of advantages to a long-term relationship, like not having to shave your legs as often," Karen told him with a stilted smile.

"I never noticed."

"That's why I could get away with not shaving them as often."

"You should have told me, so I could have asked for some compensation," Rick responded in a flippant manner. "I should have been able to skip buying birthday cards for you. I was never any good at picking them out."

"I apologize for getting more out of our relationship than

you did," Karen answered bitterly. "The bad thing about being with someone for so long is that it hurts that much more when the time comes to leave them. You've lost your perspective. I can't play Bonnie to your Clyde, Rick. I just hope they put you and Binny in the same cell. Then you won't have to deal with Bubba. Goodbye, Clyde."

"I care about you. We can...."

Karen abruptly left the apartment in tears, slamming the door behind her. Rick almost ran after her but realized that any attempt to persuade her to adopt his point of view would be futile. A briefly awakened conscience implored him to abandon the plan, but the temptation of starting a new and very different life was too strong for it to overcome.

"I know I might wind up being brutalized in some dark prison. But this is worth the gamble. Because if Binny's plan works, I'll have the freedom to do anything, or nothing, whatever I please," Rick said to no one.

Despite his outward self-assured demeanor his inner continence was like a raging sea in the middle of a great tempest. Rick slept sporadically that night. He had strong feelings for Karen and putting their relationship in jeopardy was a very high price for him to pay for his ill-gotten wealth. Yet even that was not enough to dissuade Rick from pursuing this opportunity. Even an incredibly real nightmare about being incarcerated with Binny could not shake his resolve.

"At least they let us take our toys to prison," Rick said aloud after waking up and observing the *Dungeon and Dragons* figure on the nightstand next to his bed. "Which means I'll have Bowmarc to protect me. It's just you and me, pal."

R ick Gaines sat in a lounge chair on Seven Mile Beach. The perfectly clear turquoise waters surrounding the Cayman Islands leisurely approached the shore, as if to accentuate the unhurried pace of this paradise. Attractive women in revealing garb walked by him, their bodies seemingly sculpted from nature's most sensuous stones. More than one of them flashed a smile as they went by, which proved to be more alluring than the most irresistibly seductive song. He picked up his margarita and took a long sip. This idyllic setting had put a spell on him, and he optimistically considered this afternoon at the beach a dress rehearsal for the rest of his life.

Yet Rick knew he would soon have to reluctantly return to reality.

Oscar was also on the island. Instead of staying on a hotel near the water he had opted for a bed and breakfast in town. They were to meet here shortly, to discuss their plans for the evening. Rick kept reminding himself that his future was at stake. Having played an integral part in Binny's scheme, the former white-collar worker was putting his freedom at risk for thirteen-million-dollars.

"We can't screw up now, pal," Rick said to Bowmarc, who currently resided in the beach bag next to his lounge.

Rick closed his eyes. The gentle breeze that whispered through the palm trees had almost induced him to fall asleep when a shadow suddenly engulfed him. He looked up and saw a seaplane traversing the sky above him, its occupants most likely on their way to one of the nearby islands.

He took Bowmarc out of the bag and said, "That's the way we'll be traveling from now on."

Rick returned the warrior to his current abode and then shut his eyes once more. When the darkness returned Rick opened his eyes and saw Oscar standing there in a bathing suit. His long lean legs, having been deprived of sunlight for years, were as white as the sand he was standing on. The bookie's belly was substantial.

"You made it," the Oscar said while extending his hand.

"I sure did. Any news from Binny?"

"We're in the money, Ricky. He wired it a couple of hours ago. It should be in the casino's bank account by the end of the day."

Rick tried to control his emotions, but the idea of his being independently wealthy gave him pause. His partner recognized this and smiled at him before saying "We'll meet with Petey Bonellie tonight. He's going to treat the money like it was an investment in his place. Then he'll pay us each a very generous dividend, right away, so the whole thing looks legit."

"Do you know this guy?"

"I know some people in New York that recommended him. He's a square guy, don't worry."

"But where did we supposedly get this money?"

"We found an abandoned ship at sea. And it just so happened that the casino wanted one to bring people from Little Cayman Island and Cayman Brac Island to the casino. So they bought the ship from us and we told them to keep the proceeds in the business in exchange for stock."

"That sounds convoluted enough."

Oscar could not comprehend his response.

"It'll be hard for anyone to follow the money," Rick explained.

"Exactly!" Oscar said with a grin. "That's how you launder bucks. I don't think for a minute that we're going to get caught, but I want to have a story in case we do. That's where most people foul up. They're so confident, they forget to cover their asses."

The mention of being caught put a pall over Rick's excitement. Oscar reassured him by revealing the origin of the plan.

"My lawyer Terry Manson thought this up. It can't miss. We'll...."

Oscar's cell phone rang, and he answered it. Rick tried to remember why the name Terry Manson sounded so familiar.

"Yeah babe," Oscar said. "What? Oh, the fruit this morning. Yeah, I just can't eat that for breakfast. Because I can't, it's not natural. Cereal and eggs and all that crap is what you eat in the morning. Of course there are lizards here, we're in the tropics. Well, offer him some fruit and he'll run out of the room. I'll see you soon."

Oscar put his cell phone away and then smiled at Rick.

"That's my wife Sylvia. We're staying in town at a less expensive joint. I didn't want to lay out too much money after buying lunch the other day and then buying the plane tickets to come down here. That out of pocket stuff really adds up after a while. There are a bunch of these little lizards that keep coming in the room. Sylvia's convinced they're planning an invasion, so she's staying there to chase them away."

But we're about to get thirteen-million-dollars Rick thought incredulously. *Why are you worried about the cost of the hotel?*

"So you came down here by yourself?" Oscar asked him.

"Yes, the woman I've been seeing couldn't make it," Rick answered in a disappointed tone.

"That's too bad. But you'll see a lot of desirable babes tonight. We'll meet at the casino at seven o'clock."

"I'll be there."

Rick went back to his room to take a nap before the meeting. Sleep would not come, so he instead sat on the balcony and watched the ocean. There were wind surfers crossing back and forth across its sparkling surface. He made a note to add that activity to his list of things to do after the final steps in Binny's scheme were completed. The calypso music from the hotel lounge wafted up to his room. Rick decided to extend his stay on this island paradise.

"But first things first," he thought aloud. "We have to get the money."

Rick started tapping his fingers on the arm of the chair as he contemplated the meeting at the casino.

"There are so many things that could go wrong," he said aloud with despair. Then the first-time thief found his resolve. "Oh the hell with it. I won't get to enjoy one cent of the money if I spend all my time thinking negative thoughts."

Oscar and Rick arrived at the Mash It Up Casino precisely at seven. A man named Jorge greeted them at the door and escorted the two men to Petey Bonellie's office. As they walked through the establishment Rick observed the well-dressed customers dancing to the loud reggae music. He also glanced at the gamblers that were patronizing the slots and other gaming attractions. There was an excitement in the air, a care-free energy that would be sapped away from many of these people when they left the casino with empty wallets early the next morning. Rick noticed a slender woman alone at the bar, making a mental note to look for her on the way out.

Petey's office overlooked the gaming area. He was watching the activity below, his eyes moving back and forth across the casino floor, intently seeking any gambler who might be attempting to alter the odds in his or her favor. Oscar cleared his throat loudly to get the casino owner's attention. Petey turned and shook his hand, doing the same with Rick before directing them to a table with comfortable leather chairs.

"Your package arrived, gentlemen," the stocky casino boss said triumphantly as they sat down.

"That's good to hear," Oscar responded without the hint of excitement in his voice.

Rick was too entranced by the thought of having millions of dollars to say anything.

"So you want your money to be wired to the Reefer Bank."

"That's where we're going to park it, Petey," Oscar responded.

Rick gave Oscar a questioning look. The bank's name made it sound like a financial institution that catered to drug smugglers. He then realized that his reason for being here would put him on a par with such individuals in many people's eyes, especially those in law enforcement. His partner patted his arm to reassure him.

"So how's Frankie and Gino been?" Petey asked the bookie.

"Pretty good, but things are changing. It's tough to make ends meet in the city these days."

"They should come down here," Petey suggested with a grin. "But I think they'd miss New York food."

"At least there's a pizza place in town," Rick, who was looking for an opening to join the conversation, said.

Petey gave Oscar an exasperated look.

"Rick knows there's nothing like New York Pizza," Oscar told their host. "He was just surprised to see a pizzeria here."

Petey nodded, as Rick tried to recover from his faux pas. All three of them picked up a menu from the table and read silently. Rick chose a local dish and put his down. The other two did so in short order. Jorge came in to take their orders.

"So what will you have, sir," he asked Rick.

He was in the mood for something different, so Rick replied, "The marinated conch with herb roasted pumpkin."

Petey looked at him as though he had just disrobed before asking "What the hell is a conch?"

"It's a mollusk," Rick explained.

"I have to start paying attention to what those screwballs in the kitchen are putting on the damn menu in this joint. How long have you known this guy?" he asked Oscar.

"We go way back. Ricky is a stand-up guy, believe me."

"And what would you like, sir?" Jorge asked him.

"No doubt about it-I want the New York Strip Steak," Oscar replied.

"Now this man knows how to eat," Petey said with a grin. "Bring me one too, with extra mushrooms. You want extra, Osc?"

"You only live once, eh Petey," he replied in the same fashion.

"I have to check on my business. You guys relax and I'll be right back."

"Maybe if we stay here all night I'll eventually say something that doesn't offend him," Rick remarked in frustration.

"Don't sweat it. He's just a meat and potatoes guy," Oscar's description of their host being validated by Petey's paunch. "When he lived in New York the guy only ate at chophouses. He's also homesick."

"How do we know he won't keep our money?"

"For one thing he's getting a nice piece of change out of this. And if we get screwed we might tip off the cops. There's also Frankie and Gino. They're good friends of mine, and they can be pretty nasty. So we won't have any problems with Petey."

Their host returned with Jorge and the food. They exchanged pleasantries while eating, though Rick only spoke when spoken to. After dinner Petey offered them cigars, which Oscar accepted and his partner declined, despite the disapproving look from the casino manager. Rick quickly concluded that he had gained nothing by not accepting the cigar, since he breathed in nearly as much smoke by just sitting next to the other two as he would have by smoking one himself.

"So the minister of finance will get his cut," Petey told them. "That should keep the authorities off our backs."

"Did you find a boat?" Oscar asked him.

"Na, I can't really use one. I mean getting people from the other islands to this one would be a pain in the ass. I'll be in court for weeks the first time some drunken asshole falls off of it and drowns. But there's a wreck a little ways off the beach. If anyone wants to check out our story, I'll say that I bought the boat from you guys and then it sank in a storm."

"Sounds good, Petey. We'll be at the bank tomorrow afternoon."

"It's been a pleasure, Osc. Give everyone back home my best."

Petey enthusiastically shook his hand, and then tepidly did the same with Rick. He told them to see the cashier for some free chips before returning to his station by window. Oscar and Rick went downstairs to the casino.

"We're almost there," Oscar said. "I'll call Binny and tell him that the money's here."

"Do you want to have a drink to celebrate?"

"I'll take a rain check. I better go back to the room to make sure the lizards haven't eaten my wife."

"Did you tell the manager about them?"

"Yeah, but nothing's happened. I guess he's waiting for one of the local witch doctors to show up and put a spell on them. I'll see you tomorrow. We'll both be on easy street by the end of the day."

"That sounds good," Rick said as they shook hands. "And by the way, I changed my alias to Jesse Gleason."

"Why did you do that?"

"I just thought that it sounded better."

"That will be no problem. The guy we're meeting with tomorrow won't ask for any id."

It sounds like we're doing business with a tightly run outfit Rick thought sarcastically.

"I'll call the guy in the morning so he can change your paperwork before we get there. Have a good night, Ricky."

After Oscar left his partner went in search of the svelte woman he had seen at the bar. She was still there, tapping her foot to the lively music. He sat down on the stool next to her and ordered a drink.

"They sure like their music loud down here," Rick remarked.

"It's got to be loud, my mon, or there be no party," she replied in a surprisingly deep voice.

"My name's Jesse Gleason," he told her.

"I know."

"How do you know that?"

"You met with Mr. Petey. Don't worry. Everybody knows everyting about everybody on tis island. But nobody cares."

She told him her name was Honey Brown, pronouncing the first word as *Oney*.

"Can I get you another drink?"

"You want me to meet with *your* Mr. Petey?" Honey responded with a smile while glancing at his crotch. She then requested a stripe from the bartender. He produced an ice-cold bottle of Red Stripe beer and poured its contents into a glass.

"So what do you do back in New York?" she asked him.

"I thought you knew everything about me?"

"Now how could I know such a ting," she replied as a smile appeared on her broad lips. "I've never been to New York, my mon."

"Well, I'm kind of between jobs right now. What do you do?"

"I work at a hotel. But I live for reggae. Let's dance."

Rick accompanied the slender woman to the dance floor. Her skin was the most delicious shade of brown, and he was quickly mesmerized by the bold but graceful movements of Honey's long legs. They seemed to be getting an unusual amount of scrutiny from the others on the dance floor. Rick began to feel paranoid but managed to resist the temptation to leave.

"You're a champion!" she said after they sat down.

Rick gave her a quizzical look.

"You're a good dancer," she clarified.

"Oh. Do you know that feeling you get when you do something for the first time?" Rick asked her.

"Like making love?"

"That's always for the first time. I'm talking about doing something you'd never even thought about doing before. Rolling the dice and putting your ass on the line. I feel so alive right now, like I've become a different person."

"I do tat every night," Honey said with a laugh. "I memba the first time I saw a television," Honey continued, in an effort to respond to his musings, though they had eluded her understanding. "I thought the little people on the screen were real. I say where did they find tose tiny people?"

They laughed and then spent several hours at the bar. Rick refrained from any further remarks about his current state of mind, having realized that the words might inadvertently reveal something about the true purpose of his trip to the Caymans. They went out on the dance floor several times, each using the physical movements of the other to learn about their partner's unspoken wants and desires. The void that had been created by Karen's departure was being filled for one evening at least. Rick was very reluctant to have it end, but Honey insisted.

"My man, Oney has to put on her shows and go now," she said firmly. "I can't be late for work."

Rick realized that *shows* were shoes after she put them on.

"It was nice meeting you," he said. "How about dinner tomorrow?"

She looked at him carefully, and then put her large hand on his shoulder.

"You have it, my mon. I'll be here at six thirty."

She smiled and walked away. Rick had a few more drinks before going to his room. He watched the other people in the casino, wondering if they would believe that a fortune was waiting for him at the Reefer Bank. Rick decided they probably would not since he could not completely comprehend it either.

Oscar knocked on Rick's hotel room door before noon the next day. The largest man he had ever seen accompanied the bookie, who was dressed in a crisp new suit.

"This is Kareem," Oscar told him. "He's in charge of security."

"Security?" Rick questioned him as the dark stranger nodded at him.

"There's a lot at stake, so I want to be sure the man we're meeting with knows that you and I mean business."

Oscar and Rick, with their protector, took a cab to the bank. The brilliant afternoon sun illuminated the buildings of George Town, Grand Cayman's largest city. Every time they approached an office building Rick anticipated arriving at the financial institution that held his millions. They did not come upon it, however, until the cabbie turned off the main thoroughfare and drove down a narrow street. They stopped in front of a building that was little more than a shack, with no sign upon it.

"This is it," Oscar said. "Wait for us, will you mack?"

The cabbie nodded as Kareem struggled to get out of the cab. Rick looked at the building in amazement.

"This is the bank?"

"Yep. It doesn't have a sign, but this really is a bank."

"The only sign I'd expect to see on this dump is one that said *condemned*. I bet my gift for opening a new account is a joint," Rick said while wondering why he had worn a suit.

Oscar slapped him on the back and said "We're going to be fine, partner. People avoid coming to this part of town. We won't find a better place to keep our money. It comes highly recommended."

I don't doubt that the person who recommended it was high Rick thought to himself.

Kareem opened the door for them, and they stepped inside. There was a short counter that apparently served as the teller's area, though it had no windows. A small man dressed in shorts and a cabana shirt with bright flowers on it stepped from behind a very large desk with a low fence around it. He extended his hand.

"I'm Demery Dixon," the banker said with a smile, which suddenly disappeared after he glanced at Oscar's security man.

"I'm Steve LaSalle," Oscar told him as they shook hands. "This is Jesse Gleason."

"Have a seat, gentlemen."

Demery sat down behind his desk once more. Oscar and Rick occupied the two chairs in front of it, while Kareem stood behind them with his massive arms folded across his chest. The ramshackle building made the computer on the bank president's desk seem out of place. Rick was very surprised to see it, almost as surprised as he was that they had deposited their millions in this financial institution.

"Gentlemen. I have printed out the forms with all your pertinent information on it. You will please review them and then use my machine to create a password that only you know. You will use it to access your money."

"Do you have many depositors in this....bank?" Rick asked him.

"Yes we do, Mr. Gleason. Our clients are very secretive individuals, so I can't name any names. But your money is safe here. We are affiliated with a very well known and respected bank. But in order for it to stay that way, our relationship with that bank must be kept out of public knowledge."

"Jesse is the detail man in our operation," Oscar explained. "He always asks a lot of questions. But since Petey recommended your establishment to me, I'm sure there'll be no problems."

Kareem glared at the diminutive manager, and he almost fell out of his chair. There were three accounts set up under the Boat Guys Corporation. Oscar took the sheet with Binny's information on it. He would deliver it to him in New York. The bookie then leaned over the fence to set up a password for his nephew before creating his own.

Rick stood up and started to climb over it to do the same. Demetry put up his hand and said "No!"

"I just want to use the computer," Rick explained.

"Bank regulations forbid anyone other than myself from coming inside the barrier."

This bank has regulations? Rick silently responded. He then leaned over to reach the computer as Oscar had done. He typed his password on the keyboard. Rick chose the word *affordable,* with the idea of remembering how this money had come to be his every time he accessed the account. He also found it appropriate because there were many things in this world that had suddenly become that way for Rick Gaines.

"Would I be able to get ten thousand in cash?" he asked Demetry.

"Certainly."

He walked over to an old safe in the darkest corner of Reefer Bank. The door on it squeaked as the bank manager opened it. Demetry removed the money and handed it to Rick, who looked at the stack of bills in wonder. He mechanically signed the withdrawal slip and put the money in his pocket. After another round of handshakes they left the bank.

Oscar's cell phone rang as the cab driver drove away.

"I don't need to wear a hat Sylvia," he told her. "Yes, I know I'm bald on top, but the cab I'm sitting in isn't. We did it, babe. We're home free. I'll be there soon. Don't worry about them; we'll be back in the Bronx before you know it."

Rick paid the cab driver after they arrived at Oscar's hotel. Kareem shook Rick's hand, his menacing glare now replaced by a good-natured smile. Oscar handed him two hundred dollars while thanking the big man for his help.

"Who was that guy?" Rick asked after he had left.

"He's a cab driver from Cincinnati. Kareem's down here on vacation. I thought he'd make the man handling our money think twice about trying to play any games with us."

"That must be a very large cab," Rick remarked with a grin. "Do you want to grab a drink to celebrate?"

"I'll have to take another rain check. My wife is waiting for me. She's declared a lizard alert and needs my help. Sylvia is in the hotel room using a broom to shoo them away. Between you and me, I always knew she was a witch. Besides, we're catching an evening flight out of here, so I have to pack. It's cheaper."

"But you have millions of dollars," Rick said in an excited whisper.

"Yeah, but I'm still out of pocket for a lot of stuff."

"Let me pay for Kareem," Rick offered as he took the money out of his pocket.

"Thanks."

"Bringing him along was a great idea."

"Thanks again. Are you going to stay here long?"

"I was thinking of spending a week on the beach."

"It might be better if you go home for a while. You don't want to disappear at the same time the money did. You never know who might notice. Hang out in New York for a couple of weeks, and then tell everyone you're relocating."

So much for doing anything I want whenever I want Rick thought. Then aloud "You're right. I'll just stay for the night."

"And by the way, that... broad you were dancing with last night...she has something in her shorts that no woman should have."

"What do you mean?"

"She's a guy."

"No. No way."

"Well, I'm sure when he's in costume, in his heart of hearts, the man thinks otherwise. But Honey Brown is a transvestite."

"How did you know that we were dancing?"

"I talked to Petey this morning. He mentioned it to me."

Another mark against me!

"Everyone knows everything about everyone down here," Oscar said with a smile.

"And nobody cares."

"But I thought you might. Have a good time."

Rick went back to his room, determined to find another place to spend his money that evening. Feeling embarrassed about being taken in, he had no interest in seeing Honey. Yet as the afternoon wore on Rick began to remember the pleasant conversation and energetic dancing they had engaged in. She, or more precisely he, was exceptionally good company. Since nothing physical had occurred between them, Rick's consternation over having been fooled faded quickly.

He went to the casino and found Honey waiting for him in

the dining area. Rick greeted his dinner companion pleasantly, though it was obvious he was now aware of Honey's true gender.

"Kiss mi neck," she said with a smile.

"Well, I...." Rick tried to find an answer to the request.

"That just means I'm surprised to see you. With all the labrish about you and me I'm sure you know wat I am now. My mon, if you're ashamed to be seen with me, I will go."

"Well, no, not really. In fact, I think I'm through with worrying about what other people think. I'm just very surprised. Why do you dress up like that?"

"I feel free wen I wear tese clothes, like everything inside me is tere for all people to see. You can't be knowing what I mean, this is true. But when I'm Oney Brown, my soul can escape from my body. This is really me."

Rick smiled at her.

"Let's get a table."

"I don't know if I can sit down. I worked my backside off today."

They laughed and then sat at a table near a large window. The two of them silently watched the sun begin its descent into the sea for some time before speaking.

"I'm thinking of having the New York Strip steak," Rick said, hoping to rehabilitate his image in Petey's eyes, if he was watching. He then realized, with an inner grin, that his choice of a dinner companion would more than offset his selection of an entrée. "How about you?"

"I thought you'd be wanting some caviar after today," she responded with a knowing smile.

"How did you know about that? No, don't tell me. Everyone knows everything about everyone down here."

"And nobody cares. I think I'll have a steak, too."

Rick and Honey spent all night in the casino, tomorrow being the female impersonator's day off. They didn't dance on this occasion but did manage to go through all of Rick's money, though the now wealthy unemployed American never gave it a second thought.

The two of them walked along the beach at sunrise. They strolled past a large woman with the darkest eyes Rick had ever seen. She wore a necklace with red and black beads on it. The rising sun shone on them, creating a ring of fire around her thick neck.

The woman turned and looked at Rick, saying in an ominous tone "It is yours to lose, if you be a fool. Tere is no kama. You must make your destiny."

Rick stopped momentarily, becoming lost in her fathomless eyes. He then wrestled his gaze away from her and caught up with Honey, who had continued to walk on.

"Who was that?" he asked in an unsteady voice.

"An Obeah woman, my mon. She practice what you call voodoo, what we call guzam."

"She spoke to me."

"What did the woman say?"

"Oh...I'm not sure," Rick replied, believing that revealing too much was one way to become the fool.

"Are you a teif?"

"No, I just had some business to take care of down here," Rick replied uneasily.

"With Mr. Petey for a pardner, well I don't know. A lie? But no matter. Share mi spliff with me and you nuh watch nutten."

"What does that mean?"

"You'll ease up, relax-no worries. No freteration."

Rick took the marijuana cigarette from Honey as they sat down on the white sand. He had not smoked the substance for a long time, which greatly enhanced its effect. After each of them had taken a long drag they watched the waves approaching the shore for what seemed like the entire day. Yet the sun was barely above the horizon when his companion stood up.

"How beautiful it is to do nothing and rest afterwards," Rick said thoughtfully while trying to remember where he had heard that expression.

He arose, and Bowmarc fell out of his pocket. Honey looked at the action figure, and then smiled.

"My confidant, and friend," he sheepishly explained.

"Be careful back in New York," she said in a thoughtful tone while taking his hands in hers. "Up tere if tey know everyting about you, tey do care."

Honey bent down and picked up Bowmarc before saying "And I don't think this little mon can do nothing about it. Listen to the Obeah woman. I don't want nuthin to happen to my key."

"Key?"

"That means friend, my mon."

"I'll watch my step," he said after Honey handed him the toy. "And you do the same."

Rick went back to his room. He undressed, removing Bowmarc from his pants pocket before taking them off.

"We did it, my man," he told his companion before placing him on the nightstand.

He went into the bathroom and then disrobed after coming out.

"This" Rick declared in a loud voice while collapsing on the bed, "is me."

CHAPTER

5

Binny Jenkins walked to the Internet Café. The preoccupied computer wizard bumped into a few of the passersby along the way. Oscar had called from the Caymans, and after complaining about his travel expenses, told him that the package made it to Reefer Bank. That was the signal for his nephew to carry out the final step in the plan.

He went inside and sat down at a computer. Binny accessed the pc belonging to John Moore and quickly located the program that he had covertly installed on it. He then used it to instruct the computer to access the Elmendorf Bank computer and erase his addition to the partitioned section of the hard drive. That was to be done ten minutes after he logged off. Binny did so, and then went to the fast food place next door for a burger. When he returned the hacker confirmed that the computer had performed its task. He had to restrain himself from cheering out loud.

I'm so glad I sent that email to Lauren!

Binny had one more program to eliminate, which was the

one on Moore's machine. He was about to delete it when someone tapped him on the shoulder.

I'm a dead man, he thought before turning around. Instead of seeing an officer of the law, however, Binny found Wispy Soul standing there

"Hey you!" Wispy said with a heartfelt smile after he turned to face her.

"Hey! How are you?"

"Great. What about yourself? I mean, it was so wrong of them to fire you!"

"Well, I was a little out of line, I guess. But things are going great now. I'm doing consulting work."

"Super. Do you have time for a latte?"

"Sure. I can finish this later," said Binny, his focus suddenly shifting to Wispy.

Binny logged off the machine and accompanied his former co-worker to the counter. They sat down at a table with their beverages.

"I couldn't believe they gave Rick the boot, too," Wispy said after taking a sip from her cup. "Stephens is such an asshole. Have you heard from Rick?"

"A couple of times. He's thinking of relocating to find work. There aren't many jobs around here."

"That sucks. You know I found the most amazing new philosophy. It's called *Nada Prodigalidad,* which means waste nothing. The idea behind it is that everything in the universe has value, no matter how insignificant or even repulsive it may appear to be. Everything fascinates me now, because it all matters, Binny. We shouldn't waste even one amp of electricity, one tender feeling or one morsel of food. That's why I'm thinking of becoming a Freegan. They get their food from the dumpsters behind restaurants. It's still fresh, so it doesn't taste bad. There's no reason to let all that protein go to waste."

Binny looked into her large brown eyes and saw the truth. Wispy was dressed in a plain brown sweater and a skirt that were both showing their age. To anyone else in the café her attire would have been unremarkable, perhaps even qualifying as homeless garb to some. Yet to Binny the outfit served only to accentuate her simple, but beautiful soul.

"You're absolutely right. Why shouldn't we use all our resources. I just might go Freegan myself," Binny said with feigned enthusiasm as he imagined digesting the leftovers retrieved from a dumpster.

They talked for several hours and exchanged phone numbers before parting company. Binny went home in a state close to a stupor, dreamily contemplating his next encounter with Wispy Soul. As he lay down to sleep, the computer geek suddenly realized that the second program had not been deleted. Binny sat straight up in bed, putting his head in his hands.

"I blew it!" he almost screamed. Then after a long while Binny looked up and saw his Albert Einstein poster. The professor's image helped him regain his composure.

"There's no reason to panic. I can do it in the morning. Moore is never going to find that program anyway."

He tossed and turned all night. Binny was waiting at the Internet Café when the doors opened for business early the next morning. He quickly accessed the Pittsburgh pc, but could not locate the program. Binny spent hours looking for it before finally giving up. He called Oscar, who could not understand what his very agitated nephew was telling him. The bookie set up a meeting between the three partners in the clearing, believing that Rick would be able to decipher Binny's ramblings.

The former human resources professional had come back from the Grand Cayman Islands feeling invincible. Several calls to Karen had gone unanswered, but Rick believed this was a temporary situation. As per Oscar's advice he had told his neighbors that there was no work for him in this locale. Rick gave the landlord notice and began anticipating the beginning of a new life. Then Oscar called.

"Binny had a problem with the computer," he began the conversation.

A chill went through Rick's body. This feeling of dread, he

realized, was the price one paid for acquiring thirteen-million-dollars in an illegal fashion.

"What kind of problem?"

"I can't say for sure. I didn't really get what Binny was talking about, but that's nothing new. We have to get together."

"I'll be there."

Now he sat in the clearing, eating a roast beef hero and listening while Binny explained the problem. Rick resisted the temptation to panic when he had finished.

"Maybe you did delete the second program," he calmly suggested. "That would explain why you couldn't find it. Wispy had you so distracted that you probably don't remember doing it."

"No, I wouldn't forget that. I'm sorry, guys."

Rick could hear Karen saying *I told you so!*

"So you screwed up, Binny. You fucked up, you loused up, you hashed up..." Oscar started to run on.

"We get the point," Rick interrupted him.

"But it just means you're human," Oscar added sympathetically.

A human screw up Rick thought. Then he said aloud "so what happens if Moore comes across it?"

"I'm sure the guy won't know what it is, so the odds are, he'll do nothing. But if the bank somehow finds a way to trace our transaction back to his computer...it has the account number that we wired the money to on it."

Rick finished his sandwich and took a long drink from his can of beer, despite the mild nausea that had been brought on by Binny's description of their problem. There seemed to be only one solution, though it could result in complications, if they were caught.

"We'll have to try to get his computer," Rick said reluctantly.

"We don't need the whole computer. Just the hard drive," Binny told him.

"It'd be better to make it look like someone was robbing the house at random," Oscar pointed out. "So we should take the whole thing."

Now I know how Nixon felt Rick thought.

"I'm sorry, guys," Binny said once more.

"We all make mistakes, nephew," Oscar pointed out. "One time I…"

"We've got to come up with a plan guys," Rick interrupted him again.

"I can get into the house," Oscar told them. "But this guy Moore might have more than one computer." The bookie started to laugh and said, "Moore has more."

"You're sure you can get into the house?" Rick asked him.

"Yeah," Oscar responded in a disappointed tone. Rick and Binny didn't seem to appreciate the accidental humor in his previous statement. "But I won't know which computer to take, if this guy has more than one. So Binny will have to come with me."

"Let's do it," Rick said with a confidence he really did not possess. "Book the flight, Binny."

"Fly?" Oscar asked in a concerned tone. "Let's drive. It'll be a lot cheaper."

"And a lot slower," Rick responded. "I want to get his done."

"But I'm already out of pocket for the Caymans, the lunches…"

"Say no more," said Rick pleasantly before handing his credit card to Binny. "This one's on me."

"That's really good of you, Ricky," a relieved Oscar responded.

I like to do things for cheap people Rick mused.

They flew to Pittsburgh. Rick rented a car under his original alias and drove them to the Moore residence. Evening had fallen, and they watched as the occupants of the home went about their weekday routine. Rick noticed a sticker on one of the windows that said *Goring Alarms.*

"How are we going to get in now?" he asked in a dejected tone.

"They might not have much of a system," Oscar pointed out. "There might not even be an alarm. Some people just put the sticker on the window to make everyone think they're protected."

"If I can hack into Goring's database, I'll be able to find out what they've got," Binny told them.

"Let's find a motel," Rick said.

Binny discovered that the Moore's home was protected by Goring. There was no surveillance equipment, just a system that alerted the company if a door or window was open when the alarm was set.

Both John Moore and his wife worked, and their children attended school during the day. That was when the three thieves returned to the deserted home.

"Be quick about it," Rick, who was to be the lookout, said.

"No problem, Ricky," Oscar assured him. "Just call us on the cell phone if anyone shows up."

Binny and Oscar walked around to the back of the house. The bookie took out a glass cutter and made a large hole in the sliding patio door.

"Put these on." Oscar handed his nephew a pair of latex gloves.

"What for?"

"We don't want to leave any prints."

"Of course! You'd think I never saw a movie about burglars!"

The two men climbed through the hole. The Moore household was a very neat and orderly affair, with numerous pictures of the family hung over the living room sofa.

"I'd like to see their pictures from the Amazon," Binny said.

"Where is that?" Oscar asked him.

"In South America."

"A friend of mine went to the Amazon to get a Dean Martin CD. He must have really wanted it bad."

"I think your friend probably meant that he bought it on Amazon.com. That's an internet site where you can buy just about anything."

"No shit."

They looked around the Moore's home until finally locating John's office. Binny sat down at the computer and began typing on the keyboard.

"This isn't the machine I used," he said in a concerned tone.

"Let's check out the other rooms. There must be another computer around here."

They searched the entire house and did not find one.

"This must be the machine," Oscar said after they went back to the office to have another look at the computer.

"It's not, believe me."

"Could this be the wrong house?"

"No way."

"Let's get out of here. There's no point in looking for something that isn't here."

They left the Moore's residence. Oscar saw a baseball on the lawn and picked it up. He dropped it in front of the patio door and then used a small hammer to rough up the edges of the hole in the glass.

"They'll think some kid broke the window with his baseball," he said triumphantly.

Rick was carefully scrutinizing the quiet neighborhood around him. All the homes were silent, a sign of these times when two incomes were often necessary to support a family. He wondered what the etiquette was for a lookout. Should he drive away after alerting his partners if the police suddenly appeared, leaving it to Binny and Oscar to escape on their own? He could not deter an armed police officer, so what would his remaining at the scene accomplish? Yet they were in this together, and escaping alone seemed disloyal, no matter what the practicalities of the situation were.

Rick was thinking these thoughts when he glanced in the rearview mirror. A police car had pulled up behind him. His heart suddenly raced uncontrollably. After this moment, he would never doubt the strength of the now hyperactive organ in his chest. The officer stayed in his car for a while. Rick took out his cell phone and was about to call Binny when the law enforcement agent emerged from his cruiser. He walked up to the driver side door of the vehicle parked in front of his own.

"Good morning," he said to Rick. "Can I see your license and registration?"

Rick was paralyzed for a moment. His hand rested over Bowmarc, who was currently residing in the pocket of his pants.

Time to draw your sword, my friend.

Suddenly a being he did not know existed took control of the situation. The straight arrow he had been all his life watched as this new entity answered for him.

"Sure thing, officer," he heard someone say. "This is a rental. I can show you the agreement."

The officer was aware of that fact, having looked up the plate number with the database link in his car. He examined the license, a very impressive forgery that Oscar had acquired for his partner.

"So what brings you to Pittsburgh, Mr. Close?"

"I'm meeting with John Moore to discuss a business venture," he replied in a stress-free voice. "I'm early, which is unusual for me, so I have to wait for him to come home."

The officer carefully scrutinized Rick and found nothing out of the ordinary.

"Okay Mr. Close. I've been keeping an eye on this neighborhood lately. We've had a few break-ins. Good luck with your business."

"Thank you, officer. Have a good day."

Rick took a newspaper from the backseat and pretended to read. The policeman left, and the thief almost exploded as the tension inside him was finally released.

"I'm good at this!" he told Bowmarc.

Binny and Oscar, who had anxiously watched the scene from behind some bushes, ran to the car. Rick, who had not quite recovered from his encounter with the police officer, came close to jumping through the roof when their frantic footsteps startled him.

"Is everything all right," Oscar asked him as they got into the car.

"My life expectancy has been shortened by about thirty years, but other than that, everything's fine," Rick replied as he drove away.

"You're really cool under pressure, Ricky," Oscar complimented him.

Then why am I sitting in a puddle? He asked them "Where's the computer?"

"I don't know," Binny replied in a concerned tone. "We found one in there, but it's not the same machine."

"How could that be?" Rick questioned him.

"I don't know. But it isn't, trust me."

"They must have gotten rid of the computer you used," Rick suggested as the three of them discussed the situation after arriving at the motel.

"That's why I couldn't find the file," Binny said.

"Why would they dump the machine?" Oscar asked.

"I don't know. But I have a way to find out. I'm calling the Moore's tonight. What kind of a computer did you use, Binny?"

"A Dell 3000."

"I'll say I'm taking a survey for Dell, and I want to know if they're satisfied with their computer. Let's get the Moore's phone number."

Rick placed the call later that evening. Mrs. Moore answered the phone.

"Hello, this is Justin Pitt from Dell Computers. How are you this evening?"

"A little tired. We just got back from South America. It was a fascinating trip, but a very long one. On the first day..."

"I'm calling to see if you're satisfied with your computer," Rick, who had no intention of listening to the details of their journey, cut her off.

"Oh, well, we were, but it was John's birthday, so we bought him a new one. Now some people might say the trip was enough of a present, but that man works so hard..."

"I'm sure he does, Mrs. Moore. What did you do with the 3000?"

"We donated it. John's originally from Morgan Town, New York. He gave the machine to the elementary school there."

"Thank you, Mrs. Moore. Tell John that all the folks at Dell wish him a happy birthday."

Rick hung up the phone and looked at his fellow thieves.

"Apparently the trip to the Amazon wasn't enough of a birthday present for John Moore," Rick said in an annoyed tone. "They had to buy him a new computer too."

"The first thing they did after getting back from the Amazon was buy a new computer?" Binny asked incredulously. "I would have gotten prints made of the pictures I took. I really wanted to see them."

"Maybe the next time you break into their house the pictures will be framed and hung on the wall," Rick responded with sarcasm.

"What happened to the old machine?" Oscar asked him.

"It was donated to a school in Morgan Town, New York."

"So where does that leave us?" Oscar asked.

"Binny?" Rick looked at the techie.

"Well, I suppose they'll erase the hard drive, which would seem to mean that we're home free."

"Seem to?" Rick questioned him.

"I would think so. But we can't be positively sure that the hard drive will be erased. And if some really good programmer comes across my program, he or she might get curious about it, which would be very bad for us. That's because the program has the number of our offshore account."

Rick closed his eyes. The chances of the computer orchestrating their downfall were so remote it seemed foolish to waste the energy required to even worry about it. Yet there would always be the tiniest bit of doubt, a small but dark cloud on the horizon that would never go away.

"I don't know about you guys, but I'm the kind of person that looks both ways before crossing a one-way street," Rick told his partners. "I'd like to know that there's absolutely nothing that can link us to that bank."

"We'd be taking a big chance," Oscar warned him. "If we

get caught trying to lift the machine, they might put the whole thing together."

"I'm with Rick," Binny said. "I'd like to have peace of mind."

"Then you shouldn't have robbed a bank," said Oscar with a grin.

"If we can get to that damn thing we're home free," Rick added. "We have to take a shot at it. Let's find out where Morgan Town is."

■ ■ ■

Sara Simpson stood in front of her fourth-grade class, watching the excitement on their faces as they examined the computers donated by the alumni of Morgan Elementary School. Hers was the first classroom to be so equipped. Sara would have liked to think that her class was chosen because of her teaching prowess but knew there was another far more important factor involved in making that decision. In her mid-twenties, she was by far the youngest teacher on the Morgan Elementary staff. That, in the opinion of the man who was in charge, made Sara the logical choice, since the other teachers, as he put it, still preferred to use an abacus.

He was sitting in the room, watching with interest as the children settled in for their first lesson. Lionel King's long, thick blonde hair harkened back to a much earlier era. His secretary, Tracy Hawa, sat next to him, wearing a pink dress with purple polka dots. She had organized the program, working many extra hours with the principal to bring it to fruition.

"Okay, before we begin, let's give a nice round of applause for Principal King and Miss Hawa."

The children obliged her. Principal King maintained his usual stern countenance. Tracy smiled while unsuccessfully trying to suppress a giggle.

"Now who can tell me what the best thing about using a computer is?" Sara asked them.

The children squirmed in their seats.

"I'll give you a hint. No more papers, no more books…"

"No more teachers, dirty looks!" Buddy Myers finished her sentence.

The class erupted in laughter. Their reaction drew a stern glare from the principal. Tracy observed them with a stoic expression on her face in deference to her superior.

"Well, not quite, Buddy," Sara said pleasantly. "I'll still be here: with my dirty looks."

Sara contorted her face to create an absurd expression, which resulted in another hilarious response from her students. She knew a reprimand from her boss would likely be forthcoming but felt that hearing the sound of the children's laughter was worth it.

"We wouldn't want you to go away," Rex Thompson, a red-haired boy, told her after the laughter subsided.

"Why thank you, Rex," Sara said as she smiled at him.

The other students looked at him and rolled their eyes.

"The best thing about using a computer is we won't need pencils and paper anymore!" Sara told her students enthusiastically. "You can do your work on the computer. And as for books, well the machine in front of you contains an unlimited library. Your computer has a lot more memory than the one in the spacecraft that landed on the moon! We measure the computer's memory capacity in megabytes."

Tracy suddenly burst out laughing, to the surprise of Sara, and the chagrin of the principal.

The teacher looked at her and said "Well, I guess it does sound like something you'd buy at McDonalds."

Tracy did not respond to her remark.

"How many of you have used a computer before?" Sara continued.

Most of the children raised their hands. Sara started to walk towards the blackboard. She had been standing with her foot on the baseboard radiator and did not realize that her heel had become lodged in it. The slender young woman fell to the floor, eliciting an amused response from everyone in the room except the principal and his secretary.

Sara stood up, pulling her shoulder length brown hair back to reveal a sheepish grin. After retrieving her shoe, the young teacher instructed the children to turn on their machines. Sara then walked around the room to be sure the task was accomplished.

"Okay, everyone's up and running. Now take your mouse and move the arrow to the icon that says internet. Click on it."

The computers used by several of the children responded sluggishly to the command. Rex Thompson's machine was not one of them. Sara delayed any further instructions until everyone was logged on to the internet. Rex used this lull to explore the web. He glanced through some articles, not understanding most of the information they contained. As boredom overtook him, Rex typed the words *Miss Simpson smells* as he chuckled to himself.

He liked his teacher, and in fact had a crush on Miss Simpson. Yet the temptation to treat an adult like a peer was too great to resist. The computer suddenly displayed a strange looking screen. The words *connecting to Elmendorf Bank* were at the top of it. This was John Moore's machine. Binny's program had been activated.

Rex panicked, fearing that his disrespectful description of Miss Simpson would be discovered. He turned off the computer.

"Having trouble, Rex," Sara asked as she came up behind him.

"I...I turned it off by mistake."

"By mistake? How did you do that?"

"I hit the wrong...thing. I'm sorry, Miss Simpson."

"We'll get you going again. Just push that button."

Rex did so, and the machine came to life once more. He clicked on the internet icon.

Sara returned to the front of the room and said, "Okay children, now we're going to use the computer to find out where Morgan Town is."

■　■　■

Miles Gouveia sat at his desk, contemplating the dismissal of an Elmendorf Bank employee. As the Vice President in charge of security he was responsible for all matters relating to the safety and well being of the people who worked for the bank, and for safeguarding its considerable assets. Firing someone was not something that gave Miles pause under most circumstances. In this case, however, the individual's indiscretion had made him a hero in the eyes of many.

A man had approached his window and handed him a note. The short correspondence instructed the teller to hand over all the money in his drawer. After he read it the would-be robber gave him a glimpse of the revolver inside his jacket. Bank policy dictated that the request be honored to avoid any possible harm to the bank employees or its customers.

"I'm sorry sir," the teller had responded instead. "But I'm not authorized to comply with your demand."

The man with the gun was perplexed, having not anticipated such a response. He had been nervous throughout the encounter, which had not gone unnoticed by the teller. The doomed employee breathed a sigh of relief when the man ran out the door, only to be captured later by the authorities.

"I'm sorry son," Miles said aloud as he signed the memo ordering the dismissal of the teller. "But rules are rules."

"Good Morning," Tom Becker, his assistant, said as he walked in.

"Same to you. What's going on?"

"You're not going to believe this, but the fed thinks we owe them fifty-million-dollars."

"Why?"

"They're claiming that we took an overnight loan for that amount on Tuesday."

"And we don't agree?"

"There's no record of it on our side."

"Those guys deal with so much boodle it's a wonder they don't lose track of it more often. Stay on top of it and let me know what happens."

"Will do. I'll see you later."

Miles spent the day at a suburban branch which had been the target of an overnight robbery attempt. The security system had detected the activity and alerted the authorities.

"That's a hell of a set up you've got here," one of the detectives told him.

"It can detect a flea coming through the air conditioning vent," Miles said proudly. "And it should be able to, given what we paid for it."

"It sure makes our lives a lot easier."

"Mine too."

Miles was sitting in his office the next morning when Tom appeared once more.

"I have an update on the fifty million."

"When you don't say good morning, I know we've got a problem. Have a seat."

"The fed is sticking to their story," he said after occupying the chair in front of Mile's desk. "Our people have looked at every transaction from that day. They just don't see it."

"What do you think?"

"I'm beginning to wonder if one of our employees made a withdrawal."

The VP looked at his assistant with a stern expression on his face.

"How could someone do that without leaving a trace?"

"Maybe they manipulated the computer's operating system."

Miles stood up and walked over to the window. He watched the pedestrians walking by below, realizing that anyone of them could be planning to compromise the bank's security. At moments like this he felt as though everyone in the world was his enemy. Miles turned and faced his subordinate.

"I recently convinced the board of directors to spend ten-million-dollars to upgrade our security system, which included beefing up our cyber safeguards. I cannot go to them now and say someone compromised the computer system. Are we clear on that?"

Tom nodded, though he wondered what other option Miles would have, should it turn out that the money was pilfered through the computer.

"Get them to go through everything again. I want an answer, damn it!"

Tom stormed into Mile's office a day later. The security head was in the middle of a phone call and was not pleased that he had to interrupt it.

"Someone tried to hack into the system!" Tom exclaimed while ignoring Mile's glare.

"What!"

"They were trying to copy the backup copy of our software. Gary, our head programmer, thinks they were going to use it to steal from us."

"Did our system detect it?" Miles asked, hoping that the new security measures had been effective.

"Well, no, actually. Gary just happened to be setting up a test for a new program. He uses the partitioned part of the hard drive for that. That's where the hacker was going to put the software he or she copied. Gary could see the hard drive being accessed by someone on the outside."

"So if he wasn't doing that..."

"They might have gotten away with it. This could be why the fifty million is missing."

"Did he get any information about these bastards?"

"They ended the communication. Maybe they realized that we were on to them. But he did manage to get their Wi-Fi information. He's finding out who they are right now. I guess we have to call the FBI."

"Close the door."

Tom did so.

"I've got ten years of my life invested in this institution," Miles said solemnly. "I'm not going to lose my job, and my career, over this if I can help it. If we go through official channels the board of directors will have to be informed right away. I'm going to go another route. Let me know when you find out who these pricks are."

"You're taking a big chance, Miles."

"And you're going to obey my orders. Dismissed. Close the door on your way out."

Miles picked up the phone and dialed. His friend Dan Gartner answered after several rings.

"Howdy Miles. Ready to do some fishing next week?"

"Well, actually, I'm going to have to cancel my vacation, Dan. We have a crisis at the bank. It looks like someone stole fifty-million-dollars from us."

"That's a lot of greenbacks. Do you know who did it?"

"We've got a lead. I'm hoping we can resolve this pretty quickly."

"Well, the bureau is usually pretty good at finding these people. I'll make a call and ask my fellow employees there to look into it if you'd like. You might even get to go on your vacation after all."

"Well, the thing of it is, I don't want to involve the bureau just yet," Miles replied while leaning back and clasping his hands behind his hairless head. "I was the one who pushed for the new security system. And if I have to tell the directors that it failed…"

There was only silence in response.

"Are you still there, Dan?"

"Yes I am. As a former FBI agent, you know what needs to be done. You have to call the bureau."

"We both know that even if you guys find out where the money went, it won't be there now. I'm just hoping that if we find the people who did this, they'll give the money back. Then neither the FBI, nor the board of directors, will have to get involved."

"And if you don't find them?"

"That's negative thinking. Since our trip is off, maybe you could help me out with this. In an unofficial capacity, of course."

After another long period of silence Dan answered.

"I guess I could, since my vacation has been ruined too. I mean who wants to go fishing alone."

Tom knocked on the door, and Miles gave him permission to enter after putting his friend on hold. He told his superior where the attempt to copy the bank's software had originated from. Miles thanked him and sent his assistant away.

"So what do we have to do first, partner?" Dan asked after Miles had picked up the phone again.

"We have to find out where Morgan Town is."

The three bank robbers drove from Long Island to Morgan Town, arriving there several hours after darkness had fallen. This picturesque New York Hamlet was built upon rolling hills that were a child's delight in winter, the terrain being ideally suited for riding a sled. At this time of year the landscape was transformed into a myriad colored painter's palette, with the tree's autumn leaves providing its striking colors. The occupants of the bookie's sedan saw none of this, however. Night had stifled the breathtaking canvas while hiding the land's swells. This was no loss to the men in the car, because they would not have been interested in observing them in any case. Their only reason for coming to this place was to cover up a crime.

"Turn left at this corner," Binny, who was getting the directions to the school from his iPhone, told Rick.

Morgan Elementary was in the heart of residential Morgan Town. There were some scattered security lights around the red brick building, but for the most part this quiet, uneventful neighborhood had made the authorities somewhat complacent about the school's security. Rick slowly drove into the parking lot after dousing the headlights.

"They must have an alarm," Oscar said. "How the hell are we going to get in there?"

"I could try to find out what security they have by hacking into the school's computer," Binny suggested. "It might take a while, though."

Rick got out of the car. He walked around the parking lot, searching the school's windows and doors for a weakness. He identified several but realized that the virtually certain presence of an electronic sentry made his effort academic. Then Rick looked up, and a smile suddenly appeared on his face. He got back into the car.

"We'll go in through the air vent on the roof," he said.

"What about the alarm?" Binny asked.

"I don't think it will be connected to the alarm."

"Well, I'm game, but I'm not much of a climber," Oscar said.

"You can be the look out," Rick told him. "Do you know how to text?"

"What's that?" Oscar asked.

"Instead of calling someone, you type a message and send it with your cell phone," Binny explained.

"What will they think of next," Oscar remarked. "Why can't I just call you if somebody shows up?"

"Because they might hear us talking," Rick told him.

"I can set up the phone to send a text. Then all you'll have to do is press the send button," Binny told his uncle.

"I'll get our *ladder* ready," Rick said.

He got out of the car and quietly moved the dumpster up against the school building. Rick then grabbed a small picnic table from the playground and put it on top of the waste receptacle. Binny joined him shortly after.

"Does Oscar know what he's doing?" Rick asked.

"I set it up to send a message that says *trouble*. Uncle Oscar just has to push a button to send it. The only question now is do you know how to get into the school through the air vent."

"I've had previous experience. I broke into my elementary school as a kid. Which, come to think of it, made no sense at all. It was the one place I always hated to be, yet I wasted a whole Saturday afternoon getting in there."

"It might turn out to be worth it now. Are you sure about the alarm?"

"As sure as I am about anything. The school I broke into all those years ago didn't have their alarm connected to the air vent. And while it's been a long time, I just have a feeling that things haven't changed all that much. Sometimes you have to follow your instincts."

"Wispy would agree."

Great, now I'm thinking like a woman who walks around in a toga. But I want to get this over with, so here goes nothing. Or everything.

Rick easily pulled himself onto the roof. Binny was anything but athletic, but with his partner's help he made the climb. Rick quietly removed the cowling on the vent, and the two of them crawled through the air duct. The narrow air passage was just barely wide enough for them, and Rick worried about his partner getting stuck in it. They reached a vent in the auditorium's ceiling, and squeezed through it, each executing a clumsy landing on the stage there. Rick stood on a table to put the vent's cover back in place. After reaching the hallway Rick and Binny peered into every classroom they came upon. There were no computers in any of them.

"This must be the wrong school," Binny said dejectedly.

"The lady didn't lie to us. Let's keep looking. We'll find it."

"I hope we find a bathroom, too."

"I'll get you a lavatory pass," Rick said with a grin.

After a fruitless search of two more corridors Rick began to have his doubts. Then they came upon classroom number thirty-four. Binny peered through the window on the wooden door and pumped his fist in the air.

"There she blows!"

"The door's locked," Rick said with concern after trying to open it.

"Not a problem."

Binny took out his wallet, removing a slender screwdriver from inside it. He inserted it into the lock and opened the door. They stepped inside.

The techie took a small flashlight from his pocket, and examined the machines being used by Miss Simpson's class. He knew the brand name of the one that had provided them with access to the bank's computer. On that basis the hacker narrowed his search down to five possibilities. He sat down in front of the first one and turned it on. The screwdriver in his wallet began to dig into his thigh, so he took out his billfold and placed it on the computer.

■ ■ ■

Oscar waited for his companions to emerge from the school. He had parked a half block away from the building, in a spot that gave him an all-encompassing view of the area around it. There was no activity to be seen there, and as the time passed his mind began to wander. He suddenly remembered that one of his biggest clients had not yet placed a bet on the upcoming weekend's football games. The bookie hit several keys on the cell phone in his hand before reaching the main screen. He then dialed the client's number.

"Vic. Oscar here. How are things?"

"Not bad. The wife and I went to the Coppa Cabana tonight. I danced like a fool. I'm lying on the couch in front of the tube now trying to recover from it."

"You interested in Raiders versus Forty Niners?"

"What's the juice?

"Raiders by six."

"Oh, I don't know. That sounds steep, especially since I got my ass kicked on Monday Night. What do you think?"

"Healy hasn't got it anymore. So Oakland won't do shit."

"What's the matter with him?"

"The lucky suit he always wore to the stadium on game day got ruined by the cleaners. The man has no confidence now. Oakland's quarterback is going to be a basket case for the rest of the season."

"Where do you hear this stuff, Oscar?"

"I know people who know people. I just wanted you to know about it, too."

"Put me down for a grand. Just make sure the bastard doesn't get cured by one of those high-priced psychiatrists before the game."

"Will do. I'll talk to you Friday."

He ended the call just as a police car with two civilian vehicles behind it drove into the school parking lot. Oscar looked at the phone in his hand, searching for the message intended for Binny, but it was no longer displaying the text screen. The bookie slapped his forehead and then watched helplessly as the occupants of the automobiles ran into the school.

"I fucked up," he mumbled to himself.

■ ■ ■

Binny had three more computers to examine. He began to type a command into one of them when the cars arrived. They could see them through the windows that comprised the parking lot side of the classroom. Rick motioned for him to turn off his flashlight and the pc just as they heard footsteps coming towards Miss Simpson's classroom.

Rick and Binny ran to the emergency escape window. The hacker awkwardly climbed out first, and his accomplice began to follow. Rick had one leg through the window when he suddenly hesitated.

"Your wallet," he said in a whisper. "I saw you put it on the computer. Did you take it with you?"

Binny, who was now standing outside, ominously shook his head.

"Give me the flashlight."

Rick searched for the wallet. The modest beam of light was barely powerful enough to illuminate the area where Binny had been working, but it was enough to reveal the hacker's billfold. Rick ran over and picked it up, just as two policemen approached the door. He lip-synced the words *run away* to Binny just before entering the coat closet. The classroom door opened slowly, and then the lights were turned on.

"I told you there'd be no one here," Officer Tommy Oslifer said with relief as he holstered his pistol.

"You can't be too careful," his brother, Officer Larry Oslifer replied. "Remind me to chew out Sara for not locking the door."

At least they didn't notice that we broke in Rick thought to himself.

"We're all clear in here fellas," Larry told the group waiting in the hall.

Miles Gouveia walked into the room, accompanied by several members of his staff. Lionel King walked through the door next. They looked around the classroom and saw nothing amiss.

"One of these machines contacted our bank's computer," Miles told Principal King.

"With all do respect, Mr. Gouveia, that doesn't seem plausible," he responded.

"Where did you get these machines?"

"They were donated to us. I'll have to find who the donors were later in the morning, since the people who possess that information are probably sleeping right now, just like I was," King said in an irritated tone. He had been awoken by the police at the behest of Gouveia.

"We'll wait."

"Perhaps you'd be more comfortable in my office. I know I would be."

"Thank you, Principal King."

"We'll stay here to make sure nothing happens," Larry said.

"Good idea, Officer Oslifer," King said. "I'll have my secretary make some coffee for us as soon as she comes in."

Rick remained in the closet, wondering how he would ever

make his escape. The two officers discussed the implications of what was the first major crime in Morgan Town that either of them could remember.

"So those guys from the bank are saying that someone tried to rip them off using one of these machines. Who in this town would try something like that?" Tommy wondered.

"I don't know. It couldn't have been one of the kids, could it?"

"Maybe someone tricked one of them into doing it."

"It could have been one of the teachers," Larry suggested. "I know we're getting way ahead of ourselves, brother. But.... well, this is Sara Simpson's class. She might know something about it."

"No, not Sara."

"We have to think about all the possibilities," Larry said with gravitas as he sat down in the teacher's chair.

Tommy tried to squeeze his abdominous body into a student's desk, abandoning the attempt when his internal organs began to vehemently object. The two officers were silent for the next hour. Larry was trying to solve the mystery, while Tommy was anxiously waiting for the school cafeteria to open.

"I'll get us some doughnuts," he said with relief after sixty minutes had finally passed, an interminable period for the officer's palate to wait.

"Those things will kill you," Larry, who was in excellent physical condition, warned him.

Rick thought about trying to escape. He could not see the remaining police officer but dodging one of them was certainly preferable to evading the pair. The novice criminal began to slowly open the closet door, just as Sara Simpson walked into the room.

"Larry. What are you doing here?" she asked pleasantly.

"Hi Sara. You're not going to believe it, but someone tried to rob a bank with one of these computers."

"What? When?"

"Yesterday. There's a Mr. Gouveia here from the Elmendorf Bank. He's in Principal King's office right now."

"Do they know who did it?"

"I don't think so. But it could be terrorist related."

An hour later the children entered the classroom en masse, their high-pitched voices suddenly falling silent when they saw Officer Oslifer.

"Put your coats away and take your seats," Sara instructed them.

Rick had postponed his dash for freedom when the teacher entered the room. Now the students were approaching his refuge. He could hear Karen saying I told you so once again and envisioned the stern-faced judge who would pass sentence on the former human resource director. Then Rick noticed a blanket on the shelf next to him and used it to cover himself. The children, distracted by the presence of the policeman, failed to notice the large lump on the closet floor.

"Miss Simpson," Lionel King said as he walked into the classroom, his presence eliciting absolute silence from the students. "We seem to have had an incident here two days ago. I'm told that something very unusual occurred on one of these computers." He looked at the children and asked, "Do any of you remember seeing something strange on your computer's screen?"

The principal, and the bank vice president who was standing behind him, anxiously waited for one of the students to speak. Sara, however, knew her students well enough to detect a non-verbal response. The ones who had nothing to tell would immediately look around the room, trying to find a classmate that did. Any child that knew something about the incident would look down, hoping to avoid the principal's scrutiny. Rex Thompson was the only one who did so.

"Rex, didn't you tell me that there was something funny on your computer screen the other day?" Sara asked him.

The red haired, freckled faced boy had never made that statement, but by saying that Sara gave Rex an opportunity to voluntarily provide the principal with the information he desired.

"Well, there was a lot of writing that I didn't understand," Rex said hesitantly. "And I didn't see it on anyone else's computer."

Gouveia walked over to his desk. The young boy felt intimidated by the bald stranger.

"So this is the machine that contacted our bank," he said.

The closet door had been left slightly ajar by the students. Rick could see where Rex was sitting. Now he knew where the computer containing Binny's program was.

"Did you understand any of the words, son?" Gouveia asked in a kind, but firm tone.

"I think Rex already answered that question," Sara answered for him as she walked over to protect her student. "You might be expecting just a little bit much from him. We just started using the computers."

She gave Rex a reassuring pat on the back.

"Hi Principal King," Tommy said when he returned with the doughnuts.

"You make a very convincing stereotype, Officer Oslifer," the principal said sarcastically. Then to Sara "This is Mr. Gouveia. He's with the Elmendorf Bank."

` "It's nice to meet you." Sara shook his hand.

"Same here. Several of the bank's computer people will be here shortly. They'll want to examine that machine."

"My class goes to the gym at eleven o'clock and then to lunch right after it. Your people can have the room to themselves for a couple of hours."

"That's perfect. Thank you, Miss Simpson."

"I have to interview an applicant for the custodian's position," King said to Gouveia. "I'll see you when I'm through."

Sara followed the two men into the hall.

"Principal King, could you ask the policemen to wait outside? It's very distracting to have them in the room when I'm teaching a lesson."

"Do you have command of your students, Miss Simpson?" King asked in a stern tone.

"Under normal circumstances, yes. But this has been a very unusual day."

"I suppose you're right. Having to watch Tommy Oslifer eating his doughnuts would be a sore trial for anyone, especially a child. Don't use the computer that contacted the bank."

Sarah returned to the classroom and began her lesson. The students were instructed to start up the machines. The girl sitting next to Rex was asked to share the one she was using with him. This was not to the liking of either child.

"Miss Simpson, Sissy won't let me touch the keyboard," Rex complained.

"He just wiped his nose with his hand, Miss Simpson. It's disgusting."

"Go wash your hands, Rex. And the next time use a tissue."

What a fun job that woman has, Rick said to himself.

The light coming through the partially opened door shone on the blanket, or more precisely quilt, that had hidden him from the children. His means of escaping detection consisted of many small, square pieces of fabric with writing on each of them. Rick began to read the words.

The Pacific Ocean is the deepest ocean in the world was written on one square.

I didn't know that, Rick thought to himself.

After Rex returned from the boy's room Sara instructed the children to key in the words *Mount Everest* on their computer. A picture of the forbidding peak appeared on their screens.

"This is the tallest mountain in the world," Sara told her class. "It's so high that the people who climb Mount Everest have to take oxygen with them. There's not enough of it at the top of the mountain for the explorers to breath."

The children stared at the picture in awe.

"I'm never going there," a boy named Rusty said adamantly.

Smart kid Rick thought with a smile.

Sara continued the lesson, which ended with her students finding Nepal on a map of the world. She then asked if there were any questions.

"If I'm never going to that mountain with no air, why do I have to know where Nepal is?" Rusty asked after being called upon.

"Can anyone answer his question?" Sara asked the rest of the class.

"Because we are citizens of the world, and we should know about all the places in it," Darlene Yeats volunteered.

She must be the class brain, Rick observed. *I always hated those kids.*

"Very good, Darlene. Today we learned that Mount Everest, or as some would call it the mountain with no air (she smiled at Rusty), is the tallest mountain on earth. We'll put that fact on our learning quilt."

Rick suddenly felt like a trapped animal. There was nothing else in the small coat closet to hide him. His was to be the shortest criminal career in history.

I wonder if they'll put that on the quilt, too he thought.

Rick took Bowmarc from his pocket, wistfully thinking that the stoic figure would defend him with his axe and sword.

It's up to you, pal.

"But first, it's time for the gym," Sara told her students. "And you'll be going to the cafeteria right after it, so bring your lunch with you."

Thank god for physical education, Rick thought gratefully.

He was about to take his leave after Sara and the children had gone, only to be stopped by the arrival of the bank computer technicians. Rick watched anxiously as they examined the computer donated by the Moores.

"There's a program on here I'm not familiar with," one of them said.

"It must be the one that contacted our operating system two days ago."

"And before that, too, only we didn't detect that incident."

"Right. Gouveia wants us to leave the machine intact, in case they try to run the program again. If they do we might be able to find out where they are."

"Okay."

They completed their task and left the classroom. Rick was about to do the same when Sara and the children returned. Later, as the children prepared to end the school day, Tommy Oslifer came into the room.

"Eh, Sara, we have to go now. We're late for work."

"Oh, right, you two have more than one job."

"Clay and Josh, the guys who are supposed to relieve us, haven't shown up yet. They went to the high school by mistake. Do you think you'll be all right without any police protection for a couple of minutes?"

"I haven't seen any desperate characters around here. I'll lock the door when we leave."

"Thanks."

The children retrieved their coats, once again failing to notice the quilt on the closet floor. Then they filed out of the room and lined up in the hall, with Sara right behind them.

Now's my chance the intruder decided.

The class began to walk towards the school exit. Rick silently stepped out of the closet. He was about to grab the computer that had robbed Elmendorf Bank when the sound of hurried footsteps coming down the hall reached his ears. Rick left the machine where it was and made a break for the classroom door.

Sara had neglected to lock it and was moving quickly down the hall to remedy her omission. Just before reaching room thirty-four she turned her head to say hello to a student emerging from the door of another classroom. Sara did not see Rick coming out of her classroom, and she ran into him. The slight Sara Simpson bounced off the thief, landing on the floor in a heap. The children were accustomed to seeing her in that position and responded with their customary laughter.

"Are you all right?" Rick asked, trying to act as though he belonged there.

"I'm fine. Are you okay?" she asked as he helped her up.

"You took quite a tumble."

"That's nothing new for me," she answered with a self-deprecating grin. "Can I help you with something?"

"Well, yes, I'm...here about the custodial position." Then to himself: *I am good at this.*

"Do you have an appointment with Principal King?"

"Oh, no, I just heard about the opening."

"The administrative offices are down the hall. You should see Tracy Hawa. She's Principal King's secretary. Good luck."

"You be careful now."

"I've been doing that for years," Sara answered with a smile. "And I still wind up on the floor."

Sara tried to lock the classroom door, but the damage caused by Binny's screwdriver made that impossible. She left it unlocked and escorted her students to the school exit.

Rick walked to the administrative offices, thinking about what he would say to the principal's secretary. As his intention was to get out of the building as quickly as possible, Rick had meant to leave without inquiring about the job, but Sara was standing nearby chatting with another teacher. Her suspicions might be raised if he did not take the time to see the secretary.

Rick went in and was directed to the principal's office. Tracy was sitting at her desk outside King's door.

"Can I help you?"

"My name is Jesse Gleason. I'm here to apply for the custodian's job."

"Did you submit an application?"

"Well, no, I just heard about it yesterday."

"Let me get you one."

Tracy stood up, and Rick had to force himself not to stare at her outfit. She wore a short black sequenced skirt with an orange top that had yellow butterflies on it. The secretary's large eyes had a generous amount of eye shadow around them.

She's either late for Halloween or early for Mardi Gras.

Tracy handed him the application and said "here you go. And you're in luck. The applicant who was supposed to meet with Principal King…well you're not going to believe this…he never showed up."

She laughed hysterically while Rick politely smiled and thought *she sounds like a deranged hyena.*

"I'll see if he's available now."

Tracy left the room while the applicant scrutinized her outfit one more time.

Thirty minutes later Rick found himself sitting in the Principal's office for the first time in thirty years. Lionel King sat at his desk, exhibiting his customary stern expression as he assessed Jesse Gleason. The applicant reciprocated, exhibiting an appropriately serious expression on his face. King's thick blonde mane was his most distinctive feature. At first Rick thought it was a wig, but then concluded that nature had bestowed it on the man's head.

"So you haven't filled out the application. Normally I would be irritated by this deviance from customary procedure. But I'll assume that your technical expertise is up to speed, for the moment. There's a larger issue here, Mr. Gleason. Do you know what it is?"

"Well, honestly no, Mr. King."

"That's *Principal* King, sir." He stood up and walked over to the window, observing a group of children on the playground before continuing.

"We must never, never forget our obligation to the boys and girls that attend Morgan Elementary School. The staff here, no matter what their function may be, holds not only the minds, but the hearts and souls of these young people under their sway. This country must revive its Puritan work ethic. Morgan Elementary, and the other schools in this great nation, will begin its resurrection. We must be a hard working, frugal people. Never spend money if you don't have to. That's why I decided to use donated machines instead of buying new ones."

I'm so glad you did. We never would have met if you weren't so cheap.

"I ask you Mr. Gleason, can you accept that responsibility?

Are you as good a human being as you are a custodian? If not, you could be the most proficient person on the face of this good earth at unclogging toilets and removing bubble gum from the underside of a desk, and still be unqualified for this position. How say you, sir?"

Principal King delivered those words with such fervor that Rick suddenly felt like he was about to join a religious cult. Had he answered the question honestly, the response would have been no, not at this juncture of his life. Rick, however, had one goal in mind: gaining access to the computer.

"I can live up to that responsibility, Principal King. I can do the work and have a positive influence on the students." *Should I say so help me God?*

King turned and looked at him intensely. Then he nodded and said "I believe you can, Mr. Gleason. Fill out the form. If everything checks out, you'll have a job."

Rick shook his hand and returned to the reception area. Tracy smiled at him.

"How did it go?" she asked.

"Pretty well, I think. I'm going to fill out the form and return it tomorrow," he told her.

"Good. If you get the job, I'm going to call you Lucky. The guy didn't show up to see Principal King. Can you imagine that?!"

The secretary laughed hysterically once more. Rick wondered about the mental stability of this woman and hoped he would not have to spend too much time with her.

He walked into the hall and encountered Sara again, though without any physical contact on this occasion.

"Did you see Tracy?" she asked him.

"Yes. She sure likes to laugh."

"Between you and me, I refer to her as Lady Ha Ha," Sara said with a short chuckle of her own. "But not to her face, of course. If I ever become a standup comic, I want Tracy in the audience."

Rick laughed and then said "I interviewed for the job. If they like what they hear from my references, I've got it."

"I'm impressed. Principal King can be a little overbearing."

"Just a tad," Rick said with a smile. "My name is Jesse Gleason."

"Sara Simpson." She shook his hand. "Are you from around here? If you say yes, I'll faint. I didn't think there was anyone in this town that I didn't know."

"I'm from Schenectady."

"I'll bet you're looking for a place to stay. I saw a house for rent advertised in the *Town Crier*. Let me rip out the ad for you."

Sara had an armful of papers which were soon on the floor, the result of her efforts to locate the *Crier*. After Rick helped her pick them up, she found the ad and tore it out for him.

"I'm surprised that the Gutners are renting their house," Sara said. "They don't seem like the type that would want strangers in their home. The house is on Street Street."

"Street Street? Did they run out of names here?"

"Actually, it was called Henry Street. But during a storm one half of the street sign blew away, leaving only the word *Street*. People started calling it Street Street, and the town council eventually decided to officially rename it."

"I guess that was the practical thing to do. It saved them the cost of a new sign."

"Exactly. I'll see you around, hopefully."

"Thanks for your help."

Rick walked past the classroom again, observing the policemen who had arrived to stand guard over the computer. He then left the building and paused to gather himself. What could have been a disastrous episode had turned out to be a beneficial one. He now knew which computer had Binny's program on it, even if there seemed to be no way to reach it at that moment. Rick looked around and spotted his fellow thieves in the car, a block away from the school.

"I fucked up, Binny," Oscar lamented to his nephew for the umpteenth time.

"I know, Uncle Oscar, but it'll be all right. I'm sure Rick will find a way out."

"Do you know how much it will cost for his lawyer? We'll have to help pay for it. And I've already got a lot of out of pocket expenses for this scam, Binny. Not to mention what our own lawyers will cost if he squeals. I messed up Binny."

"We all took a chance," his nephew, who was on the verge of madness due to his uncle's constant repetition, said in an exasperated tone.

The back door opened and both men froze, expecting to hear a policemen's voice telling them to surrender.

"Well, that was interesting," Rick said.

"Hey, you made it!" Binny exclaimed.

"I'm so sorry, Ricky. I screwed up! I loused up! I muffed it!"

Binny was about to slap his uncle, but Rick put an end to his apologies before he could.

"It's no problem, Oscar. In fact, my being stuck in there may have done us some good. I know which machine has the program on it. Unfortunately, the people from the bank do too."

"We'll break in again and grab it," Binny said.

"There are cops watching the classroom," Rick informed him.

"I can't believe they found the machine," Binny said despondently. "When I copied the bank's software onto the partitioned part of their hard drive they must have detected it."

"Actually, according to what one of the techies said, the computer contacted the bank again two days ago," Rick told him.

"What! How did that happen?" Binny asked incredulously.

"I don't know. But that's what he said. Apparently, they didn't notice what your program was doing the first time Moore's computer contacted the bank. But when it contacted Elmendorf Bank a couple of days ago, the computer people did notice."

"We're so screwed," Oscar said dejectedly.

Rick took out the application from his pocket and looked at it carefully.

"What's that?" Binny asked him.

"Believe it or not, I had an interview for a custodian job

at the school. A teacher caught me trying to sneak out of the building and I told her I was there to see about the position."

"That's it! You take the job, and you'll be able to get to the machine," Binny said triumphantly.

"There're just a few problems with that idea," Rick replied. "In the first place, they want references."

"We'll make them up."

"But what if they contact them."

"I'll just go online and get into the database of some schools. I'll make up a history for you. It's easy. How do you think I got the job at Affordable."

"You little cheat," Rick said with a laugh.

"I'll make all the school references old ones, so the people there will have to check the database instead of relying on memory."

"What about recent history?"

"Oscar can give you a reference. You've been working for him for the last six years."

"I don't think they'll hire a bookie's assistant," Oscar pointed out.

"I'm not talking about your real business. We'll make one up."

"Could it be a restaurant? I always wanted to own a restaurant."

"You got it, Uncle Oscar." Binny said as he patted him on the back. "We'll give them your cell phone number, which has a different area code. They'll think they're talking to someone on Long Island."

"What about doing the job? I'm no good at fixing things," Rick said.

"It won't matter. By the time they figure out you're incompetent, we'll either be out of here or in jail," Binny pointed out. "But I'm sure it will be the former instead of the later. Because you're stumbling onto this job has to be because of karma! We can't lose."

Who's Carman? Oscar thought to himself.

"I wish I could believe that," Rick said with a thoughtful expression on his face.

"We should find a place to stay," Oscar said. "There must be a hotel around here."

"The teacher gave me a listing for a house that's for rent. Living there would make my story seem more plausible. The only thing is I don't have much cash. And I can't use my credit cards, because they've got my real name on them. I also can't get a cash advance off them either, because I used up the available balance in the Caymans."

"What about the Reefer Bank money?" Binny questioned him.

"I don't think we should access that until we get rid of the hard drive," answered Rick.

"You're right," Binny concurred. "I don't have much cash either, and I've never had a credit card."

"Well, I guess it's up to me. I don't want to use my credit cards around here either. But Sylvia can bring some cash up here for me. Of course this means I'll be out of pocket again."

"It's for thirteen-million-dollars each, Oscar," Rick reminded him.

"I'll give her a call. I saw a greyhound bus stop when we drove through town. She can take the bus here."

"A plane would be faster," Rick said.

"Yeah, but it's so expensive."

Rick was about to suggest paying for the airline ticket from his share of the bank's money, but then thought better of it. Oscar was determined to remain frugal, and his partner sensed that even if he had billions of dollars instead of mere millions, this would always be the case.

"I'll need a fake driver's license with the name Jesse Gleason on it," Rick said.

"No sweat," Oscar said confidently. "I'll call my friend Marty and have him make one up. He can give it to my wife before she leaves. I'll have to pay him for it, of course."

"Did you know that Garfield died from an infection, not a gunshot wound," Rick asked them.

"You mean the cat?" Oscar asked him.

"No, President Garfield."

"What made you think of that?" Binny inquired.

"I hid in the coat closet for most of the day. I used a blanket to cover myself up when the kids went into it to hang up their jackets. It had all kinds of facts on it. That was one of them. It actually would have been an interesting experience if I wasn't shitting my pants the whole time."

"You learn something new everyday," Binny observed.

"Now let's learn where the nearest hotel is. I need a shower," Rick suggested. "This belongs to you, I believe."

He handed Binny his wallet.

"Thanks. I was wondering if I'd ever see it again."

"It's a little light. I had to bribe a hall monitor to let me leave the building," Rick said facetiously.

"Give a kid a badge...." said Binny with a laugh. "But it's money well spent."

They pooled their remaining funds to rent a hotel room for the night. Oscar raised a minor objection to this expenditure but was the first to fall asleep on one of the large double beds in the room. Binny created Jesse Gleason's past as Rick watched a basketball game. The computer maestro then used the hotel's fax machine to send the application with the fabricated references to the school the next morning. Rick was offered the job, and he accepted. The principal never called Oscar for a reference, but he did request a copy of Rick's driver's license, which the new employee was able to provide on his first day of work.

"Report to Henry Pabst at six o'clock Monday morning," Principal King told him over the phone. "And remember, you're now a member of an institution that is charged with shaping the young minds that will determine the future of this great country."

"Yes sir," Rick replied enthusiastically before hanging up, feeling as though he had just volunteered to save the world.

I wonder if he's that demanding of the cafeteria ladies.

"I'm in," he told Oscar and Binny.

"Good. Now let's go pick up Sylvia."

They drove to the bus terminal. Sylvia arrived on time, but with an exasperated air about her. She still managed a smile for Binny. The bookie's wife also had one for Rick, after being introduced to him. Oscar and Sylvia sat in the front of the car while Rick joined Binny in the back. She was in front of the janitor, her antiquated beehive hairdo making it impossible for him to see out the front window.

I guess she believes that style will come back one day. I think it'd have a better chance of being revived if people didn't have to look at it, though.

"I'm famished!" Sylvia informed the other occupants of the car. "Do you believe they didn't serve any food on the bus?"

"How are they going to serve food on a bus?" Oscar asked her. "The only one who could do it is the bus driver, and he's too busy driving. It would have taken you three years to get here if he had to stop every time someone wanted a sandwich."

"They should take out one of the seats and put in a vending machine with sandwiches," Sylvia suggested.

"But then they'd lose a fare. The bus company can't do that. They'd go out of business."

"Losing one fare would put them out of business? What, do they charge a hundred-thousand- dollars a seat?"

"You don't understand how a business works."

"I know more about it than you do, Mr. Losing one fare can kill a bus company."

"You're killing me," an exasperated Oscar told her. "Did you bring the fake id from Marty?"

"Yes I did," she produced an envelope and handed it to her husband. "And it created a great deal of stress for me. I don't like carrying illegal things."

"What's the big deal?" Oscar said dismissively as he handed it to Rick. "It's not like you were carrying heroin."

"What if the bus crashed and I was unconscious? The police might have found it when they went through my purse to look for my id. Then I'd be arrested for carrying a fake driver's license."

"You'd just tell them that you found it and were going to mail it back to Jesse Gleason."

"How can I tell them that? I'm unconscious!"

I'm starting to wish you were unconscious now, Rick thought to himself.

"I meant when you woke up, which probably would have been just before they were about to give you the electric chair for carrying a fake id," Oscar said sarcastically.

"I have to eat," said the thickset Sylvia without responding to his remark.

"There's a burger joint up ahead. We'll stop there."

"Now that stuff will kill you," she pointed out

"Having one burger can't kill you. Do you know how many people in this country have had at least one fast food burger in their lives? If just one could turn a person into a stiff, most of the people in the world would be dead."

"But one fare can kill a bus company. Stop here. I'll get a chicken sandwich at Subway. Though God knows what the stuff they put in their sandwiches really is."

"You'll have to eat it there," Oscar said as he parked the car. "I'm selling the car to Ted Jacobs, and I don't want to get any food stains on the interior."

"You can't sell this car to anybody!"

"Why not?"

"Because we lease it. We don't own it."

"It's just a matter of coming up with the right paperwork. I'm sure the car company has offices full of people who can straighten things like that out. Ted told me that if I ever wanted to get rid of this car he'd like to buy it."

"So buy it from the leasing company, and then sell it to Ted. Or have him buy it from the leasing company."

"I don't have time for all of that. I'll just sell it to him directly."

"But then you'll have our next-door neighbor's money, and

he'll have to pay the leasing company to keep the car. You can't sell it to him. Ted and Francine are nice people."

"You always hated Francine."

Sylvia ripped the overly large sunglasses off her face and said "I never hated that woman. I did say she was a little bossy when we were putting together last summer's block party."

"I heard you use the word hate."

"I might have. As in I hate the way she bosses everyone around. But that doesn't mean I hate her. It's very irresponsible of you to go around telling people that I hate Francine when I said it was her behavior that I didn't like."

"I don't go around telling people that you hate Francine. Frankly, the subject never comes up, unless I'm talking to you about her."

"You're killing me, Oscar. And I'm starved, so let me get my artificial chicken sandwich before I die," Sylvia told him. "Do you boys want anything?"

Binny was hiding a smirk as he shook his head. Rick had been numbed by the Anastas' bickering. He also responded with a silent no.

"Do they always carry on like that?" Rick asked Binny after the couple left.

"No. They're usually much worse," he responded with a laugh. "But Aunt Sylvia is tired from her trip, so she doesn't have the energy to really argue."

The Anastas' went inside and stood behind a young girl as she ordered. After requesting virtually every toping Subway had to offer on the sandwich, the teenager asked the man behind the counter to cut off a small piece of it for her to sample. He obliged, and she chewed it slowly, which tried Oscar's patience. He gave the girl an exasperated look. After she approved the sandwich they ordered their meal and sat down at a table to eat it.

"Why did you give that kid a bad look?" she asked her husband between bites.

"She had to taste the sandwich before accepting it? I mean,

where did the girl think she was, in a fancy restaurant ordering a bottle of fine wine?"

"Maybe she wanted to see if it needed anything else on it."

"The guy making the sandwich couldn't have put anything else on it! The thing was already ten feet thick!"

"That's a ridiculous statement."

"How could she possibly taste any one particular topping with so many of them on it?"

"Maybe the girl asked for a piece of it because she was very hungry, like me."

"You mean the girl waited until she was on the verge of starvation before coming to Subway for a lousy sandwich? I have to wonder about these kids."

"I have to wonder about you!"

Oscar and Sylvia emerged from the fast food eatery. Rick was hoping that the process of digesting the food would quell her appetite for any more contentious conversation. That, however, was not the case.

"Why do I need an alias?" Sylvia asked indignantly as the two of them got into the car. "You guys are doing this job. I just delivered some money to you. I don't have to get involved."

"You are involved," Oscar corrected her. "Remember the fake id?"

"Don't remind me! But now that I've gotten rid of it, they'll never trace it back to me. I'm clean."

"Do you want to go home?" Oscar asked her.

"No. I think our house is haunted. I heard a lot of strange noises last night, and I sensed the presence of a poltergeese."

Do the poltergeese fly south for the winter? Rick thought with amusement.

"You mean poltergeist Aunt Sylvia," Binny told her.

"Whatever. It was very nerve racking. I don't want to be in the house alone."

"You don't want us to go to jail, right," Oscar said.

"Of course not, babe. But no one has to know who I am. I don't have to give anyone my name."

"Someone might hear one of us call you Sylvia if you're living in the house. Then they might be able to figure out who you are after we leave. But if we call you Lori LaSalle, they'll never find out who you are."

Sylvia looked at him skeptically.

"Lori LaSalle? Where did you get that name?'

"I'm using the name Steve LaSalle. And you're my wife, so it made sense to give you the same last name. And as for Lori, well it starts with the same letter as LaSalle, so it's easy for me to remember."

"Darling, have you looked in the mirror lately? You do not look like a LaSalle, or even a Steve for that matter."

"What is a Steve LaSalle supposed to look like?"

"Like more of an outdoorsy type. You look more like a tall Danny DeVito type."

"What the hell kind of a thing is that to say to your husband!"

"It doesn't mean you're not attractive, in a very basic way. You're just not LaSalle material."

"And what name do you think suits you?"

"Victoria Swanson."

"What?"

"It's a classy name, and that suits me. A lot of people have said that I'm a classy babe."

"Name one."

"You did."

"I was trying to woo you."

"That wasn't wooing. I could tell by the look in your eyes that you meant it."

"When someone's wooing you, everything sounds sincere."

"You mean you were full of shit when you were romancing me? You're scum, you son of a bitch."

What a classy babe Rick thought to himself. Then he said aloud to Sylvia, "We've already gotten used to calling him Steve LaSalle. I think things would go a lot smoother if we didn't start changing names."

"You're right, Rick," Sylvia agreed with him. "I'll do whatever it takes."

"Victoria Swanson," Oscar said with a laugh as he drove away.

They followed the directions Oscar had gotten from one of the Subway workers. The house was located on a block of uniform, middle class homes. Rick got out of the car and observed the quiet neighborhood. He suspected that the people here would be leery of any strangers that invaded their domain.

I just hope we can wrap this up quickly, before these nice people run us out of town on a rail.

The ad said that the real estate agent who was showing the property could be found in the house next door. Rick walked onto the porch of that simple abode and rang the doorbell. There was no answer. After waiting several moments, he turned to say something to his associates in the car. There was a lady in a housedress standing behind him. She had appeared out of thin air, apparently born of nothing.

"Oh, I'm sorry, did I startle you?" she asked him.

"No, not at all," Rick was barely able to say, his nerves having been stretched to the limit by her sudden appearance.

"My name is Mary Popkins. I take it you're here to see the Gutner place."

"That's the house for rent, right?" Rick responded in a stronger voice, while observing the unusually thick lenses on her glasses. *They're thicker than Principal King's hair.*

"Yes."

"That's why I'm here. My name is Jesse Gleason."

"It's nice to meet you. Shall we take the tour?"

He signaled the others to join them. The three of them walked up to the house wearing latex gloves, which Sylvia had brought at her husband's request.

"This is my family," Rick said, while trying to ignore the gloves.

"Well, looks like you're related to a bunch of germo-phobes," Mary observed pleasantly.

"I'm Steve LaSalle," Oscar told her. "I'm Jesse's uncle."

"My ass you are," Sylvia mumbled.

"And this is my wife Lori, and our son, Ralph."

"It's nice to meet you all," Mary said. "Let's take a look inside."

"What's a germo-phobe?" Oscar whispered to Sylvia.

"I think it's someone who's afraid of Germans," she answered in kind.

Rick followed Mary inside, with the others close behind. The house was a well-kept, simple affair. The big screen t.v. caught Oscar's eye, while the expensive looking stereo lured Binny over to have a look. Rick noticed the case with military artifacts in it. He wondered why anyone that was renting their home would leave such precious items on display.

"Mr. Gutner and his family went on a six-month tour of Europe."

"That sounds like a great trip," Rick said.

"Yes. I've thought about going to Europe, but Timmy and I are happy where we are. There's no place like Street Street."

I hope I'm that contented someday, Rick thought.

"Is Timmy your son?" Sylvia asked her.

"No, he's my dog. Mr. Gutner has a sentimental reason for going, He was in World War II, you know. The rent is fifteen hundred a month."

"Can we see the upstairs?" Rick asked her.

"Absolutely," Mary responded pleasantly.

They followed the short haired retiree up the stairs. There were two bedrooms on the second floor, one being a loft, with the open side facing the front of the house.

"We'll use this one," Sylvia announced. "It seems nice and airy."

"It looks like they were too cheap to put up four walls," Oscar observed.

"Can we have a moment alone?" Rick asked the real estate agent.

"Sure thing," said Mary. She went downstairs.

"This is perfect," Binny spoke first.

"I don't know," Rick said. "I think the neighbors are going to be very curious about the four strangers that are moving into their neighborhood. And that could be *very* inconvenient for us."

"We'll just have to keep a low profile. We won't do anything to attract attention to ourselves," said Oscar confidently.

"You mean like wearing latex gloves?" Rick responded.

"We can't leave prints," Oscar pointed out.

"You're right," Rick conceded. "I'll get a pair of work gloves to wear at the school. I'll use the latex gloves here. Maybe people will believe that we're just afraid of germs."

Oscar and Sylvia looked at each other with an expression that said *so that's what germo-phobe means.*

"It sure beats staying in a hotel," Binny observed.

"Okay, we'll do it." Rick agreed.

He walked down the stairs to find Mary. She was not there, and Rick turned around with the intention of searching the second floor for her. He discovered that she was standing right behind him once more. His heart did not race quite as fast this time.

Another Ches, he mused.

"Oh, I'm sorry, I did it again," she apologized.

"We'll take the place," he told her.

"That's wonderful. We're going to be neighbors. It'll be really handy for you to have the real estate agent living next door."

Rick's instincts told him that *handy* might not be the best word to describe this arrangement.

Sylvia gave her the cash, and after a very long goodbye, Mary left her tenants alone.

They carried in the luggage and retired to their rooms. Binny took the other upstairs bedroom and Rick chose the one on the first floor. He was again surprised by the personal items left on the bureau. There was a gold watch, cuff links and a bottle of expensive perfume, all there for the taking.

"What trusting souls," he thought aloud.

Binny gave Rick a quick tutorial on how to erase the

incriminating program on the Moore's machine, using one of the Gutner's two computers to demonstrate the necessary commands to type in while writing them down for his partner. After convincing his instructor that he was up to the task Rick ate a fast food dinner and went to bed. Lying in bed, the novice thief wondered if he was up to the task of impersonating a custodian, given that his skills as a repairman left much to be desired.

"I'll just give it my best shot. There's really nothing at stake here; just the rest of my life."

"Let's switch sides tonight. I want to sleep on the right side of the bed."

Rick sat up and looked around, expecting to see Sylvia in the room. Then he realized that her voice had carried downstairs because the Anastas' were in the open loft. The door in Rick's bedroom would not shut tightly because the doorknob was broken. He could hear the conversation taking place in the loft.

"I always sleep on the right side of the bed," Oscar said adamantly.

"That's your problem. You're too rigid!"

"I'm definitely getting there," Oscar responded, now in a seductive tone.

"I'm not in the mood," Sylvia replied.

"Oh, right, I'm always full of shit when I try to romance you," a now irritated Oscar said.

"You're taking that out of context."

"Context my ass. Well at least you know I'm sincere," Oscar said with a grin as he turned to display his profile.

"You're killing me!"

Rick covered his head with a pillow. Their discussion continued in the same vein for several hours. He managed to listen without going mad by chanting what would become his Morgan Town mantra.

"There is no easy money."

CHAPTER 7

S ara Simpson jogged to the park early the next morning. The young teacher was taking advantage of the unseasonably warm weather, wearing shorts and a tee shirt. Morgan Park was deserted when Sara arrived there. She sprinted down the path that led to the meadow, pausing after reaching her destination to enjoy the peaceful Saturday morning. Then she started to work.

The object Sara was looking for was supposed to be buried in this area. She took a GPS receiver from her knapsack. After ascertaining her position, Sara checked the co-ordinates that were written in a small notebook. Then she slowly walked in the direction indicated by the device. Sara became engrossed in the changing numbers on the GPS display, and as a result failed to notice the garbage can in her path. She fell over the barrel and hit the ground hard, which resulted in a loud thud that echoed throughout the silent park.

Larry and Tommy Oslifer had parked their patrol car in a stand of trees at the end of the meadow. Sara's mishap awoke the two officers. In a stupor, the brothers tried to comprehend where they were. After fully regaining consciousness, Larry and Tommy looked around to find the person who had so rudely interrupted their sleep.

"Is that Sara Simpson?" Tommy asked in a still groggy tone.

"Yeah. What the hell is she doing here at this hour?"

They watched as she stood up and resumed her search. Sara located the exact spot where the object she sought was supposed to be buried. Taking a small shovel from her knapsack, the teacher started to dig. A smile appeared on her face as she removed a small container from the ground. That quickly disappeared, it being replaced by a disappointed expression after she opened it.

"Sara dug something up," Larry said. "It must be something from the terrorists."

"We don't know that."

"We've got to do something."

"Do you know who her father is? He owns this town. If we piss him off, we'll be deported."

"You can't be deported from a town."

"Then maybe we'll be exported."

"Look," Larry said calmly. "She dug a hole in the park. Now that's illegal. So we'll just question her, and go from there."

"I guess there's no harm in doing that. But do me one favor first."

"What's that?"

"Leave your gun in the car."

"I'm not going to shoot her!" Larry said indignantly.

His brother gave him a skeptical look, so he complied with the request. The patrol car emerged from the trees. Sara saw it just as she put the lid back on the container. After driving across the open field Tommy and Larry stepped out of the car, looking disheveled.

I guess they sleep here, Sara thought with amusement.

"Good morning, Sara," Larry said.

"Good morning, Officers Oslifers," Sara responded pleasantly. "It's a pretty day, isn't it?"

"That it is," Tommy agreed. "So what brings you out here so early?"

"I have a lot to do today, so I needed to get an early start."

"We couldn't help notice that you dug a hole, Sara," Larry said. "I was wondering if you could tell us why. I'd also like to know what kind of device that is."

"This is a GPS receiver. It tells you exactly where you're standing."

"Why would you need one of those?" Larry asked, with hands on hips.

"For a school project."

"What's in the plastic container?" Larry questioned her further in a suspicious tone.

"This is what I was looking for. Is there a problem, officers?"

"Well, technically, you're not supposed to dig holes in the park," Tommy answered.

"I think you'd agree that this looks a little unusual," Larry pointed out. "I mean with what's going on at the school, you can see why we need to find out what you're doing. What exactly are you doing, Sara?"

"Geocaching," she replied.

"Is that the name of the person who buried the box?" Larry asked her.

"No, it's the name of a game," Sara explained.

"None of this is a game, Sara," Larry told her in a dramatic tone.

"Give us a second, okay Sara?" Tommy asked politely.

"No problem."

The two men walked back to their car, with Larry keeping an eye on Sara as they did so.

"We could get screwed if we piss off a Morgan," Tommy whispered to him.

"But we could also ruin our careers if we just let her go

and it turns out later that she was up to something," Larry countered.

"Let's call the chief. He should be in by now."

"He won't be at the station for another half hour. And you know how he hates to have his breakfast interrupted."

Tommy scratched his head. In his opinion, it was far too early in the morning to resolve such a conundrum.

"Look, let's ask her if she'll come in for questioning." Larry suggested.

"Okay, but only if you give me your handcuffs."

"Oh, all right."

They walked over to their suspect.

"Look, Sara, if you don't mind, we'd like to take you in for questioning," Tommy said apologetically. "I mean, you can understand that, right?"

"Well, Officers Oslifers, on any other day I'd go with you. But like I said before, I have a lot to do today."

"We'll be fast, but thorough," Larry assured her.

"I really don't see the point," Sara told them.

"It's really just to cover ourselves," Tommy explained. "If the chief found out that we didn't pursue this, we could lose our jobs."

Then you'd only have three, Sara thought before saying "What the heck then. I'll take a ride."

"You can just follow us in your car," Tommy said.

Larry was about to object when Sara made his objection unnecessary.

"I jogged here. So I guess you'll have to give me a ride."

"You jogged all the way from your place? You must be in great shape." Larry was impressed.

"I try."

Sara got in the back of the patrol car. As she did so Larry reached out to push down her head, to be sure the suspect did not hit the roof while getting in the car. Given that Sara was not manacled this gesture was superfluous, but the officer had seen it done on many police shows. He was not going to pass up an opportunity to emulate the TV cops.

They drove through the town, giving many of the early morning shoppers a chance to see Edgar Morgan's daughter riding in the backseat of a patrol car. When they arrived at the police station several passersby witnessed Sara being escorted inside by the men of many occupations.

Sheriff Tim Reinhart had arrived early that day, his vacation having invigorated the highest ranking official of Morgan Town's Police Department. The Oslifers brought Sara into an interrogation room and then, after grabbing a cup of coffee, went into their superior's office.

"Hey boss," Larry greeted him. "How was the trip?"

"Great. There are some mighty interesting places to see in Turkey. I take it you boys managed to stay out of trouble."

"Sure," Tommy said in a halting voice. "You know what's been going on over at the school."

"Yes I do. What's the latest on that?"

"I think we broke the case." Larry said with pride in his voice.

Tim twirled the ends of his handlebar mustache for a moment before responding. He did not think his two most dedicated, but also most inept, officers capable of such an achievement.

"How so?" he asked, and then waited in dread for the answer.

"We caught Sara Simpson digging a hole in the park," Larry informed him.

"Digging a hole?"

"Yes sir," Tommy answered.

"How is that related to the school?'

"She dug up a box," Larry told him. "And she was going to meet someone named Geocaching."

"Now wait a minute, Larry. She said that was the name of a game."

"Football is a game. Baseball is a game. Geocaching sounds like the name of a foreigner. And Sara sounded like she was trying to hide something from us, boss. You can see for yourself. We took her in."

"You arrested Sara everyone knows her real last name is Morgan Simpson!"

"No, we asked her to come in for questioning. Tommy wouldn't even let me use the cuffs on her."

"I've always wondered which one of you two was the brightest. Now I know. Congratulations, Tommy."

The sheriff went into the interrogation room with the Officers Oslifers right behind him.

"Sara," he said with his warmest smile after entering the room. "It's so good to see you. I hope you haven't been inconvenienced."

"No, not at all Sheriff Reinhart."

"Call me Tim. My guys were just a little confused by what you were doing in the park."

"It's called Geocaching. You use a GPS receiver to find the box, or geocache. There's nothing valuable in it. I wanted the kids to do it because they've been learning how to use maps and other means of navigation."

"Now that makes sense," the sheriff said with a nod.

"What's in the box, Sara?" Larry said in a slightly intimidating tone.

"Let's have a look," she responded.

Sara opened the plastic box. There was a log inside with a list of the people who had found the container. There was also an empty tape dispenser and a spool of string.

"Like I said, nothing of value," Sara told them with a laugh.

"I'd say so," the sheriff agreed.

"Can we see the log," Larry asked her. "I'd also like to take a look at your notebook."

The sheriff was about to overrule his subordinate when another officer entered the room. She whispered something to him. Tim nodded and then addressed Sara.

"We have to speak with someone else for just a moment. This won't take long. Would you like some coffee?"

"Do you have any juice?"

"Find some juice for Miss Simpson," he told the officer who had delivered the message. "Oslifers, come with me."

They went into the sheriff's office, where Miles Gouveia and Dan Gartner were waiting for him.

"Nice to meet you," the sheriff said after shaking their hands. "I hope our officers have been helpful."

"Absolutely, sheriff," Miles replied. "They've given the computer round the clock security. I understand the teacher was acting suspiciously in the park."

"We're just getting to the bottom of that now," Reinhart told him. "It seems that she was playing a game called Geocaching."

"I've never heard of that," Gouveia said in a dubious tone.

"Neither have we," Larry concurred.

"I have," Gartner said. "My son has played it before."

"Can we see the box she dug up?" Gouveia asked.

"I'll see if Sara will agree to that," Reinhart told them.

"Ask her for the notebook, too," said Larry.

Tim left the room and returned several moments later with both items. Gouveia opened it and thumbed through the log. He did the same with Sara's notebook.

"We should go through the log," Larry suggested. "We can round up the people listed in it and find out what they know."

"Let's just concentrate on the ringleader," Reinhart responded sarcastically.

Gouveia handed the items to Gartner.

"My guys are going to drive Sara home now," the sheriff told them. "There's no reason to keep her here."

"It's your call, of course," the Bank V.P. responded. "But we might learn something from her if the teacher believes she's a suspect."

"But Sara isn't a suspect," the sheriff pointed out. "She's just a schoolteacher that wanted to educate her class about how to find things. Sara's going home now."

"As I said sheriff, it's your call. Let's have lunch some time."

"That sounds good to me."

Gouveia and Gartner left the police station.

"She's in league with someone," Gouveia said confidently as they got into the car.

"I'd say that someone is the village idiot, judging by what was in the box. And the log is just a list of the people who have dug up the box."

"What about her notebook? It looks like it was written in some kind of code."

"It was in shorthand. Miles, I think you're looking at the wrong person here."

"I can't believe that kid would be able to do this without her support."

"The kid? You think he ripped off the bank?"

"No, but I do think he knows more than he's telling us. Do me a favor. Check out the park. Maybe you'll find something there. Those cops could miss the elephant in the room and a couple of whales, too."

Gartner gave his friend an impatient look.

"This is my ass, Dan," Miles implored him

"I walked through the park yesterday. And I saw a bunch of kids fishing, which is what I should be doing right now. Only they weren't doing it in water. There were going after wooden fish that were lying on the pavement. They had rings on them where a real fish's mouth would be, so you could hook them. I think I'll join them. That way I'll be able to say that I caught some fish on my vacation."

"I owe you big time, buddy."

"And then some."

■ ■ ■

Rick Gaines stood in the Gutner's home office and watched as Binny struggled to gain access to the school's computer system. The techie had defeated so many security schemes over the years that his success, at least in Rick's eyes, seemed inevitable. Yet as the moments slipped by the frustration on Binny's face grew.

"I guess they have a lot of safeguards on their system," Rick said.

"Yeah, they're really looking out for the kiddies. But it's nothing I can't handle-if I have enough time."

Which I suspect is the one thing we don't have a lot of Rick thought. Then he said aloud, "I'll check back with you later. Good luck."

"Thanks," Binny replied in an unoptimistic tone.

Rick opened the door and was startled to find Mary standing there.

"Hi. Do you have a minute?"

"For you, of course." *Just give me one to recover from my latest coronary.*

"Your Uncle Steve has created a turkey shortage in Morgan Town."

How could there be a shortage of turkeys in this place? Then aloud, "What do you mean?"

"Mr. Travota, he owns the supermarket, said that your uncle ordered fifty turkeys. He wasn't sure why."

I bet Sara calls that guy John Travota. Then aloud he said, "My uncle is a very generous person."

"I understand."

"He was going to donate them to an agency that feeds those in need. He's a good man."

"What about me?" asked Sylvia, who was in the loft. She believed that a wife was entitled to share in the credit for her husband's good deeds.

"You too, lord," Rick responded to the voice from above. "You're the best. And by the way, I always knew you were a woman."

Mary looked at him with a puzzled expression on her face.

"I'll talk to him about it," Rick assured her. "He didn't know it would cause a problem for everyone else."

"Did you hear that Sara Simpson has been arrested," Mary told him.

"The schoolteacher? For what?"

"I'm not sure, but the Officer Oslifers said they caught her doing something suspicious in the park. There's a rumor going around that it had something to do with a bank robbery."

"Any idea what the something was?"

"No. But they took her to the police station in a patrol car."

"I'm sure it's a misunderstanding. Do you know where she lives? I want to thank her for recommending this house to us."

"She's over in the Anderson Apartment building. I'll see you soon."

"I'm sure you will."

Oscar came home soon after the landlady had left.

"I found a great place to watch the ballgame," he told Rickie triumphantly. "It's a little pub over on Main Street."

"That's great, Oscar. What's going on with the turkeys?"

"I bought them for my clients," he explained. "I always do that on Thanksgiving."

"Well apparently you've created a turkey shortage in Morgan Town."

"I didn't think of that. Where we live no one would miss fifty birds."

"Especially if they were pigeons. You can't draw the local's attention to us."

"I have to keep the business going. What if we can't keep the money? I need something to fall back on."

"It won't be an *if*, if you make the people suspicious. Then the only thing we'll have to fall back on is the cot in our cell. Call the store and tell them you'll get them elsewhere. Please."

"I could get them from the grocery store I usually buy them from," Oscar decided. "You don't have to worry about me, Ricky. I'm going to keep a low profile from now on."

"I'm going to see Sara Simpson."

"Who's she?"

"The teacher that has Moore's computer in her class. According to Mary, she's been arrested for doing something suspicious in the park."

"She's a pervert?"

"I said suspicious, not perverted. I'll see you later."

Sara Simpson sat in her apartment with her roommate Maya, discussing the events of the day. The teacher had initially considered her predicament to be comical in nature, something that she would enjoy revisiting in the years to come. After Sara left the police station, however, a feeling of dread suddenly enveloped her.

"You can't take this too seriously," Maya tried to reassure her. "This town is full of mental munchkins. This is Moron Town."

"I just want to teach the children," Sara said. "And I'm starting to feel like this thing with the computer is going to take that away from me."

"Drink a bottle of wine and chill out."

"Me? I get drunk at the salad bar."

"I keep telling you, we need to be elsewhere. Come to New York City with me. You'll find plenty of kids to teach there."

"There's also a lot of violence in those schools, from what I hear. I wouldn't be able to function in that environment."

"That's a defeatist attitude. Think of it as a challenge."

"If I want that kind of a challenge I'll join the army."

"I have to go shopping. Do you need anything?"

"Maybe a character witness," Sara replied with a smile.

"I'll be happy to do that for you. You're one of the biggest characters I know."

Sara smiled at her friend as she left the apartment. Then the teacher picked up a pile of papers to grade and began to work. A knock on the door interrupted her. Sara stood up and answered it.

"Remember me?" Rick asked with a smile.

"Vaguely," Sara replied in the same fashion. "I suffered a concussion when I collided with you. Come in and help me regain my memory."

Sara offered him a drink, and he accepted. They sat down in the living room.

"I just wanted to thank you for showing me the ad about the house," Rick began the conversation.

"My pleasure. It's a nice neighborhood. Did you hear anything about the job?"

"Yes, I was hired."

"Excellent!"

"How old were you in that picture?" Rick asked her after noticing the framed photograph next to the lamp.

"Seven or eight. The boy standing next to me was my best friend in those days. His name is Haji. The infamous Haji."

"Why the infamous Haji?"

"My dad always thought he was evil. It could have something to do with the fact that he's from India. A foreigner, you know. Or it could have been the *Star Trek* script we wrote together. In our story the transporter malfunctioned. McCoy wound up with Spock's ears, Kirk got Uhura's boobs, and Nurse Chapel had Kirk's manhood, or wienny as we referred to it back then. She started chasing Spock all over the ship because he had her vagina. We sent it to NBC, but never heard back from them."

"I can't imagine why," Rick said with a laugh.

"I think it was because the show had been cancelled years before. It couldn't have been the material. It was inspired. My dad found our script and didn't see it that way, though. He blamed Haji for corrupting his little girl. Anyway, I truly believe that someday, probably long after I've left this world, someone will find it and appreciate our very imaginative script. It'll become a hit."

"Post humorsly," Rick said.

"Right!" Sara responded with a grin.

I like her.

"It's the same thing with my poetry," Sara added. "Like Emily Dickenson, I won't be appreciated until after my time."

"Let me hear one."

"He put his head on her perfect breasts, his lover's skin as soft as a cloud. He was enveloped in her beauty, and his heart was revealed by this lovely soul named Lenore."

"That's great!"

"Thank you."

"I hear you had a run in with the law," Rick said, in as casual a fashion as he could manage.

"Oh, that. It was just a misunderstanding. They had just never heard of Geocaching. Have you?"

"Yes. I read an article about it a while back."

"I was...."

She was interrupted by another knock on the door. This time it was her father.

"Hi Dad. Come on in," she said to Edgar Morgan with a smile.

He entered the tiny apartment, without bothering to hide his displeasure at the fact that his daughter had chosen to live there.

"This is Jesse. He starts working at Morgan Elementary on Monday. This is Edgar Morgan."

"What do you teach?" her father asked with a notable lack of interest.

"I'm a custodian."

"Really? We have a toilet in our home that just won't stop running. Are you any good at fixing them?"

"I've fixed them before," Rick told him.

"Good. We can discuss it at church tomorrow."

Church?

"You will be at church?" Edgar asked when he saw the surprised expression on his face. "Anyone who works for Principal King must be a God-fearing soul. And you look like a Catholic to me. It the surest way to gain job security."

His daughter nodded.

"I'll be there," Rick, who had sensed that Sara's father wished to speak with her alone, said as he stood up to leave. "Thanks for the beer, Sara."

"My pleasure, Jesse. I'll see you tomorrow."

"Sara, I understand that you were involved in an incident

today," her father said after reluctantly sitting in a well-worn chair.

"It was just a misunderstanding. I was preparing for a game of geocaching, and the police officers thought I was doing something suspicious."

"Thought? You mean to tell me that digging holes in the park isn't a suspicious activity?"

"Well, no, it's how the game is played. And it was only one hole."

Edgar let out a long sigh before continuing.

"No one I know has ever heard of that game you described to the sheriff. And that includes your mother. She's so distraught about this incident that I couldn't get her to drive over here with me. The poor woman is afraid to be seen in public."

"Mom doesn't want to be seen in public with you?" Sara, who knew that was not the case, asked innocently.

"Not with me per se, but in public generally, even if she's alone. Because her daughter was carted off to the police station."

"I'm sorry Mom's so upset. But I didn't do anything wrong. I'll call her and explain."

"You can't. She took several sleeping pills and went to bed. Sara, what's gone wrong here?"

"Nothing. I mean this whole thing is just because the school board was too cheap to buy new computers. It really has nothing to do with me. My life's fine."

"Is it really? You think teaching in an elementary school is the best way to realize your full potential?"

"Yes. I'm doing something important."

"You could have a management level position in my company. In several years you'd be an executive. And you'd be living in a first-class condo, or even a home."

"Teaching the kids is important. Years from now I'll be able to look back and say that I contributed to their development."

"So get married. Start a family. You'd be able to say the same thing, and without having a police record."

"I don't have a police record. I was just asked to come in for questioning. And it was worth it, because I got a free bottle of fruit juice."

Edgar stood up and took his daughter's hand.

"Honey, I know you mean well. But you can have a real life. Don't throw it away on some idealistic myth about the nobility of sacrificing something that's in your own best interest to help others. You've been hiding from the name Morgan. That's why you're in this predicament. Take what's yours, or you're liable to lose it," he said in an ominous tone.

Her father walked out the door.

"He's going to bail on me," Sara thought aloud, in disbelief. "And I didn't do anything wrong."

■ ■ ■

"How did it go?" Binny asked Rick after he arrived at the house.

"I didn't find out anything. She was just about to start talking about what happened at the park when her father showed up. He took over the conversation, so I left. I have to go to church tomorrow."

"Why?" Oscar asked as he entered the room with Sylvia.

"Sara's father suggested I go, to get in good with the principal. That wouldn't have been enough to get me to go, but during the drive over here it occurred to me that I might get a chance to talk with Sara after the mass. So I'm going."

"We should all go," Sylvia told him.

"I haven't been to church in years," Oscar responded.

"Me neither," Binny said.

"Well, it wouldn't hurt for the two of you to do a little soul searching," Sylvia said. "I think you guys should start to come to terms with the moral implications of the robbery."

"You're involved in this too, Miss holier than thou. I don't think the good lord will start doing handstands when he sees you walk into the church," Oscar retorted and then added a derisive laugh.

"This is your scheme. I had nothing to do with it," Sylvia pointed out.

"Oh yeah. Who bought Ricky the fake id?"

"I'm the only one who has to go," Rick interjected.

"I didn't know what you were going to do with it. Besides, I always consider the moral implications of the choices I make. I reflect on my life."

"I've never seen you reflect on your life."

"Well, of course not. You can't see someone reflect on something. It's all on the inside."

"Right," Oscar said skeptically. "The next time you're reflecting, let me know. Maybe I'll see an aurora around you."

"You mean aura, genius," Sylvia corrected him.

"We'll do it together, Ricky," Oscar said cheerfully while ignoring his better half.

Why don't I find that encouraging, Rick thought to himself.

The four of them emerged from the house the next morning, in what they hoped would pass as their Sunday best. Rick wore casual slacks with a dress shirt, as did Binny and Oscar. The men's clothes had been purchased the night before. Sylvia was dressed in the pants suit she had worn on the trip to Morgan Town.

"Good morning," Mary Popkins said as she walked by the house with her dog.

She had planned to stop in after the animal had been exercised, but the tenant's early departure had prevented her from raising Rick's blood pressure once again.

"Hi Mary," replied Rick. "You look very nice. I like your haircut."

"Thank you. It can never be too short, as far as I'm concerned. I'm on my way to church. I had to give Timmy a chance to relieve himself first."

The people here give their dogs a name like Timmy. And they name their kids Rex and Buddy. They're whacked out, Rick mused.

"What kind of a dog is that?" Oscar asked her.

"A Pekinese. It took years and years of breeding to develop their unique appearance."

Oscar observed the wrinkled, compressed face of her pet.

"I could have done that in a second. It would only take one good hit with a shovel."

"What?" Mary asked as she cringed.

"He has a weird sense of humor," Rick explained. "That's a beautiful animal."

"Timmy certainly is," a somewhat mollified Mary agreed. "I'll see you at the church. Let's go home, dear."

"You shouldn't have said that to her," Sylvia chastised her husband.

"It's just a stupid dog."

"People like her love their dogs."

"How can you love something that you can't even have a conversation with?" Oscar questioned her.

"I've asked myself that question on many occasions," Sylvia said in a biting tone.

"What's that supposed to mean!"

"Guys, it's time to get into happy family mode," Rick told them. "We have to act like the locals now."

"You're right, Ricky," Oscar said while nodding his head. "We'll be just like the other people in this jerk water town."

That's what I'll be praying for, Rick thought to himself.

They drove up to the Old Hope Church just as the congregation began to arrive. The white building with the majestic steeple was over one hundred years old, though the diligent maintenance it had received over the years made the church appear to be of contemporary origin. Father Joseph stood on the steps in traditional garb, greeting his parishioners.

"Good morning Violet," he said to a middle-aged woman. "How are you?"

"I'm distraught, Father. Becky's in the rehab clinic again. She just can't get herself straightened out."

"She's a wayward soul. I think it might be time for you to give up hope for her."

Violet nodded solemnly and went inside the church.

"Hello father," Rick greeted the pastor.

"Welcome to our parish."

"You were kind of rough on Becky."

"People like that deserve no sympathy," the priest said sternly. Then he laughed at the incredulous expression on Rick's face. "Violet likes watching soap operas. Becky is a character from one of her shows."

Rick smiled before saying "This is my Aunt Lori and Uncle Steve. This is my cousin Ralph."

Binny, for just an instant, looked around, wondering who Rick was referring to. Then he remembered his alias and shook Father Joseph's hand, who was wondering if the person sitting behind Sylvia would be able to see over her up do hair style.

Mary arrived with her dog in tow.

"Good morning, father. I hope you don't mind if I tie Timmy to your tree."

"The lawn can always use more fertilizer."

"I was going to leave him at home. But Timmy looked so depressed when I walked out the door that I just had to bring him with me. I'm ready for my Corinthians reading."

"They wrote a book, too?" Sylvia asked her.

"What?" Mary responded.

"You said you're reading something by the Kardashians, right? I watch that show all the time."

"She said Corinthians, Aunt Lori," Rick quickly corrected her.

"Oh, I'm sorry. I'm sure the Corinthians are just as entertaining."

"That's why they're a regular here," Father Joseph said with a smile.

The Morgans arrived. Sara saw Rick and moved quickly through the crowd to speak with him. Just as she began to say hello, Timmy lunged away from Mary, which put his leash in the schoolteacher's path. Sara tripped over it and landed face first on the grass.

"Oh, I'm sorry, are you all right?" Mary bent down to help her up.

"I'm fine."

"Sara, I don't think I'd recognize you if you weren't lying on the ground," Father Joseph told her. "Go into the rectory and wash your face, dear."

"Thanks," she replied sheepishly. "That new sod you put in is really doing well."

The rest of the people went into the church. There were potted plants in the vestibule with tags on them that read *stolen from Sanders Nursery*. Rick read the tag twice before letting out a laugh.

"Humor is one of his gifts," Father Joseph said to him with a grin.

The priest began the mass after Sara joined them. Rick remembered most of the hymns and responses, though his *family* did not fare as well. Fortunately, the passionate voices of the people around them hid their many mistakes, though Oscar's applauding after the singer finished her first song drew stares from the entire congregation.

"I'd like to welcome Jesse and his family," Father Joseph said at one point. "Our church, and community, is made stronger by the addition of such upstanding people."

The irony of his statement was not lost on any of the four. They received a polite response from the parishioners. Rex, who was sitting in the pew in front of the newcomers, pointed a toy gun at Rick and pulled the trigger. A stream of water hit him in the chest. Rick smiled as he took the gun away from him and lip synced the word *confiscated*.

"My friends in Christ, today's gospel is a reminder to us that the best road to take is not always the easiest one to travel upon," Father Joseph began his sermon, his words echoing through the cavernous cathedral. "We must work for the things we want in life. Those possessions that are acquired under false pretenses will never bring us happiness. The true reverends in our world, those who are most worthy of being revered, are the people who go out into the world every day and earn a living."

Karen's been talking to this guy! Rick mused.

"Those are the people who have accepted the challenges that laboring for the things they desire present. These citizens of our community can, as Peter once wrote, rejoice in their suffering, for they have taken the noble path."

That guy Peter sounds like a lot of laughs, Rick silently observed.

Father Joseph's sermon was brief, much to the delight of his audience (and especially the newest members of the congregation.). The mass proceeded, and the collection basket was passed. Rick only had a dollar in his wallet but thought his meager donation might be excused given that he had just started his job. A woman in the pew across the aisle passed the basket to Oscar. He dropped it on the floor and bent down to pick it up, deftly taking twenty dollars of the parishioner's donations while doing so. Only his partners noticed the theft. The bookie then casually put the money back before passing the basket on to Rick, giving the appearance of having donated a respectable sum to the church.

I've got you covered, Oscar lip synced the words to his partners.

That guy is smooth, Rick thought as he put his dollar away. Binny, who had no money to donate, simply grinned at his uncle. Sylvia shook her head.

The mass continued, despite the squealing protests of several babies that were in attendance. The time to offer each other a sign of peace had arrived. Rick happened to glance over at Oscar just before the priest instructed the congregation to do so. He was staring up at the roof of this hallowed building, as if the gates of heaven could be seen there.

He's really getting into this.

Principal King's wife was in the pew in front of Oscar, and she turned around to shake his hand. The bookie responded by pulling out a gun and pointing it at her.

"What on earth!" she exclaimed before swooning.

"What the hell was that," Rick whispered to Sylvia, who was seated next to him.

"He fell asleep," she responded in kind. "Sometimes Oscar sleeps with his eyes open. She woke him up. That startled him, so he took out his gun."

I should have known he was sleeping. He wasn't arguing with you.

Rick saw Father Joseph moving towards the prostrate woman. Oscar had put the weapon away so quickly that only King's wife was able to catch a glimpse of it. Rick took Rex's water pistol out of his pocket and slipped it into Oscar's hand.

"He had a gun!" Ellen King blurted out after regaining consciousness. "He was going to shoot me!"

"It was a joke." Oscar showed her the toy weapon. "I'm very sorry, ma'am."

Father Joseph gave him a disapproving look before saying, "We take our celebration of the Eucharist very seriously in this parish, sir."

"I'm sorry, father."

"Are you all right," the priest asked Ellen.

"I think so. I've never in all my life witnessed such boorish behavior!"

"Let's conclude our mass," the priest told his flock

Rick and his partners left the church quickly after the final blessing.

"Why are you carrying a gun?" Rick asked in an exasperated tone as they drove away.

"I have it in case we get into a jam," Oscar replied. "I mean, we are stealing the bank's money. If they figure out who we are, I want a chance to get away."

"You've never fired that thing at anyone," Sylvia pointed out.

"I've used it for target practice."

"Was the target breathing?" she asked him. "Was it flesh and blood? You couldn't shoot anyone."

"I don't know about that," he said while giving her his most menacing look, which was more comical than frightening.

"You don't scare me, mister," she responded with disdain. "It was a stupid thing to do!"

"I admit that, okay. I shouldn't have taken my gun to church."

"Didn't you say that we wouldn't do anything to attract attention to ourselves? Carrying a gun around in this town is not a good way to avoid attracting attention to yourself. It makes you as conspicuous as Beethoven would be if he was playing in a punk rock band. Now we've got the priest wondering about us. I'm sure he thinks we're all in league with the devil. And the principal's wife is going to think that we had something to do with the robbery. That was not a good move, Oscar."

"I know Ricky, I know. I messed up. I screwed up. I fucked up. I...."

"We get the point!" Rick exclaimed.

"That priest sure looked pissed off. I hope he doesn't put a curse on us," Oscar said with a concerned expression on his face.

"He's not a warlock," Rick pointed out.

"I won't do it again. From now on I'll watch my p's and q's."

Now why don't I believe that, Rick thought dejectedly. *Give me strength, Bowmarc.*

CHAPTER

8

R ick arrived at Morgan Elementary School the next
morning. He went to the head custodian's office, wondering
on the way there if his performance as Jesse Gleason
the custodian would be a convincing one. For encouragement,
Rick kept reminding himself that his time here would be brief,
providing he could quickly find a way to reach the computer.
For just a moment, a sense of nostalgia came over him as he
remembered his own elementary school. The sometimes erratic,
yet promising pictures created by the students that were hung
on the walls reminded him of the ones he had drawn as a boy.
Rick almost wished he could regain the innocence of those days.

He walked into the office and found his new boss, Henry
Pabst, reading the paper while sipping a cup of coffee. He
was a burly individual, with graying hair that attested to the
many years he had been in his current position. Henry did not
acknowledge Rick, so he cleared his throat.

"I know you're there," was the response he received. "But
I'm not done with this article yet. Have a seat."

Rick sat in the chair next to Pabst's desk. He looked around the room, observing the photographs on the wall that spanned Henry's thirty years as the head custodian. After what seemed like an interminable time, he finally put the paper down.

"So what are we going to do about Iran?" Pabst asked Rick.

He had been so absorbed in his own affairs the news of the world had escaped his notice. Rick was also caught by surprise because he had expected his new boss to be reading the sports section. Henry's physique suggested that he spent many hours in front of a television with a beer in his hand watching other people play games.

"I say nuke em," Rick, attempting to be flippant, answered.

"It could come to that. The Israelis just might panic and push the button. I hope you're not going to suggest the same solution for a clogged sink, though," Henry said with a laugh.

Rick followed him into the custodians' room. His boss opened one of the lockers and pointed to a uniform hanging there. Rick put it on while Henry glanced though the fictitious background that Binny had created for him. He seemed satisfied with his qualifications.

"It seems like you know your stuff."

Things aren't always what they seem, Rick thought.

"I'll tell you what I tell everyone who works for me. It's all about time. I expect you to get your ass here on time every morning. I also expect you to get your work done in a reasonable amount of time. You do that, and we'll get along fine. If you don't, we have a problem. And if that happens, I might have to *nuke* you. And you don't want the Pabst pushing the button. You read me?"

"I understand."

"Good. Now here's your first job. The doorknob on room thirty-four has to be replaced. The teacher broke her key in the lock. Here's the new knob."

"I'm on it," Rick said enthusiastically.

"I'm not the one who started calling myself the Pabst, you know. It's a nickname the other guys gave me."

"Right."

Rick left the custodian's office and walked towards his destination.

"Mr. Gleason," the bold voice of the principal caused him to stop suddenly.

The new custodian reluctantly turned around to face him.

"Is your Uncle's behavior typical for all the members of your family?"

"No, Principal King. My Uncle Steve has had a difficult life. We moved here in the hope that this setting would help bring him around. Our family just can't give up on one of our own."

"That's commendable," King responded, in a voice that indicated he had been moved by his employee's loyalty. "Carry on, Mr. Gleason."

I am good at this.

Rick continued down the hall as the students filed into their classrooms. He followed the numbers on the doors until he reached the one in need of a new doorknob. Much to his satisfaction, this was Miss Simpson's room. Rick opened the door and went inside. He was delighted to discover that it was deserted. Taking out Binny's written instructions from his pocket, he approached the computer containing the information that could put him in jail. Just as Rick was about to turn on the machine he heard someone walking towards the door. The newest member of the custodial staff quickly took the new doorknob from its box. He put it on the desk with the incriminating machine and pretended to be assembling it when the door opened.

"Oh, hi," Sara said. "How's your first day going?"

"So far so good. The first thing I get to do is fix your door."

"I'm such a klutz. Somehow I broke the key off in the lock when I tried to open it this morning."

Rick felt a twinge of guilt, since he knew the lock had been damaged when Binny picked it.

"What happened to your students?" he asked her.

"There's an assembly this morning. I took the children to the auditorium and came back to meet with the Lion King."

"The Lion King?"

"That's what I call the principal, but not to his face, of course," Sara explained. "Someone used one of the computers that were donated to the school to rob a bank. Now the bank is trying to find the money, and the thieves, so they've sent their people here to examine the computer. They're supposed to have a big meeting at the school this morning."

"I'll try to stay out of the way," Rick said.

"Just do a good job on the doorknob. I'd hate for all those people to be stuck in my classroom because they couldn't open the door. I want things to get back to normal. And congratulations, again. Not everyone can survive an interview in the Lion King's lair. That's how I refer to his office."

"Do you tell the students that you'll send them to the Lion King's lair if they misbehave?" Rick asked her with a smile.

"No, because if I did, I'm sure I'd wind up there. And I'm a coward, at heart," Sara replied with a laugh.

She sat down at her desk while Rick began to work. He removed the broken doorknob and read the instructions for installing the new one. The pseudo custodian was almost knocked over when Miles Gouveia burst into the room, pushing the half open door out of his way as he entered. Lionel King followed with the two policemen that had come to relieve the Oslifers, who had left for one of their other jobs.

"Good morning Miss Simpson," King said in greeting. "I believe you've met Miles Gouveia. He's the Vice President of Security for Elmendorf Bank."

"Yes I did. So what have you found out so far?"

"I'd prefer to wait for...ah, here they are," Gouveia said as two other men entered the room. "This is Gary Knowles, one of our computer people. And this is Dan Gartner. Let's fill everyone in on what we know."

"Well, first of all, I don't think John Moore, the man who

donated the computer, had anything to do with the theft," Gartner, a non-descript individual, began.

"Excuse me, what is your position at the bank?" the principal asked.

"Dan is a... consultant on our most difficult security issues," Gouveia answered for him.

"As I was about to say, I doubt Mr. Moore would have donated a machine that he used to rob a bank, at least not without erasing the hard drive. In fact, I'm sure he would have destroyed the entire machine."

I'd go with that option Rick, who was working behind the door in an effort to be unnoticed, thought to himself.

"Is there anything unique about this machine?" Miles asked Gary Knowles.

"Not at all. It's just your typical p.c. with 256 bytes."

A fisherman would be envious, Rick mused.

"So someone used this machine to steal the money," the security V.P. asked. "Did that someone break into Moore's house?"

"I don't think so," Knowles responded. "My guess is that someone hacked their way into his computer. They could have installed and ran their program without his being aware of it."

"Especially since he was in South America at the time," Gartner added.

"South America?" Larry Oslifer questioned him as he entered the room with his brother.

"You're out of uniform, gentlemen," King said in a disapproving tone.

The two officers were dressed in their pizzeria attire.

"We were working at the Don's," Larry explained. "The sheriff wants us to take notes at this meeting. He wants to get up to speed on the case as quickly as possible."

"I could have taken the notes," one of the officers on duty interjected.

"Yeah, but you weren't at the station when he found out about the meeting," Tommy Oslifer pointed out.

"Neither were you," the other officer countered.

"But Charley was, and since he knew we were on this case from the beginning he called us right away," Tommy told him. "Because this is important!"

"And we can't handle something that's important? The sheriff asks us to do a lot of things..."

"With all due respect, I think you're drifting away from the point of this meeting," Gouveia interjected in an irritated tone.

They're just like me, Rick thought with a smile. *They would have asked where Lauren got the machete, too.*

"Why was this guy in South America?" Gouveia asked.

"He took a trip down the Amazon River," Dan told him.

"Why would anyone in their right mind go all the way to South America just to take a boat ride?" Miles Gouveia wondered. "That sounds suspicious to me. Can you pursue that any further?"

"Excuse us. I have to speak privately with Miles for a moment," Gartner told the others.

The two men went to the boy's room.

"If you want me to formally question Moore, you have to report this incident to the FBI," Dan said to his friend.

"I'm not talking about a formal investigation. This is technically still a discrepancy between our records and the Feds, not a theft."

Gartner looked at him skeptically.

"Maybe you could question the guy in person, and be a little, just a little mind you, intimidating," suggested Miles.

"Out of the question. I'm taking enough of a chance just being here."

"And I really appreciate it, Dan. We'll assume, for now, that this guy is just queer for rivers. Let's go back inside."

They returned to the classroom.

"I think, based on what Dan just told me, that Mr. Moore is an unlikely suspect," Gouveia said. He then looked at Knowles, and noted his shoulder length hair, which could not have been in greater contrast to his own barren head, before saying "That means someone else instructed Moore's machine to take the money. Is that possible, Gary?"

"Yes. This person, or persons, sent the program that copied our software to Moore's machine via the internet. Then this person, or persons, activated it, and the computer took the money."

"And they tried to do it again, after the computer was donated to the school," Gouveia added.

"I'm not positive about that," the computer expert responded. "It could have been activated by someone in the school, either accidentally or intentionally."

"Intentionally! You better have proof, sir, before you begin casting aspersions on the good people of Morgan Elementary!" King told him in an indignant tone.

"He didn't mean anything by it, Principal King," Gouveia tried to placate him. "Where's the little boy who was using the machine when it contacted the bank again?"

"He's in an assembly," Sara answered.

"Please bring him here," King told her.

He watched her walk out the door and for the first time noticed Jesse Gleason standing behind it.

"I'm glad to see you're on the job, Mr. Gleason," he said encouragingly.

"Thank you."

Sara went to the auditorium and retrieved her charge. At any other time, Rex would have been delighted to miss his classmate's rendition of *Stars and Stripes Forever*. On this occasion, however, he sensed that something ominous was behind his removal from the concert, despite Miss Simpson's pleasant demeanor.

"Would you excuse us?" King said to Rick after the boy and his teacher entered the room. "And close the door on your way out."

Rick obliged him, knowing that he would not miss anything that was said inside the classroom. Since the doorknob with the broken lock had been removed, there was a hole in the door. He could stand out in the hall and hear their conversation.

"Don't be alarmed, Rex," King told him after the student sat down in a chair next to his teacher's desk. "We're still trying to ascertain what happened on your computer a couple of days ago."

Rex gave Sara a questioning look.

"Ascertain means figure out," she explained.

"Oh," he said. Then to the principal "I just turned it on, like Miss Simpson told me to."

"Rex, my name is Miles Gouveia. Your computer contacted the computer at the Elmendorf Bank. Did you do anything to make that happen?"

The boy nervously clasped his hands together, and then looked away.

"Rex, don't be afraid," Sara said kindly.

"I think this young man is holding something back from us," said Gouveia in a suspicious tone.

"Maybe this *young man* just feels uncomfortable," Sara snapped at him.

"I think that's enough for now," King said. "Miss Simpson, why don't you take Master Thompson back to the assembly. We'll continue this meeting in my office."

Rick acknowledged Sara and Rex as they left the room, and then did the same with the others. He thought for a moment that the computer would be left unguarded when the meetings participants went to the principal's office, but his hopes were dashed when the two policemen who had relieved the Officers Oslifers remained in the classroom. Rick hastily finished installing the new doorknob before going to King's office.

Tracy Hawa was walking out as Rick walked in. She wore the shortest skirt he had ever seen. He wondered how the principal could tolerate its affect on the young minds of tomorrow.

Probably, Rick thought, *because of its affect on his own.*

"Oh, hi," she said with a smile. "Can I help you?"

"I...happened to notice that the light over your desk wasn't very bright," Rick told her. *And that, to me, seems fitting.* "I thought I'd take a look at it."

"That would be great. I have to leave early today. My uncle died unexpectedly. I'm going to his wake."

"I'm sorry to hear that."

"You know, it just goes to show how even the most terrible things can have a positive aspect to them. Now get this: if Uncle Bill had died one day earlier, I wouldn't have been able to go. But because this is the anniversary date of my employment at the school, I get another year's worth of personal time. I had used it all up before today. Sometimes things just fall right into place."

Tracy let out a laugh, and Rick managed to produce a smile while wondering if this woman would be able to avoid cackling at the wake. After she left he took a chair and stood on it, removing the cover from the light in the ceiling. Rick was standing right next to the principal's office, which, fortunately for the thief, had walls that were paper thin. He could hear the discussion going on inside.

"So you're convinced that the man who gave us the computer had nothing to do with robbing the bank," King said.

"Yes," Gouveia said as he glanced at Gartner.

"So someone else used his machine to perpetrate this crime," King continued.

"I think that's likely," Gouveia responded.

"What about terrorists?" Larry Oslifer interjected.

Lionel King shot an annoyed look at the man in the white outfit and said, "I think that's a little far-fetched."

"They need a lot of money to operate their organization," Larry told him. "And what a great way to steal it without being caught."

"This sounds like a sophisticated operation to me," Tommy added. "It seems really complicated. It must have been planned by terrorists."

Tying your shoelaces probably seems complicated to you, too Rick thought to himself.

"Besides, who else would want fifty-million-dollars," Tommy continued.

"How about anyone and everyone," the principal retorted.

"I see no evidence of terrorist involvement," said Gartner firmly.

Miles had never thought about the possibility that such an organization had been responsible for the theft. Now he considered it. The vice president didn't embrace the officer's theory because it seemed likely: it was because the powers that be at the bank might overlook the failure of the security system he had recommended if they thought the bank had been victimized by such desperate, and clever, individuals.

"I think we should allow for every possibility," he said in an emphatic tone.

The FBI agent looked at his friend incredulously.

"I noticed that the schoolteacher was very protective of the boy," Gouveia continued. "Almost as if she wanted to keep us from learning anything from him."

"So Sara's involved with the terrorists," Larry said in a satisfied tone.

"Miss Simpson is dedicated to her students," the principal interjected. "I'm not surprised that she would object to having Rex interrogated by a stranger."

"I wouldn't want to jump to any conclusions," Miles Gouveia told the officers. "I'm just trying to think of all the possibilities. Do you think we could question the boy without his teacher being present?"

"I suppose," King responded. "But I won't let you run rough shod over him."

"That's not my intention, Principal King."

Lionel King walked out his office door and found Jesse Gleason working on the light over his secretary's desk.

"I see you're still on the job, Mr. Gleason."

"Yes, sir. I thought the light over Tracy's desk was a little dull," Rick responded with an inner smirk.

"I like observant people. Carry on."

"I didn't become an FBI Agent to harass children," Dan said to Miles after King left and the Oslifers took their leave to use the bathroom.

"You're not here as an FBI Agent. You're a consultant. And I'm not harassing the boy, I'm just trying to find out if he knows anything."

"We should be on the lake catching fish that we'd claim were twice as big as they really were," Dan said.

"A V.P. of Security that goes on vacation when their employer is missing fifty-million-dollars winds up fishing for another job," Gouveia pointed out.

The assembly was over, so the principal walked down to Mrs. Simpson's classroom, peering into the other ones he walked by on the way there. The suddenly attentive expressions that appeared on the faces of the students in those rooms when they caught a glimpse of their principal gave King a great deal of satisfaction. He arrived at room thirty-four and went inside, interrupting Sara's geography lesson.

"I'm sorry to intrude, Miss Simpson, but we need to ask Rex a few more questions in my office."

The boy looked petrified. Sara was tempted to say no but knew that refusing a request from the Lion King could result in a school employee being unemployed.

"I see," she said. "Let me get someone to watch the class, and we'll come down to your office."

"That won't be necessary. I'll escort Master Thompson to the meeting."

"Well, this is a very important lesson, Principal King. I'd hate for him to miss it."

"He'll be back in the wink of an eye. Come along, Master Thompson."

Sara watched helplessly as her pupil went with the principal, the youngster displaying the demeanor of someone who was about to face his doom. King tried to make casual conversation with Rex as they walked to his office, but the boy could not focus on his words. As the two walked by him Rick saw the expression on the youngster's woebegone freckled face. The thief wanted to rescue Rex, who reminded him of himself at that age, but he could not.

They entered the office, and the subject of their interrogation was told to have a seat. Rex fidgeted in the chair, his eyes darting around the room in the hope of locating a friend.

"Young man," King began. "There has been a very substantial theft from Mr. Gouveia's bank."

"You have your own bank?" Rex responded, the paralysis brought on by the current situation being momentarily cured by the thought of anyone having all that money at his disposal.

"Not really," Miles told him. "I just work for a bank."

"Dishonesty of any kind can't be tolerated by the good people in this world," the principal resumed. "We learn that here at Morgan Elementary, don't we Master Thompson."

The boy nodded weakly,

"So if there's anything you can tell us that will help the men in this room bring these thieves to justice, it would be your moral duty to do so, wouldn't it?"

Rex responded with an even weaker affirmation.

"Son, we know you weren't involved in the robbery," Gartner said pleasantly. "We're just wondering if you saw anything on the computer screen, like a name or address that would lead us to the people who robbed the bank."

"I did. I did see a name. It was Dell."

"Dell? Is that a first name or a last name," Tommy Oslifer wondered aloud.

"It's the name of the company that makes the computer," Gary Knowles told him.

"I knew that," Larry said while rolling his eyes at his brother.

"We meant a person's name," said Gouveia with an impatient look on his face.

"I didn't see nothing," Rex told them in a shaky voice.

"There must have been something on the screen," the Bank V.P. responded in an intimidating tone.

"I think Rex has given us all he's got," Dan Gartner said while looking directly at his friend.

"Yes, if there's anything you think of later on, let us know, Master Thompson," King said kindly. "You can go back to your lesson."

The boy almost stumbled out the door.

"I think he knows something." Miles said after he left.

"He knows the word Dell," Gartner told him. "The boy just started using a computer. You think he's going to recognize a program designed to rip off a bank."

"I'm sure the boy uses one at home," Knowles pointed out. "So he's probably not as green as you think."

"Exactly my point!" Gouveia agreed.

"But I would doubt that the kid knows anything about the software that took the money," the bank's computer expert quickly added.

"Mr. Knowles," Principal King said in an indignant tone. "The students who attend Morgan Elementary are human beings, not young goats!"

Miles, who found the principal's reaction to be maudlin, said "Gary meant no offense."

"So what do you want to do now?" the far from placated principal asked Gouveia.

He looked at his computer expert.

"If the original hackers were the ones who had the computer contact the bank a second time then they know it's here," Knowles told them. "They'd have to, in order to access it, because they'd need the school's internet address. I think they might try to take it from the school, in order to cover their tracks."

"So if we sit tight for a couple of days, we might be able to nail them," Larry Oslifer said.

"That sounds like a plan," Gouveia responded, even though he was dubious about the policemen's ability to apprehend anyone. "If that's all right with you, Principal King."

"I hate to see the school day disrupted," he replied thoughtfully. "But showing the children how justice is done in this country would be an invaluable lesson. We'll play this waiting game."

"I would hope that the police can maintain a presence in the school," Gouveia said to the out of uniform twins.

"I'm sure the sheriff will agree to that," Larry assured him.

"How was his trip to Turkey?" the principal asked him."

"He had a great time."

"Why was he in Turkey?" Gouveia asked them.

"He wanted to see the ruins there," Tommy explained.

There are plenty of ruins in this country. He must be queer for ruins, Gouveia thought.

Jane Plainz, a kindergarten teacher, abruptly entered the room. The men were at first startled by the agitated teacher's entrance, and then repelled by the odor emanating from her clothes.

"Did you get sprayed by a skunk?" Larry asked as he opened a window.

"No! Someone attached a small bottle of bad-smelling liquid to the door of a stall in the woman's room. When I closed it, the bottle shattered, and the liquid got on my clothes."

"A stink bomb," Gartner said, while trying not to laugh.

"Who would do such a thing?" Jane asked the principal, while removing her glasses to rub her irritated eyes.

"Miss Plainz, why don't you go home and change clothes," King instructed her.

Don't forget to take a shower, Tommy thought to himself.

"We'll find out who did this," the principal told her. Then after she left he said, "Gentlemen, what I feared would happen apparently has happened. The presence of strangers in our midst has elicited this undesirable, and very regrettable, behavior from a student, or students. I must ask that you confine yourselves to my office until your business here is through."

Gartner was about to suggest that it was merely a child's prank, but Gouveia spoke before he could express that thought.

"We'd be happy to stay out of sight, Principal King. Of

course, we will need to return to the classroom, should the thieves appear."

"Fair enough. I must leave you now gentlemen to find the deviant who did this. Feel free to use anything in my office."

"Let's get some lunch," Gouveia suggested to the others.

"I'll pass," Knowles told him. "I'd like to take a look at the school's internet connection."

Gartner went out with his friend.

"Terrorists? Don't tell me you really believe that," he said after they got in the car.

"I'm just trying to keep an open mind."

"I think you're just trying to find some cover. The board would be a lot more understanding about the security system's failure if a terrorist organization was responsible."

"Really?" Miles replied as though that thought had never occurred to him.

"Just remember how people react to that word," Gartner, who was not fooled by his friend's attempted deception, cautioned him. "There'll likely be a witch hunt if enough people start to believe this was some kind of terrorist plot. You could hurt an innocent person, like that boy or his teacher."

"I wasn't the one who suggested it. It was the keystone cops that brought it up," Miles pointed out.

"But you didn't dismiss it," Gartner countered.

"I want to look at all the possibilities," he responded as they drove away.

■ ■ ■

Rick completed his light maintenance just as the men emerged from the meeting. Larry and Tommy returned to work at the pizza parlor, which was also the destination of Miles and Dan. Rick was walking back to the custodian's office when he saw Rex in the alcove of the school's front entrance. He looked devastated, and appeared to be contemplating his escape.

"My name is Jesse Gleason. What's going on, Rex?"

The little boy started to speak, but then hesitated.

"I'm good at keeping secrets. Why are you about to go over the wall?"

"The wall? I was gonna run out the door," the boy told him.

"That's what I meant."

Rex looked at the red-haired adult standing before him, realizing that he was once a red-haired boy like himself. The distraught youngster also noticed the empathy in the custodian's eyes but failed to interpret the self-reproaching expression on his face. Rex put his head down before confiding in Rick.

"I typed *Miss Simpson smells* on the computer. Then it went crazy, and all these words that I couldn't understand came on the screen."

Rick smiled at the boy with the weight of the world on his shoulders.

"I couldn't tell Principal King that," Rex continued. "If he told Miss Simpson what I did it would hurt her feelings."

Rick remembered having a crush on one of his elementary school teachers. Everything she did or said produced feelings within him that he did not understand. Realizations about their true nature would not come until many years later. A wistful feeling came over the thief, but he did not forget his purpose for being in the school. The words Rex had typed into the computer had somehow awoken Binny's program. Rick had learned something valuable today.

"Don't worry about it, pal. You really didn't mean it, right?"

"Oh, no. Miss Simpson doesn't smell."

"It'll be our secret, Rex."

After escorting his new friend back to the classroom, Rick returned to the custodians' room.

Henry asked him to come into his office.

"Jesse, please close the door and sit down."

Rick obliged him.

"I don't know what the deal was at the other places you've worked," his boss began. "But this is *my* school. I know Principal King thinks it's his, but he only controls the faculty and the students. The building itself is my domain. I see to it that the heat's on in the winter, so the little angels don't freeze their collective asses off. I make sure the toilets aren't backed up, so the cream of our youthful crop doesn't puke all over themselves when they have to use the john. Understand that?"

"Absolutely."

"To keep this place together, I need custodians that do the job in a timely and efficient manner. I believe I raised that point before, like when we first met. So can you tell me why it took you over an hour to put in a lousy door knob?"

"I also worked on one of the ceiling lights in the principal's office. I had noticed that it was flickering when I was in there for my interview."

"So you see a problem, and you do something about it. That's very good. But what's very bad is that you created another problem by doing it. Do you know what I mean?"

Rick gave him a perplexed look.

"You didn't tell the Pabst. Maybe I had something more important for you to do. What if one of the little tykes got their finger caught on the rim while playing a game of b ball?"

"Can these kids jump that high?"

"That's not the point."

I never seem to get the point.

"I'm just making something up. So follow me on this. We need a ladder to get the kid down without ripping his finger off. The other custodians are unavailable, and I don't know where the ladder is, because that's a small detail. I don't concern myself with those."

Rick was tempted to point out that the ladders were hanging right outside his office door but then thought better of it.

"So I need you, because you should know where the ladder is, but because I don't know where the hell you are, this kid loses a finger."

How about using the PA system.

"Because I couldn't find you, that kid has to go through the rest of his life with the nickname nine fingers. Now you see the problem."

"You're right. The next time I'll ask before I do something you didn't tell me to do."

"That's what I'm saying. So how did the light come out?"

It's much brighter than you. Then he said aloud "It's working fine."

"Beautiful! There's a cracked window in thirty-eight. Paul should be back any minute. You two guys take care of that for me."

"Will do, boss."

The day was over when Rex walked into the custodians' room. Rick was cleaning off the tools they had used to fix the window.

"Hi Jesse. You've got Bowmarc! He's awesome."

The action figure had been jabbing his thigh when he sat down, so Rick had removed it from his pocket and placed it on the shelf. He told the boy, "He's my good luck charm."

"Miss Simpson asked me to tell you that she needs a favor. And she said to make sure you bring your tool kit."

"What's the problem?"

"I don't know. But she was acting a little weird."

"I don't know if I have a tool to fix a weird teacher, but I'll give it a shot."

Rex laughed.

"I have to go, Jesse."

"Have a good night."

Rick walked down to room thirty-four. The two policemen on duty were outside in the hall. He peered through the window, and saw Sara sitting at her desk, speaking with an older child. There was something odd about her posture, though he could not discern what it was at the moment. The boy started to walk towards the door, so Jesse opened it and stepped inside.

"Now don't forget what I said, Kevin. Things like this could wind up on your permanent record," Sara reminded him just before he left. "And that will follow you for the rest of your life."

"I know Miss Simpson, I know," he responded without stopping or turning around before leaving the room.

"How's the new doorknob working out?" Rick asked her.

"Actually, not too well," Sara replied. "You put it in backwards."

Rick meekly apologized. Sara looked at him and began to laugh. Her laughter was contagious, and he could not help but join in.

"I mean it's really great, if you're not too concerned about security. I hope you do a better job on Dad's toilet," she said with a smile.

"I'll make sure of it. It's number one on my list of priorities."

"Well, actually, there's something I'd like you to do first. I'm in kind of a jam."

Rick suddenly noticed that Sara was leaning to one side. Her right arm was in the center drawer of the desk.

"I got my hand stuck in the drawer," she said sheepishly. "I'm afraid that if I try to yank it out I'll either tear up my shirt or arm or both. It's hung up on something in there."

"How long have you been like that?"

"About an hour. I managed to finish teaching the lesson without the blackboard, but I'm not too keen on going home with a desk on my arm. Do you think you can help me out?"

"That depends," Rick said as bent down to examine the desk. "If you answer one question for me truthfully, I'll set you free."

"So the truth will set me free. What's the question?"

"There's really no such thing as a permanent record, right?"

Sara laughed and said "Well, I suppose if someone checked with your elementary school when you were forty they might still have a file on you, but I doubt it. And there isn't one master file containing everything a student ever did in school following the person around like the grim reaper for the rest of his or her life. We just try to make it sound that way."

"I thought so," Rick said triumphantly as he took out the screws holding the desk drawer in place. "I got threatened with negative entries on my permanent record so many times when I was a kid I thought my life was going to be over at ten."

"What school did you go to? I'd like to check out that file."

"I'll never tell," Rick said as he removed the drawer and Sara stood up. "Now that I rescued you, I'll fix the door."

"Tomorrow will be fine. The cops are going to be here all night, so it really doesn't make any difference. I'd like to thank you. Are you hungry?"

"Sure."

"How about some pizza?"

"Well, I'm off pizza right now. But I could go for a hero. Though I'd prefer it if you could just destroy my permanent record instead."

"Now that's a tall order. I think they keep those things in the Vatican, behind one of the gargoyles. Let's get some grub."

Rick went back to the custodians' room to change, and then met Sara in the parking lot. The two of them encountered Gus Hanson there. He was the school's physical education teacher. Gus ran up to Sara and showed her an email he had received that day.

"This is it!" he exclaimed as she read it.

"A Nigerian prince has left you two-hundred-million dollars. You really believe that?" Sara questioned him when she finished reading it.

"Yes I do. My ship has come in!"

"Why would Prince Narfia leave the money to you?"

"Didn't you read it? He didn't have any heirs, so I've been chosen."

"How would the prince, or anyone else in Nigeria for that matter, know about you? Have you ever been there?"

"Sara, the world is a much smaller place today. It's a global village. Everybody knows everything about everyone."

And in this town, everyone cares because they have nothing else to do, Rick mused.

"All I have to do is pay the two-hundred-dollar banking fee, and I'm outta here."

"I think it's a scam, Gus. I don't think you should give them any money, or any of your personal information. This is Jesse Gleason."

"Nice to meet you, Jesse. Sorry I won't get to know you, but I'm about to become a rich man."

It's a great feeling, Rick mused.

"See you soon Sara, but not for long," Gus said to her before getting in his car.

"Good old Gullible," Sara said after he drove away. "Gus believes every internet scam that shows up in his inbox. He's always dreaming about leaving Morgan Town to go on Gullible's travels, courtesy of a Nigerian Prince, or some other fictional person."

"The thought of having all that money can make anything sound reasonable," Rick said knowingly.

"You sound like you'd be susceptible to something like that. Remind me to sell you the Brooklyn Bridge later."

"I'll only buy the bridge if it comes with a warranty."

"You're a tough sell."

They got into their respective cars and Rick followed Sara to the parking lot of an Italian eatery named Blando's. He hoped the name was not meant to infer anything about the fare that was served here. They stepped inside and walked up to the counter. Sara ordered two slices while Rick requested a meat ball hero.

"I'll wait for the food. You grab a table," she told him.

"That sounds good. How much is the hero?" Rick, who had suddenly remembered that he only had a dollar, asked uneasily.

"It's on me. I know that's atypical for a teacher, but I'm out to break the mold."

"Thanks. I'll return the favor sometime."

Rick walked over to the dining area to find that all the tables were taken. He was about to look for a booth when a very attractive young woman who had been sitting alone stood up.

"Excuse me, are you leaving?" he asked her.

"Yes." Then she said in a seductive voice "Aren't you going to try to talk me out of it?"

Her perfectly layered black hair and brilliant green eyes would have, at any other time, given Rick pause. On this occasion he was anxious to talk with Sara, to see if she knew anything about the bank's efforts to recover their money. Rick hesitated, and as a result, didn't get the chance to respond.

"Roomie!" Sara greeted her while handing Rick his hero.

"You know this dashing fellow?" she asked.

"He works at the school. This is Jesse Gleason. Jesse, this is Maya Baxter, my friend and roommate. Would you like to join us?"

"I sure would," she said with a quick glance at Rick. "But I just stopped in to have something quick for a late lunch. You see I'm also her father's secretary. He'll start to worry if I'm late getting back to the office. He likes my boobies."

"I really don't want to hear about my father and your boobies," Sara told her. Then she looked directly at her friend's chest and said, "Nothing personal."

"Anyway, I have to get back to work," Maya said.

"Give Dad my love," Sara said with just a hint of sarcasm in her voice.

"Sara, did you hear?" Jane Plainz asked as she approached her colleague.

"Yes. Are you all right?"

"What's happening to our school? I mean, first the parents start holding back their kids for a year so they'll have an advantage when they start kindergarten. One mother told me it was because she wanted her boy to be one of the popular kids in high school. By starting school a year later he'll be one of the first to have a license, which will win a lot of friends for him. I mean, I'll wind up teaching a bunch of twelve-year-olds at this rate. My students aren't as cute or as well behaved as they used to be. And now I can't even use the woman's room without being attacked!"

"One of your kindergarten students attacked you in the woman's room?" Maya asked her. "My, those kids are getting bolder all the time."

"Someone put a stink bomb in the woman's bathroom," Sara explained. "Jane had to go home and change."

"It took forever to get the smell out of my hair," the distraught teacher complained while patting the tightly wound bun that had been created with her auburn locks for emphasis.

"Would you like to join Jesse and me?"

"Thanks, but I ordered takeout. I just need to go home and relax. I'm just glad they didn't put any of those stupid computers in my classroom. I'd resign! I'll see you two tomorrow."

"Maybe if she gets stink bombed often enough she'll be forced to buy a new wardrobe, and wear another color besides gray, which could only help her social life," Maya observed after Jane left.

"Don't be catty," Sara admonished her.

"You're the one who calls her Plainz Jane, because she dresses like a schoolmarm from *Little House on the Prairie*. You've also commented on the fact that she's too cheap to eat anything other than tuna fish for lunch."

"It's great to have a roommate with a good memory," Sara said sarcastically.

"Nice to meet you, Jesse. I'll see you later, Sara."

They sat down and ate their food. Rick's hero contained egg plant instead of meatballs, but he ate it without complaining. Sara noticed the mistake as she wiped a bit of sauce from her pug nose.

"Didn't you order something else?"

"Yeah, but egg plant is good too."

"I'm not really surprised you got the wrong hero. Larry and Tommy Oslifer are working in the kitchen."

"That's right. They were the two police officers that were out of uniform."

"That's the Officers Oslifers. They work here and at the bowling alley too. They're determined to be millionaires before turning forty. The only thing no one can figure out is when they sleep, though I suspect it may be when they're in their patrol car."

"They must be exhausted. I'm surprised they didn't serve me one of their guns on a hero. So have they found out who robbed the bank?"

"I don't think they're getting anywhere with the investigation. The school board never should have approved the use of donated computers. I had suggested that they purchase new ones, because when you get something that's used you very often inherit someone else's problems. And was I ever right."

"What did they ask you about at the police station?"

"They just wanted to know what I was digging up. The Officers Oslifers believe that terrorists are responsible for the robbery. They thought I was communicating with the thieves through secret messages that were buried in the park. By the way, do you wear those gloves everywhere?"

Rick had neglected to remove his work gloves. Since there was no real chance of the authorities lifting his prints from the restaurant, he did so now.

"I'm just so used to having them on. I like to wear them all the time at the school to prevent my spreading any germs to the kids. Did you know that Garfield died from an infection, not a gunshot wound?"

"You mean the cat? Poor kitty."

Rick was surprised that the teacher apparently misunderstood him, but then quickly realized she was joking.

"That's on our learning quilt," Sara said after she stopped laughing. "There's a bunch of interesting facts on it. I added the one about President Garfield because I wanted the students to be aware of how dangerous infections can be. It might improve their hygiene."

"That was a good idea. It sounds like I picked an interesting time to get a job at the school."

"You sure did. I know you've only been there one day, but what do you think so far?"

"Everyone seems really nice. One thing did strike me as a little odd, though. How could Tracy be the principal's secretary? I mean she seems a little bit ditzy. And he's so serious."

Sara laughed, almost choking on her slice of pizza.

"It does boggle the mind, doesn't it? Principal King is so pious, and Sally is so...well let's just say there's been a lot of conjecture about the Lion King and Lady Ha Ha. But you won't hear anything about it from me."

"Okay," Rick said with a grin. "You're the m.y.o.b. type. I have another question for you. Who's that guy with the slicked back hair standing by the counter?"

The man Rick subtly gestured towards wore a disinterested, yet somehow intense expression on his face.

"That's Marlon Blando," Sara said with a smirk.

"Is that his real name?"

"Well, the Blando part is. His real first name is Marvin. Maya and I always called him Marlon as in Marlon Brando, because Blando sounds like Brando. And it's also because Marvin thinks he's Vito Corleone. He just loves those movies."

"But you don't call him that to his face, of course."

"Heck no, I don't want to get rubbed out. I really have nothing to worry about though because he isn't even Italian. I mean if that guy is connected, then I'm with the CIA. And I can't even spell CIA."

"I guess you wouldn't want to teach his kids. If they failed, you'd be sleeping with the fishes."

"You're right. But Marlon doesn't have any children, so that will never be a problem."

"With that expensive suit he's wearing the man looks more like the Dapper Don," Rick observed.

"You're right again. But Marlon Brando never played John Gotti, so I see Blando as Vito Corleone."

"So what name are you going to come up with for me?" Rick asked as he took a sip of his beer.

"Well, if you were heavy, I'd call you Jackie Gleason. But you're not, so I'll either have to fatten you up or think of another name."

"Actually, Gleason lost a lot of weight at one point."

"I'll take that into consideration."

"And what does everyone call you behind your back?"

"Why Miss Simpson, of course."

"Speaking of names, I forgot to tell the Pabst that I was going to your classroom. I'll probably hear about that tomorrow."

"He told you that everyone calls him the Pabst, right. And you'll notice that the only one who refers to him that way is himself. I call him the Pope."

"Now I'm in trouble with the Pope. I better make sure I watch my step with Marlon Blando, too. I'm not going anywhere near his non-existent children."

"You're getting the hang of this place, Jackie Gleason. Welcome to Morgan Town. Would you like a Tic Tac?"

"Sure."

` "Do you know how you tell if it's a tic or a tac?" Sara asked as she put the mint in his hand. "If it starts sucking your blood, it's a tic. If you step on it in your bare feet and it hurts you, it's a tac."

"That's the most useful thing anyone ever told me," Rick said with a laugh.

"Oh, oh," Sara said ominously.

"Did you get bitten by a tic?"

"No, someone just walked in that I don't need to see."

"Miss Simpson," Lana Landers said as she came over to their table.

"Mrs. Landers. How are you?"

"Just fine. I want to commend you on the wonderful job you're doing with your class. Guinevere is learning so much."

Here comes the "but" Sara thought as she thanked her for the compliment.

"But there is one small problem. As you know, for the first years of her life we called our daughter Gwen. Then she discovered that Guinevere, which is her real name as I'm sure you're aware of, was a princess. So we started addressing our daughter by her full name. However, it seems the students in your class refuse to make the transition."

"I'm aware of that, and I have tried to get their co-operation, but children that age are notorious for being contrary."

As are people of any age, Rick chuckled to himself.

"I think the issue will work itself out over time," Sara told the girl's mother.

"I don't know if you understand how important this is. We want our daughter to find her inner princess."

You've already found your outer asshole, lady, Rick thought.

"I know you're trying to resolve some legal issues at the moment...."

"I don't have any legal issues to resolve. That was a misunderstanding. A child has to learn to deal with frustration. The people they encounter in their lives aren't always going to do what they'd like them to do," Sara pointed out.

"I respect your opinion, Miss Simpson. I hope you don't mind if I discuss this with Principal King. I'll see him at the annual Knights of Columbus dinner tonight."

"Not at all, Mrs. Landers. And enjoy the dinner. My father is going too, and he told me that it's one of his favorite events of the year."

Lana Landers paused for a moment before responding.

"You know, on second thought, I think we'll try it your way. I'm sure Gwen; I mean Guinevere, will persuade her classmates to use her full name over time. Keep up the good work, Miss Simpson."

"She sure changed her tune quickly enough," Rick said after Lana left. "Is your father connected?"

"No," Sara told him. "He's Edgar Morgan. He owns the biggest business in Morgan Town. People are very intimidated by him, because a lot of them get their weekly paychecks from Morgan Widgets."

"What's a widget?"

"A device that controls other devices. Dad would never tell me what the other ones were since the company makes the widgets for the military. Top secret, you know. They probably operate the t.v. in the officer's club. Widget. That always sounded like the name of a teenybopper from the sixties to me."

"You remember Gidget?" Rick asked with a smile.

"Thank God for reruns. Anyway, I really hate to drop his name like that, but I'd rather spend my time coming up with ways to reach the children, not using it to debate the best way to find one little girl's inner princess. It would be great to teach in a place where the education of the students is all that matters. A place where your efforts are appreciated, for the right reasons."

"If your dad is a Morgan..."

"Then why am I a Simpson? It's because I got tired of people being intimidated by the name Morgan. It seemed like people were always walking on eggshells when they were around me, because I might report something negative they said about my father's company to him. So I started to use my mother's maiden name."

"One more question, if you don't mind. When I was in school I had an English teacher named Mrs. Iglio. She used to stick students in the head with her pencil when they misbehaved. In fact, since they used lead pencils back in those days, I think I might have lead poisoning of the brain as a result."

"You must have been very bad!"

"I'll take the fifth on that one. My question is, are you that kind of teacher?"

"Hell no. This is the twenty-first century. I use a taser."

"You're not serious, are you Miss Simpson?" Ruth Childs, the mother of a boy named Benjamin who just happened to be walking by, asked her.

"Of course not, Mrs. Childs," Sara replied with a smile.

"You're doing a wonderful job with your students..."

Here comes another but, Sara thought. *I'm surrounded by buts.*

"But our Benjamin has become obsessed with using Google ever since you started teaching the children about computers. I told him last night that a boy his age should be in bed by nine o'clock and he showed me an article on the internet that said ten o'clock was satisfactory."

"What was your response?"

"I told him that when the person who wrote the article adopts you, he'll get to choose your bedtime. Until then, it's my job."

"I think that's perfect. You'll always get challenges from a child whose Benjamin's age, no matter what he's taught in school."

Just wait until he gets older, Rick thought with a silent chuckle.

Sara continued. "To not let them learn about computers in this day and age because of something like that would be a serious mistake, I think."

"I'm sure you're right," the mother grudgingly conceded. "I hope your trouble with the police isn't anything that will distract you from your work."

"Not even for a moment," Sara said confidently.

"I'll talk to you soon."

"How do you put up with those people?" Rick asked her.

"Listening to the complaints is worth it when I see the expression on the children's faces after they learn something," Sara explained.

They finished their meal and left the restaurant.

"Thanks for dinner, Miss Simpson, of course."

"I enjoyed it, Jackie Gleason. Good luck with the Pope tomorrow."

Rick drove back to the house. He was walking towards the front door when he felt a tap on the shoulder. He froze, thinking that the law had caught up with him. Then Rick slowly turned around. Mary was behind him.

My heart can't take much more of this.

"I'm sorry to bother you. But there's something I have to tell you, and I'm not quite sure how to do it," Mary said sheepishly.

"Just come right out and say it," Rick suggested. "That's usually the best way."

Mary hesitated before saying "Well, you see, I wasn't supposed to rent this house to you."

"What?"

"I hated the thought of living next door to an empty house for such a long time. It made me feel very lonely. So I put an ad in the paper and rented it."

There are other houses around yours that are occupied. You weren't going to be like Tom Hanks in Castaway, Rick thought before asking "Where did you get the keys?"

"The owner gave them to me. I was supposed to water his plants. He'll be back here on Sunday. I don't think you should be here when he comes home."

Rick just nodded.

"I'll see you soon."

"These people are all certifiable!" Rick bellowed after Mary had departed.

He went inside and found his partners congregated in the kitchen. Rick told them about Mary's revelation.

"If the owner of this house shows up while we're still in town there could be trouble," Rick said in conclusion.

"We didn't do anything wrong," Sylvia pointed out. "It's the crazy lady next door who has some explaining to do."

Takes one to know one, Rick mused. Then he said "I'm sure this guy will think that something's missing from the house. And that means the cops will want to question us about it."

"And we did do something wrong," Oscar interjected. "I mean, robbing the money from the bank would be considered wrong by most people."

"I was strictly speaking about renting the house," Sylvia responded in an annoyed tone. "You always take things out of context."

"You have to let me know that you're strictly speaking," her husband fired back. "You can't just assume everyone knows that you're not just speaking, but *strictly* speaking. I always do."

"When did you ever tell me that you were strictly...?"

"We have to find a way to get to the computer quickly," Rick interrupted her.

"I'll think about it," Binny said.

"So how did it go at the school?" Oscar asked him.

"I found out a few things," he replied.

"Good. You can tell us while we're having dinner," said Sylvia as she strained the pasta.

"I already ate," Rick told her as he opened a beer.

Sylvia put the strainer down and turned to face him, hands on hips, while looking over the top of her glasses.

"You could have called," she said in an annoyed tone.

"Well, it was a last-minute thing. One of the teachers asked me to dinner."

"You knew I'd be making dinner."

How did I know that?

"I'm sure you'll find room for Sylvia's crab cakes and spaghetti, Rick," Oscar said as he sat down at the kitchen table with Binny. "She always makes it on Monday. You'll love it!"

"He already ate," Sylvia said while busying herself at the stove.

"I had dinner with the teacher that has our computer in her class," Rick explained.

"Well, the man was taking care of business. You can't bust his balls for that," Oscar told his wife.

"A phone call. One phone call," Sylvia responded without turning around.

"I can eat a crab cake," Rick volunteered.

"They're really good," Binny said.

"No, it's not necessary," Sylvia responded as she put the food on the table. "You'll have an upset stomach from too much food."

"No way," Rick told her as he sat down at the table.

They all filled their plates, including the man who was to be constantly scrutinized by the cook for signs of nausea. Rick found her probing glances irritating, but still managed to resist the temptation to comment about Sylvia's stares.

"I found out a lot today," he addressed Oscar and Binny. "It seems the little boy that was using the computer activated your program by typing in the words *Miss Simpson smells*. That just happens to be the name of his teacher. She's the one I had dinner with."

Sylvia made an irritated sound as she cleared her throat.

"That's wild!" Binny exclaimed. "My third-grade teacher was Miss Simpson. I wrote the same thing on the blackboard when she wasn't looking. I used those words to activate the shortcut that activates the program! It's karma!"

"Why would you be thinking of your third-grade teacher when you were writing that program?" Rick asked him.

"I had just watched *The Simpsons*. And I noticed that Marge Simpson looked like my teacher."

"Did your teacher have blue hair?" Rick inquired.

"No, it was gray. But the style was very similar to Marge's. And now it turns out that the computer is in Miss Simpson's class. Karma!"

"Well, whatever's responsible, this is not a good thing. There's a guy from the bank named Gouveia who seems very determined to get the money back. He's also has an FBI Agent with him. But the guy isn't here in an official capacity. He's just helping Gouveia. I got the impression that they're friends. A couple of the local cops think that terrorists took the money. And the bank guy liked the theory. That could help us."

"Can you get to the computer?" Binny asked.

"No, there's always someone watching it. Can you get into the computer through the internet and erase the program?"

"I tried. But they've got a really sophisticated firewall on their system. They're very concerned about protecting the kids. I couldn't get through it."

"I have an idea," Rick said. "I got to know the kid who typed *Miss Simpson smells*. If you can put something on a CD Rom that will wipe out your program, I'll give it to the kid. Put a video game on there too. I'll tell him to check out the game, and hopefully he'll use the CD on Moore's computer."

"That's a great idea! I can set it up so the erasing program runs in the background. The kid will only see the video game on the screen," said an enthusiastic Binny.

"It's the best we can do, at least for now," Rick told them. "Unless you guys have another suggestion."

Neither of them did.

"I'm really surprised that Gouveia hasn't gone to the feds," said Binny. "I'm going to try to hack into his email. He might be discussing the situation with someone else. We could learn something useful. I'll use a computer at the library."

"That sounds good to me," Rick told him.

After they finished eating Binny went upstairs to create the CD. Sylvia began to clear the table.

"You've done enough," Rick said pleasantly. "And Oscar was right. That was a delicious meal."

"How's your stomach?" a somewhat mollified Sylvia asked him.

"Couldn't be better. I'll clean up the mess. You two can have your coffee inside."

"Let's have it in the bedroom." Oscar suggested.

"That's a fantastic idea," Sylvia said in a suggestive tone.

"The ballgame's on," Oscar informed her.

"So who's this Carmen?" a disappointed Sylvia asked as the couple walked up the stairs.

"I don't know. She must be Binny's friend."

Rick rolled his eyes and began placing the dirty dishes in the dishwasher. After finishing that task he turned to get the pots, and nearly jumped through the ceiling. Mary Popkins was standing behind him.

"Hi Jesse. I just wanted to make sure you didn't need anything."

"Do you happen to have a defibrillator?"

"A what?"

"We're doing just fine."

"Hi there," Oscar said to her as he entered the room. "I need another crab cake."

"Hi Steve," Mary said before giving him a curious look.

"What's the matter?" Oscar asked her.

"You look different today."

"What do you mean?" the bookie questioned Mary.

"I don't know. There's just something different about you. Good night, guys. If you need me, I'm right next door."

I have a feeling it's going to be hard to forget that Rick thought before saying "Have a good night."

"Do I look different, Ricky," a perplexed Oscar asked him after she left.

"Not to me."

"But Mary thinks I do."

"Good night, Oscar," Rick said.

"Good night, Rick," the preoccupied bookie replied.

"She appears out of nowhere," Rick thought aloud before falling asleep. "There must be some kind of magic in those glasses she wears. That lady is Mary Pop Ins. I have to mention that to Sara."

CHAPTER 9

Rick arrived at Morgan Elementary the next morning with Binny's CD in his pocket. He planned to stake out Miss Simpson's classroom in the hope that Rex would visit the boy's room at some point during that day. His boss was waiting for him with a very stoic look on his face when Rick walked into the custodian's office.

"The Pabst," he said somberly. "Is not pleased."

I'm sorry, your holiness, Rick thought to himself, remembering Sara's name for the head custodian. Then aloud "I'm sorry. I should have told you I was going to help Sara. But it sounded like an emergency, so I rushed down there."

"That young lady is always getting herself into trouble," Henry pointed out. "She can be a real dipsey doodle sometimes. If we lose our heads every time Sara has a problem we'll all wind up in the bug house."

"I hear you, boss," Rick said. "I'll do a better job of communicating, starting right now. I noticed a loose ceiling tile outside room thirty-four yesterday. If it falls off it could hit someone. I thought I'd fix it first thing this morning."

"Don't worry, these kids all have hard heads," Pabst said with a smile. "I have something else in mind for you today. It'll be your initiation."

"You'll need this," said Mike, another custodian, as he handed his co-worker a rubber suit.

"What's it for?" Rick asked apprehensively after observing the grin on his face.

"You have to clean out the grease trap," Pabst told him.

"Is it radioactive?" Rick, who was reminded of the suits worn by the workers at nuclear power plants, inquired.

"Hell, no," Mike said with a laugh. "It's just messy. You'll feel like you've been swallowed by a monster from outer space."

"One of the custodians took the snake home with him and didn't bring it back," Pabst informed Rick. "And since he doesn't work here anymore, it's gone for good. You'll have to use this."

He handed Rick a back scratcher with a small claw-like hand on the end of it.

There is no easy money Rick thought as he followed them down the hall.

Pabst and his other charge led him to the grease trap in the school's parking lot. The three of them struggled to lift the heavy lid covering the pit. After that task was accomplished Rick took his first look at the world of ooze that he was about to enter.

There is no easy money, Rick thought again.

"Put the goo you collect in this bucket." Pabst handed it to him. "When it's full, pass it up to Mike and he'll give you another one. Good luck, Jesse. I'll write your next of kin if you disappear down there."

"Tell them I was brave," Rick replied in dramatic fashion after putting on the suit.

He slid into the oily sea while fighting the urge to vomit. The aroma would have been enough to elicit that response, but there was also the sensation of being absorbed by the thick slime that had been produced by a countless number of oily french fries and other culinary delights. Rick collected the grease with the back scratcher, which proved to be a woefully inadequate tool for the job. He moved back and forth through the alien environment and handed the bucket to Mike when it was full, repeatedly resisting the urge to dump its contents on his co-worker's head after seeing the smirk on his face.

How long he spent in the trap Rick did not know, but the novice bank robber now believed he knew what being cast into hell would be like.

"Hey grease ball!" a student shouted from one of the classroom windows as he emerged from the pit.

"It's the slime creature" another one joined in. "Run away!"

"Do you want to go pick up some chicks?" a third boy asked sarcastically.

Rick removed the suit and smiled at the hecklers.

"You can take care of that ceiling tile now," Pabst said after giving him a pat on the back. "You survived the pit, Jesse. You're gonna make it here."

"Thanks, boss. It's an experience I won't soon forget."

Rick walked by Mike, who seemed disappointed that the newcomer had succeeded. He went into the custodians' office to get a ladder before entering the hallway.

"Do you want me to help you carry that?"

Rick turned around and found Rex standing behind him.

"Thanks, but I can manage. How are you doing today/"

"I'm still worried. I think they're going to keep asking me about what I did on the computer."

"I have something that might help you forget about that Rex. Come here a second."

Rick took him down the corridor leading to the administrative area where school traffic was minimal. He reached into his pocket and showed Rex the CD.

"There's a video game on here that I think you're going to love."

"Really? I'm not allowed to play video games at home anymore. I chopped the head off my sister's favorite doll."

Le guillotine!

"My parents said I couldn't play any games for a month."

This is perfect, Rick thought before saying "You can check it out here. Just slip it into the computer you're using when no one's looking."

"We have a test today, so I won't get a chance to use it, because Miss Simpson walks around the room when we're taking a test. But there are some people coming to watch us use the computers tomorrow. She usually stays up front when we have company. Then I'll get a chance to look at the game."

"Don't tell anyone where you got the CD from, okay?"

"Oh, I won't, I promise. I have to get back to class before they start wondering if I fell into the toilet bowl. Thanks Jesse!"

Thank you.

Rick ostensibly went to repair a light in the corridor outside Miss Simpson's classroom the next day, though his real motivation was to learn if Rex had used the CD. He set up the ladder and peered through the window in the door. Gouveia and Gartner were inside. They had apparently convinced the principal that their presence would elicit no aberrant behavior from the students on this occasion. The Officers Oslifers stood near one of the many windows on the parking lot side of the classroom, trying to remain unobtrusive. There was also a group of adults sitting in chairs in front of the class. One of them was Principal King, who was sitting next to a woman Rick had never met. She appeared to be a rigid, strait-laced individual. Father Joseph was seated on her right.

I hope they're not giving Rex the death penalty for typing Miss Simpson smells, Rick mused.

"Good morning class," Sara greeted her students. "You all know Principal King, of course. This is his wife, who's an advisor to our PTA. And I'm sure you've all met Father Joseph. They want to watch you use your computers. The first thing we're going to do is learn a song called *High Hopes*. We'll get the lyrics from the internet. Now let's all turn our computer on and login. If anyone needs help, raise your hands."

Most of the students handled the task with ease, with only a couple of them requesting the teacher's assistance. Rex logged on with no problem, and then began to look around the classroom like a criminal who was about to strike. He was waiting for a moment when Sara and the other adults were focused on the blackboard. As Rex had expected, Miss Simpson obliged him by walking up to it and writing the name of a website the class was to access. All eyes in the room were watching her, except the two belonging to Rex Thompson. He slipped the CD Jesse had given him into his machine and waited for the game to start.

You have to understand, she touches a primal nerve within me Principal King's voice came out of the computer's speakers and startled everyone in the room. *Tracy is a witch. She's put a spell on me. I can't resist her.*

A startled Sara Simpson stopped writing and looked at the principal. The people around him did the same, while Father Joseph managed to keep his gaze fixed on the blackboard.

He must be queer for ding bats, Gouveia thought.

Mrs. King, whose stern countenance was a match for her mate's, began boring a hole in her husband's head with her two smoldering eyes.

Principal King was speechless at first, but his silence did not last for long. He stood up after running his hands through his long blonde mane and almost sprinted to Rex's desk.

"The terrorists did this!" he exclaimed in an outraged tone while picking up the CD that Rex had removed from the computer. "They're trying to destroy the moral fiber of our school, by impugning the integrity of its leader!"

Sara, who was the target of the principal's glare, thought *why is he looking at me like that?*

What does that statement have in common with the largest reptile in the Nile River? They're both crocs, Rick mused.

"Lionel, what are you talking about!" his wife demanded an explanation.

"As I explained to you before, someone has used one of the machines in this room to rob a bank. Apparently, they want the funds for nefarious purposes. They've also decided to corrupt the minds of our young people by destroying their moral compass-namely me!"

"Where did they get a recording of you saying those things?" she asked him suspiciously.

"They probably tapped my phone," he replied. "Then they went through their recordings and found the words needed to portray me in the worst possible light. That sounds likely, doesn't it Mr. Gouveia."

"Absolutely," the Bank V.P. replied, being more than willing to support anyone who believed the terrorist hypothesis. Gartner gave them both a disapproving look.

This guy is a quick thinker, thought Rick, who was listening at the door.

"That's despicable!" Ellen King exclaimed.

And your acceptance of that explanation is incredible, Rick thought to himself. *What the hell did you put on that CD, Binny?*

"Master Thompson," the principal addressed Rex in his most intimidating tone. "Do you know where this came from?"

The boy weakly shook his head while the principal held up the CD. He now expected to get the worst in a series of interrogations by the adults in the room. Rex was spared, however, by the principal's desire to quickly end this episode and send his wife home.

"They must have snuck in overnight and put it in the computer," King concluded.

"Maybe we were drugged. That's why we didn't see them," Larry Oslifer suggested.

"These people will stop at nothing!" Tommy chimed in.

The Oslifers must have been asleep, both Sara and Rick thought simultaneously. *They didn't see the imaginary terrorists.*

"My computer people should take a look at the CD," Gouveia suggested, though he doubted that the principal would allow it.

"This vile thing cannot yield any truths, Mr. Gouveia. I'll speak to you later, my dear." Lionel King caressed his wife.

She left the room, looking at Sara with a sneer while doing so.

What did I do? the teacher thought before resuming her lesson. Rick finished fixing the unbroken light and returned to the janitor's office.

This November day was unusually mild, which allowed the children to play outside during their lunch break. Rick managed to be near the children from Sara's class, pretending to repair a non-existent hole in the fence around the school yard. A very flustered Rex Thompson came over to talk with him.

"Hey, pal, I heard there was a problem with the CD. I'm sorry about that."

"It's not your fault. It's mine," Rex said dejectedly. "I really wanted to play the game, so I used it after I got home yesterday. My parents took my Atari, but my dad has a computer in his office. I never used it before, but I thought it might be like the one at school. I had just put the CD in the machine when I heard my mom coming up the stairs. I took it out, and started to run to my room, when I knocked a bunch of other CDs off his desk. I picked them up as fast as I could. There were a lot them. I must have taken the wrong one to school with me."

"What does your Dad do for a living?"

"He talks to people. I can't remember the word for it."

He must be a talk show host.

` Principal King appeared in the school yard. He gestured for Rex to join him. The boy hesitantly obeyed. Rick watched him walk over to the Lion King and suddenly felt very guilty. Rex returned shortly after with anxiety visible in his every step.

"He wants to see me alone after school," Rex said in an ominous tone. "I'm so dead, Jesse. He wants to know where the CD came from. What am I going to do? If my parents find out that I tried to play the game, they'll kill me."

Rick thought for a moment before answering. "I think if you tell him what happened, he'll let you off the hook."

"Really? He won't tell my parents?"

"I think the principal would rather not tell anyone where the CD came from," Rick said confidently. "Just tell the truth, Rex. You'll be home free."

"Well, okay. I just hope you're right."

"Trust me on this, pal. And let me know how it turns out."

Rex appeared at the principal's office after school. There were no other people around, which only made the boy's sense of dread more acute. Yet Jesse had assured him that things would work out, and he trusted his new friend.

"Principal King," Rex said in a very small voice as he entered his office. "I'm here."

"Indeed you are, Master Thompson," King said in his much larger one as he walked up behind him. "Have a seat."

Rex climbed into a chair in front of the principal's desk. His heart was racing.

"Your father is Stanley Thompson, correct?"

Rex nodded weakly.

"I take it that you took this from him," King said as he removed the CD from his pocket.

"I wanted to play a video game that was on a CD....my friend gave me. I was using it on my dad's computer, in his office. Then I heard someone coming, so I started to leave, but my CD got all mixed up with my dad's CDs...I took the wrong one."

"Why did you leave when you heard someone approaching?"

"I'm not supposed to play video games," Rex said apprehensively. "I chopped the head off my sister's doll, so my parents said I couldn't play video games for a month. And I'm not supposed to be in my dad's office."

"I see," the principal said sternly.

Rex almost fell out of the chair. Apparently, Jesse had been wrong.

"Master Thompson," the principal said as walked over to the student. "Your egregious conduct...."

The boy looked at him with a perplexed expression on his face.

"That means you did something wrong, young man. However, I think you've suffered enough. *There are things to confess that enrich the world, and things that need not be said.* Do you know who said that, Master Thompson?"

"You did."

"Yes, but I was quoting someone. Those words are Joni Mitchell's. Always obey your parents, Rex Thompson. Let's keep the origin of the CD to ourselves, shall we."

"Yes sir!"

Principal King dropped the evidence of his infidelity into the wastebasket as Rex ran out the door without looking back.

He found Jesse still hard at work repairing the mythical hole.

"He's not going to tell my parents," Rex told him after relating the details of his meeting with the principal.

"That's great! I'm glad it worked out for you."

Jesse would have expected the boy to be ecstatic, but instead he sensed melancholy in the fourth grader.

"Is there something the matter, Rex?"

"I lied to Miss Simpson," Rex said dejectedly as he drew a circle in the dirt with the tip of his sneaker. "Father Joseph says that's wrong. But I couldn't tell her that I typed *Miss Simpson smells.*"

"Well, it is wrong to lie," Rick agreed without listening to his conscience, which now assailed him for being a hypocrite. "But you're doing it because you don't want Miss Simpson to feel bad, right?"

"Oh, yeah. I really like her. She's got the nicest eyes."

"You've got good taste, my friend. Anyway, when you say something that's not true to avoid making someone feel bad, it's called a white lie. And that's not really bad. So don't worry about it."

"Okay. I have to go. Thanks for talking with me, Jesse."

"Put it there, pal," Rick replied as he shook the boy's hand.

Rick was about to leave for the day when Sara came into the janitor's room. He was alone, the others having left early to participate in a bowling league.

"Yikes!" Sara exclaimed as she entered the room. "You wouldn't believe what happened today!"

"Yikes? I didn't know that people still used that word."

"The well-spoken people do," she informed him. "Anyway, remember what I wouldn't tell you about Principal King and Tracy when we had dinner the other day?"

"How can I remember something that you wouldn't tell me?"

"I said that many people have suggested that they might be involved, though I wasn't one of them because it's none of my business. But someone put a CD in one of the computers in my classroom that had Principal King talking about his feelings for Tracy on it. It started playing during my computer lesson today. The bank people and Principal King think it might have been created by the same people who used the computer to rob the bank. Principal King believes the people behind it are terrorists. So does that guy Gouveia from the bank."

"I could see sending a copy of it to the principal and threatening to pass the original CD around if he didn't send them the machine. But why play it in the classroom and let everyone there know about it? That makes no sense."

"It seems a little far fetched to me, too. The Lion King thinks they planted the CD to destroy his moral standing. And that's even farther fetched, in my opinion. Poor Rex had to answer more questions."

"Rex?" Rick pretended not to recognize the name.

"Rex Thompson. He's one of my students."

"That name sounds familiar. Maybe I know his father."

"He's a therapist."

Rick now understood how the CD with the principal's confession had come to be in the classroom.

"I think Rex was rummaging through his father's office. Anyway, you had to see the expression on the Lion King's face. And his wife Elsa was there! I almost cracked up."

"Elsa as in *Born Free*?"

"Yes! You remember that movie?"

"Sure do."

"That's awesome! It's always been a favorite of mine. Anyway, his wife's name is Ellen, but I call her Elsa. That woman looked like she was ready to pounce when the CD started playing."

"That had to be an awkward moment," Rick said with a smile while remembering hearing Elsa's reaction through the closed classroom door.

"I sent Rex to ask you to get my arm out of the desk," Sara suddenly remembered. "That's why you know him. I think the Lion King is seeing Rex's dad. That's how he got the CD. I had a friend in therapy, and she told me that her therapist recorded their sessions. She would give the recording to my friend so she could take it home and review it the next day. Maybe the Lion King forgot to bring his CD home. That's why Rex's dad still had it."

"You'd make a super sleuth," Rick complimented her.

"Thanks, but I was meant to be a teacher."

"Why would the boy bring it to school? Did he want to embarrass the principal?"

"I don't think so. But I'm going to find out for sure. I'll wait a while to ask Rex about it though. He's had to answer enough questions lately."

"I thought I saw the pastor coming out of your classroom today. He seems a little old for the fourth grade."

"Father Joseph never graduated from elementary school," she said facetiously. "Though the father does have a g.o.d. equivalent. He's gone back to school to get his diploma."

"G.o.d. instead of g.e.d. Very good. Does he play with the other children at recess?"

"Sure. He's the best kick ball player in the school," Sara said with a laugh. "He gets involved with some of the activities here. The Lion King feels he's a good influence on the children. Father Joseph is a really nice person."

"I came up with a name for the lady who lives next door to

the house we're renting. She seems to be standing behind me every time I turn around, just popping in out of nowhere. Her name is Mary Popkins, so I call her Mary Pop Ins."

"That's good," Sara said with a laugh. "You fit in well here. I still can't believe Gutner rented his house out. But this town is rich in the unexpected. I'll see you tomorrow."

Rick drove back to the house and saw Oscar standing in the driveway, talking with Marvin Blando. The restaurant owner was in his expensive suit, which was in stark contrast to Oscar, who was wearing his bath robe.

"The man who owns this house," Blando was telling him. "He's been my friend for many years. Out of respect for me, and our friendship, Ron has always let me use his driveway when I have firewood delivered. You have to park on the street tomorrow."

"Well, he rented the house to us," Oscar explained. "And the driveway comes with it. This is where we park our car. Why don't you use your own driveway?"

Rick drove the car onto the asphalt object of their contentious discussion and got out.

"Hi there," he said to Blando. Then to Oscar "What's going on?"

"This guy lives across the street," Oscar told him. "He says we can't park here tomorrow because the firewood he's having delivered is going to be left in this driveway."

Blando moved his head slightly from side to side, speaking with a contemplative expression on his face.

"I say you can't? As I said before, my friend, Ron Gutner, has told me that his driveway is my driveway. And if he ever needs a favor from me, I would grant it, using the full extent of my power, without question."

"Power?" Oscar asked him incredulously. "What freaking power do you have, numbnuts?"

Blando looked at Oscar with an almost sympathetic expression.

"You can ask others about me. They'll explain why I deserve your respect."

Oscar squared his shoulders and appeared ready to engage in fisticuffs with the pseudo don, who was considerably shorter than the bookie. Rick stepped between them.

"Look, Mr. Blando, we don't want to get off on the wrong foot here. If you've always had your wood delivered to this driveway, then who are we to change that tradition. We'll leave the car on the street."

Oscar glared at their neighbor, and for an instant Rick thought he was going to punch him.

"You're a wise young man," Blando told Rick. "The next time you come to my place of business, we'll drink some wine together. Salud."

"What the hell did you do that for?" Oscar protested as Rick hustled him up the path leading to the house.

"Because you looked like you were going to deck the idiot."

"That was the farthest thing from my mind."

"I'll bet dancing on a beach in Barbados with a bald baboon is a lot farther away from it."

Oscar thought about that for a moment, and then laughed.

"You got me there," he conceded.

"We don't want to do anything to attract attention to ourselves, remember? We just need to take care of that computer, and then get the hell out of here."

"You're right, Ricky. Who is that guy anyway?"

"He owns an Italian Restaurant. He also thinks he's the godfather."

"Ha! That ass is about as Italian as shrimp chow mien," Oscar said with disdain after they entered the house.

"You had shrimp chow mien!" Sylvia almost shouted at Rick as she came charging out of the kitchen. "It's beans and franks night."

"How many times do I have to tell you that it's franks and beans, not beans and franks," Oscar corrected her.

"I didn't eat dinner yet," Rick assured Sylvia.

"What difference does it make?" she asked her husband, completely forgetting about Rick's apparent transgression.

"It just doesn't sound right," Oscar told her. "Everyone says franks and beans. Binny, don't you agree."

"I forgot to wash my hands," their nephew, who had just walked down the stairs, responded. He went back up the staircase two steps at a time.

"Don't you think he's being silly?" Sylvia asked Rick.

"I haven't eaten yet," Rick repeated himself. "I can't wait to dig into those fran... dinner."

The bookie and his wife abandoned the debate. The four of them sat down to eat their meal. Rick explained why their attempt to erase the hard drive had failed as they ate.

"How did the kid get a CD with the principal admitting to his affair on it?" Binny asked.

"Apparently the principal is seeing a therapist, who just happens to be the kid's father. Rex, that's the kid's name, used the CD I gave him on his father's computer. He had to leave in a hurry, and just happened to grab one of his father's CDs instead of the one I gave him. The therapist had used it to record a session with the Lion King."

"Who's the Lion King?" Sylvia asked him.

"That's what Miss Simpson calls the principal."

"Do you know what the odds are against that happening? It's karma," Binny said after he stopped laughing. "The Lion King is being punished for cheating on his wife."

Sylvia looked at Oscar with a perplexed expression that said *who's Carman?*

"Maybe that's the name of the broad he's poking," Oscar suggested.

"It's amazing!" Binny said.

"I don't know about amazing," Rick responded. "But it was hysterical. I mean the guy's wife was there, and a priest as well. The principal is a fast thinker, though. The Lion King came up with that terrorist bullshit right away."

"So what so we do now?" Oscar looked at Binny and Rick.

"Good question. I guess Binny will have to come up with another disk. I'll try to get it into the computer. We have until Sunday to get it done," Rick said optimistically.

"I don't think so," Binny said in an ominous tone.

"What do you mean?" Rick asked him.

"I was able to read Gouveia's emails. And believe me, it wasn't easy. They've really beefed up their security."

"Maybe that's because we robbed them," Rick suggested.

"Anyway, he's been corresponding with the President of the bank," Binny continued. "Gouveia is still hoping that he can contact the robbers, and just get the money back. He'll take it with no questions asked. He's decided to wait until Friday to recover the money. If the bank doesn't have it by then, Gouveia is calling in the feds. And the first thing they'll do is go through Moore's computer. They'll find my program, and it will tell them where we sent the money."

There's no easy money, Rick thought glumly. Then he said aloud, "We need another plan. And fast."

"Maybe Ted and Felix can help us," Oscar suggested with a grin.

"Who are they?" Binny and Rick asked simultaneously.

"They hang out at that pub I went to a few times."

"You didn't ask me to go!" Sylvia interjected indignantly.

"They're in their sixties," Oscar continued while ignoring his wife. "They're widowers, and their children have all moved away. They're all alone. And they're both retired. These guys are bored out of their skulls. They'd love to get involved in our caper."

"What can they do for us?" a skeptical Rick asked him.

"You can't get to the computer because there's always cops around it. We could have these guys do something that will get the cops out of the classroom for a while. Then you can take care of the machine, and we'll be home free."

"Won't they be afraid of being caught?" Binny asked his uncle.

"That's just it. Even if they spent a few days in jail it would be a welcome change for them. Trust me."

"But will they give us up if the cops put pressure on them?" Rick asked him.

"No way. They'll say it was just a lark for them, and the cops will believe that. Everyone knows they're desperate for something to do."

"I guess it can't hurt to talk to them about it," Rick reluctantly said. "We have to get this done by Friday, or we'll be in deep shit."

"I'll talk to them first thing in the morning. I know where they eat breakfast."

Bowmarc, keep your sword handy, Rick thought.

"Do you think I look different today?" Oscar asked Sylvia as they walked upstairs after dinner.

"For the thousandth time, no! Will you stop with that crap! You're killing me!"

"The landlady said I looked different."

"I'm your wife! Who knows better, her or me?"

"You see me all the time, so you take my looks for granted. She only sees me once in a while. The landlady is likely to pick up on things you'd miss."

"I'll tell you what I wouldn't miss right now. You and your obsession with your looks. Why don't you go on a long vacation-alone!"

Their discourse continued in the same vein for an hour. Rick looked at Bowmarc, who now stood on the night table next to the bed he was using, and said "There is no easy money, pal."

R ick awoke the next morning at the usual time. The crisp November air came through the window he had left open all night. On a typical day that would have sharpened his senses, but there was no need for such stimulation now. There was a deadline to be met. Rick and his fellow thieves would be running from the law in very short order if they failed to access the donated computer by Friday. He showered and went downstairs.

Rick made coffee and took the milk out of the refrigerator. Binny, who had been up most of the night trying to gain access to the school's computer, joined him. A sleepy Sylvia soon followed. Oscar came through the door, with Ted and Felix Orpus right behind him.

"Ted and Felix have the same last name," Oscar said after introducing the gray-haired men. "And they look like twins. But believe it or not, they're no relation."

At this point I'll believe anything, including unrelated twins Rick thought. Then aloud he said "It's nice to meet you, Ted and

Felix. Help yourself to the coffee. I have to discuss something with Oscar and Binny."

"Sure thing," Felix answered for both of them.

"Do they want to help us?" Rick asked hopefully after they had gone into his bedroom.

"Yes. I haven't given them any of the details yet, but those guys hate the Oslifers. One of them gave Ted a ticket for going fifty in a thirty mile per hour zone when he sped up to beat a red light."

The nerve, Rick thought.

"The other one gave Felix a parking ticket when he double parked in front of a store that was having a big sale. He was only in there for about an hour."

How unreasonable, Rick said to himself.

"I'll tell them to create a diversion to get the Oslifers away from the school. Then you go into the classroom and do what you have to do on the computer."

"What about the bank people. Won't they be hanging around the classroom?" Binny asked.

"Not necessarily. They're usually in the Lion King's office," said Rick. "The principal insisted that Gouveia and his people stay out of sight during the school day, because the presence of strangers might upset the students. This could work. And since we have to get out of here soon, I say let's give it a shot. We'll do it this afternoon."

The others agreed. The three of them went back to the kitchen.

"You talk to them about it," Rick said to Oscar. "You seem to have developed a rapport with them. Tell them there's an unflattering picture of me on the computer that I want to get rid of."

"Will do. Felix and I talk the same language," Oscar pointed out.

"How ironic," Rick said with a grin.

"Why?" Oscar asked him.

"You've seen *The Odd Couple*, right? Oscar and Felix were best friends."

"I never saw that show," Oscar said.

"What! You used to watch it all the time!" Sylvia, who suddenly woke up, interjected.

"I never did!"

"You used to go hysterical when you watched that show. Don't try to deny it!"

"Why would I deny it? I just never saw the show! You're...."

"Just talk to them," Rick calmly interceded.

"Okay. I won't fuck this up. No dropping the ball this time. I won't screw...."

"I get your drift."

"Do you recognize those guys?" Binny, who walked into the kitchen after talking with Ted and Felix, asked Rick with a smile.

"Now that you mention it, they do look familiar."

"Their portraits are hanging in Affordable's boardroom. Those guys are the mystery twins. They started the company and sold it years ago. The two of them got tired of the city after the office was broken into for the umpteenth time."

"Tell me about it. That's what led to my demise," Rick pointed out with a grin. "If you still worked there, you'd get an extra weeks' vacation Binny."

"That would be true, if I hadn't made it up, which you're well aware of. I did the same thing when I was in high school. I told all the sophomores that they could qualify for a free pass to the school's indoor swimming pool by carrying an upper classman's books. But there was no free pass, or pool, for that matter. And if I still worked at Affordable, we wouldn't be here, with a shot at millions of dollars. It's karma!"

"When do we get to meet Carman?" Sylvia asked Oscar, who simply shrugged his shoulders.

Rick left for work while the others joined the Orpus' in the living room. Oscar took his new friends out on the porch after a brief interlude of pleasant conversation.

"There's something Jesse has to do that he doesn't want his boss, or anyone else, to know about. There's a very embarrassing picture of him on one of the computers in the school that he wants to get rid of."

The Orpus' looked at him suspiciously.

"Would this have something to do with that bank robbery?" Felix asked with a grin.

"I can't say one way or the other, if you get my drift," Oscar told them.

"So what do you want us to do?" Ted questioned him.

"I need someone to distract the Oslifers," Oscar said. "If you could do something to get them out of the school, for just a little while, it would be a big help. We'd like to do it this afternoon. And there'll be something in it for you guys, if you know what I mean."

The two men laughed simultaneously.

"Just making bigger fools out of those two jackasses then they already have on their own would be compensation enough for me," Felix told him. "I still can't believe that Sheriff Reinfart hired them in the first place."

"But then again, Christmas is coming, so a little extra in the bank couldn't hurt," Ted said. "Though to tell you the truth, being retired is the most boring thing I've ever done in my life. Just having something different to do would make it worthwhile. I mean, how many days in a row can you go fishing? Even the fish are getting tired of it: they just jump into the boat and say *let's the damn thing over with*. We'll come up with a plan and come back here around twelve."

"Sounds good, guys. Thanks."

Felix and Ted went home to devise their scheme.

■　■　■

Sara Simpson emerged from her apartment into the crisp autumn air. Wearing a sweat suit, she began to jog in the tender morning light. The streets were deserted at this early hour, with most of Morgan Town's inhabitants clinging to the final moments of their precious slumber. Miss Simpson turned onto a secluded street that went through a neighborhood of well-kept houses.

Sara started to pick up her pace. The teacher's spindly legs were surprisingly strong, and she was soon racing down the road. Feeling invigorated, Sara looked up at the clear blue sky above her and felt grateful to be alive.

Then she suddenly became airborne, landing on the hard pavement in an extremely undignified position.

The sewer pipe running under the street had been repaired the week before. A temporary patch job was done after it was finished, the town intending to have the entire street repaved in the near future. This quick fix created a deep depression in the road. Sara lost her balance after she ran over it. The water bottle in her hand went airborne, landing on a lawn across the street.

Jack Fisher was considered by many to be the most annoying man in Morgan Town. He was in the habit of doing his yard work at all hours of the day and night, always using the noisiest machines available to accomplish his task. On this particular morning he had decided to mow the lawn one last time before winter arrived. Just as he started to push his mower forward, Sara's water bottle landed in front of it. The plastic vessel became a missile when the loud machine ran over it.

Ellen King, who lived next to Jack Fisher, was also up early on this particular day. She had agreed to drive a friend to the airport, a decision she now deeply regretted. After giving her neighbor a disapproving look, Ellen got into her car and put the key in the ignition. In the next instant a plastic projectile reduced the driver's side window to an uncountable number of very small fragments.

At first stunned, Ellen did not utter a sound or make a movement for several moments. Then she saw the monogrammed water bottle lying in the shattered glass. The initials S. S. meant nothing to her, until Sara Simpson limped up to the car.

"You!" Ellen screamed "You tried to kill me! Someone call the police!"

Jack, who had come running over to see if she was all right, immediately retreated. He thought Ellen was accusing him.

"Call the police!" she screamed after him. "The terrorists tried to kill me!"

Her neighbor, who was relieved to be in the clear, obliged Ellen by making the call from his home.

"I'm sorry, Mrs. King," Sara said sincerely. "It was an accident. Are you all right?"

Ellen suddenly felt very vulnerable, being alone with the mastermind behind the plot to destroy the school, and the Kings. Her husband had already left for Morgan Elementary. She ran into the house, locking the door behind her. The police arrived quickly, finding Sara on the front porch trying to explain the incident through the mail slot in the front door.

"Are you all right Mrs. King?" Larry Oslifer bent down and asked her through the narrow opening.

"Arrest that woman!"

"What did she do?" Tommy questioned her.

"She tried to kill me!"

They both looked at Sara suspiciously.

"I was running past the house and fell. My water bottle slipped out of my hand and landed in front of Jack's lawn mower. He ran over it. The bottle shot out of the lawnmower and hit Mrs. King's car window. That's what happened, Officer Oslifer."

"That sounds bizarre," Larry told her.

"It was an accident. Just ask Jack."

He had resumed mowing his lawn, taking no interest in the police car that had arrived with siren wailing and lights flashing. Tommy went over and asked Jack to answer a few questions. He begrudgingly joined the investigation.

"So what did you see, Jack?" Larry asked him.

"Not much. I saw Sara here coming up the road, and then I bent down to start the mower. After it turned over I started mowing the lawn. I had only gone a few feet when I ran over something that shot out of the damn machine like a rocket. It smashed the window on Ellen's car, and she went running into the house, screaming like a crazy woman."

"So you don't know how the bottle came to be in front of your lawn mower?" Tommy sought clarification.

"No."

"I couldn't do that intentionally if I wanted to," Sara pointed out. "It was just a freak thing."

"She tried to destroy my husband, and now she tried to do the same thing to me!" Ellen bellowed from behind the door. "You have to arrest her!"

"I'm sorry, Sara," Larry apologized, though there was a notable lack of remorse in his voice. "But the window is smashed, and you admitted it was your water bottle that did the damage. I don't think we have a choice here."

"Maybe we should call the sheriff," Tommy suggested.

"We have to do our job," Larry responded sternly.

He took out his handcuffs, and then slapped them on a startled Sara Simpson. Though he tried to appear reluctant, she had the impression that the police officer enjoyed the opportunity to use his manacles.

"Well, I guess that's that," Jack, who was also very surprised, observed. "I'm going to finish my lawn."

"The sheriff will want to talk to you," Larry told the mail slot. "Let's go Sara."

"But I'll miss my class," she protested.

"I'm sure they'll get a substitute," Larry assured her.

Sara scrunched down in the backseat as they drove to the police station in the patrol car. Tommy suggested that they stop for bagels. Larry convinced him that it would not be appropriate, much to the prisoner's relief. She did not want to endure the stares of the curious customers there. They walked into the station and deposited the teacher in the interrogation room. Then the two officers went into the sheriff's office.

"Are you out of your damn minds!" Tim Reinhart almost

screamed after they told him about their arrest of Sara Simpson. "You know who her father is! What's the charge?"

"Assault with a deadly weapon," Larry said dramatically.

"A water bottle is a deadly weapon?"

"Well, it could be, sheriff," Tommy answered him.

"I mean, it was really moving when it hit Mrs. King's window," Larry pointed out.

"I think your brains are deadly weapons! Where's Sara?"

They went to the interrogation room. Sara was sitting in a chair, bewildered by the events of that morning.

"Take those cuffs off of her," Tim instructed Larry. He reluctantly did so.

"I wouldn't hurt Elsa, Sheriff Reinhart," she told him.

"Of course…. who's Elsa?"

"I mean Mrs. Lion King…. I meant Mrs. King."

Larry gave Sara an accusatory look.

"It was an accident," Sara insisted. "I get one phone call, right?"

"Yes. You can make it in my office," Reinhart said pleasantly, though he knew who she was calling, and dreaded the consequences. Sara left the room.

"Don't you see, Sheriff," Larry said eagerly. "Elsa, Lion King. Those are probably the code names her terrorist group uses. She was about to crack."

"You have to admit that it's all very suspicious," Tommy said.

"I think we have her on the run!" his brother added triumphantly.

"The only one who's going to be on the run after this is me," Reinhart pointed out. "They're going to run me out of town on a rail!"

Edgar Morgan arrived with a lawyer in tow shortly after.

"Mr. Morgan," Reinhart greeted him. "I believe this is all a misunderstanding. We really just need to sort out the details."

"You arrested my daughter to sort out a misunderstanding? I thought you only arrested people when they broke the law."

"Mrs. King accused Sara of attempted murder, so we did have to address her concerns," Tim told him. "But I'm sure this will all be cleared up very soon."

"We have to find out who Elsa and the Lion King are," Larry interjected.

"Who?" the lawyer asked him.

"Sara mentioned those names while we were questioning her," the officer replied. "We think they might be code names used by the group that robbed the bank."

The lawyer gave him a skeptical look.

"I want to see my daughter!" Morgan insisted.

"Sure thing," Reinhart said.

Edgar was directed to the interrogation room where Sara was waiting. She stood up and went into his arms when he walked through the door. Expecting to find comfort there, the young woman found disapproval instead.

"How could you let this happen!" her father asked in an exasperated tone. "I'm meeting with one of the senior members of the Pentagon's procurement team, and I get a message saying that my daughter has been arrested. Do you know how this looks?"

"Really, Dad, I'm fine. Don't worry about me so much," Sara answered sarcastically. "It was an accident. I fell down. That's what I do. I fall down, and then I pick myself up so I can teach the kids."

"They said you were talking in code. What's that all about?"

"They were just nick names Maya and I have for certain people."

"Don't tell me she's involved in this too? She works for a defense company, for god's sake. It's a matter of national security!"

"You can rest assured that Maya isn't involved because there's nothing to be involved in. Your widget's secrets are safe with Maya and me, Father. Although I really wonder how secret a widget can be. It's just a misunderstanding. Don't worry Dad, you won't lose her boobies."

"Don't talk to me that way, Sara," Edgar scolded her, his weighty physique trembling as he did so. "You need help."

"Yes, legal help. How about Uncle Bernie?"

"We can't ask him to get involved in such an unseemly matter."

"I'm not a terrorist! And Uncle Bernie is my godfather, for god's sake!"

"Don't use the lord's name in vain!"

"You're right, father. This is all in vain."

"The lawyer I use for real estate transactions will get you out of here. I have to get back to the plant."

He began to walk out the door, but then stopped and turned around.

"Not a word about this to your poor mother!"

"I'm fine Dad, really. The cuffs didn't hurt a bit," Sara said as he left. "I must really be a Simpson. They wouldn't do this to a Morgan," she added after her father was gone.

■ ■ ■

Rick Gaines tried to quell his sense of anticipation as he drove back to the house during his lunch break. The temporary custodian was meeting with the unrelated brothers Orpus. Obeying the traffic signals required the utmost in self-discipline by Rick. Every red light and stop sign delayed his finalizing the plan that would lead to the end of the bank robber's stay in Morgan Town, and the beginning of his life of ease.

"What's new and exciting?" Wispy Soul asked with a smile when he walked into the house.

"Nothing much," a surprised Rick answered in the same fashion.

"Have you met Ted and Felix? Those men are amazing. They have more energy than most people half their age."

"Where are they?"

"They're in the living room with Oscar. I think those guys have only one problem: they don't know how to dress. I'm sure you have lots to talk about. Binny is there, too. I'll catch you later."

Wispy walked out the front door. Rick walked into the living room where he discovered the reason for her comment about their clothing. Ted and Felix were dressed in black.

"Hi Jesse," Oscar greeted him. "The guys are ready."

"We dressed up just like a couple of thieves," Ted said enthusiastically. "We're ready to do our part in the caper. What do you think?"

"I guess you didn't realize that you'll be doing this in broad daylight. The black outfits won't be too effective."

The Orpus' looked at each other dejectedly.

"But we do have ski masks," Felix suddenly remembered. "They'll still work."

"Absolutely," Oscar responded. "They're going to steal the Oslifer's patrol car at three o'clock. That should clear the way for you, Jesse."

"Those guys will come after us like bats out of hell," Ted said confidently. "They won't want to tell the sheriff that they lost the patrol car again."

"Again?" Rick questioned him.

"About a year ago, the two law enforcement wizards left the keys in their patrol car when they went into a diner for breakfast. Somebody took it for a joy ride and left it on the high school football field. They never found out who did it. The sheriff was pretty pissed off at the Oslifers."

"Are you sure they'll leave the keys in it today?" Rick asked them. "I mean, after that experience they might have changed their ways."

"Don't worry, I know those clowns," Felix assured him. "They'll never learn."

"They were going on duty just as I left the school. I'll check out their car when I go back. I'll call to let you know if the keys are inside it," Rick said to the Orpus' as he left.

Mary practically ran into him on the porch.

"I'm sorry, Jesse," she apologized.

I wouldn't recognize you if you weren't. Then he said aloud "no problem."

"They arrested Sara Simpson again!"

"What! Why?"

"Attempted murder."

"She tried to kill someone?"

"Yes, or least that's what they claim. Sara supposedly attacked Mrs. King with her water bottle."

Elsa! "That's crazy. There's no way Sara would do something like that."

Rick heard Karen saying in a judgmental tone, *I told you someone would get hurt!* A strong sense of guilt came over the thief.

"I have to get back to work, but I'll find out what's going on, Mary. Thanks for telling me."

He drove back to the school. The patrol car was in the parking lot, and a casual peek inside it as he walked by revealed that the key was in the ignition. Rick called Oscar, and then tried to keep himself occupied until the appointed hour.

The time passed at an agonizingly slow pace. Rick was supposed to be cleaning his tools, but he frequently stood up and walked into the hall. The nervous thief was able to verify that the patrol car was still there by looking through the window on the door to the parking lot. Ted and Felix had not yet implemented their plan.

"How many cups of coffee have you had today?" Henry, who had noticed his preoccupied state, asked.

"Only three, boss," Rick replied calmly. "I always get antsy around the holidays."

"Christmas is still a long ways away, kid," he replied with a smile. "You'll burn yourself out if you keep this up."

Sara Simpson arrived just before recess after having been released on her own recognizance. She had gone home to make herself presentable for school, only to find a message waiting for her on the answering machine. Principal King wished to meet with her after the school day ended. Sara didn't need a sixth sense to know what subject they would be discussing.

"Hi there," Rick said when she walked in the door, noticing

the apprehension on her simple but pretty face. "I heard you had a problem today. What happened?"

"Oh, that," Sara tried to sound casual. "It was nothing really. That's if you consider being accused of attempted murder nothing."

Henry looked up from his newspaper.

"On the significance scale of one to ten, I'd give it a ten, so no, I wouldn't consider that nothing," Rick told her. "What happened?"

"I was jogging past the King's house and I, big surprise here, fell," Sara explained in a casual manner, though the anxiety in her eyes belied the teacher's apparently calm demeanor. "I was carrying a water bottle. When I started to fall, I stuck out my arm to regain my balance, and the water bottle slipped out of my hand."

Sara acted out her movements as she spoke. The jacket she wore had a Velcro strip on the sleeve, which was used to adjust its width. When she extended her arm it stuck to the Velcro strip on a vinyl cooler that Henry used to carry his lunch. Sara then raised her arm to disengage it from her sleeve. Henry's lunch chiller was lifted off the table and, after breaking free from Miss Simpson's coat, flew out the door.

"Heads up!" Henry yelled.

Ellen King had just arrived at the school to attend the meeting. As she walked past the janitor's room the cooler sailed past her head, impacting a picture drawn by one of the third graders.

Ellen screamed, and ran to the principal's office.

"I'm so dead!" Sara said dramatically.

"It was an accident," Rick tried to reassure her. "If you need someone to back you up, I'll be happy to do it."

"Me too, Sara," Henry offered.

"All I want to do is teach," she said in a defeated tone.

Sara went to the inquisition.

When the clock in the janitor's room read ten minutes to three Rick stood up and casually went into the corridor. The others in the room were busy, so they did not notice him walking out the door. The thieves would be home free, if the unrelated brothers could lure the Oslifers away from their post. Rick forced himself to walk at a normal pace, despite the urge to run down the hall. He was even more anxious now to leave Morgan Town, as the guilt he felt about Sara's predicament was starting to play on his mind.

The school choir was rehearsing in the auditorium. Their sweet, simplistic sound made Rick nostalgic for the innocence that one loses in the process of becoming an adult. All during his childhood he had been told that stealing was wrong. That preachment now weighed heavily on his conscience. For a moment Rick became disoriented, his mind desperately seeking an acceptable explanation for his current surroundings.

"How the hell did I get here?" he asked aloud.

Then Rick saw his reflection in the glass window on a classroom door. That lost feeling passed quickly after seeing himself as Jesse Gleason.

These are different times. You have to grab what you can, or someone else will beat you to it. You have to do whatever it takes to survive. The only truly innocent beings on this planet are the ones that are still in the womb and besides, this is the most exciting thing I've ever done.

A sense of urgency took hold of him.

"This is what I am now," he said aloud.

Rick refocused on the plan. He walked up to the door that provided access to the parking lot and peered through the small window in it.

The unrelated brothers had arrived on time. They got into the patrol car and started the engine. Ted was the driver, and he looked through the windows into Miss Simpson's classroom, where the Officers Oslifers guarded the computer. The retiree waited patiently for at least one of them to notice that their vehicle was being stolen. When Larry stood up and ran towards the window Ted slowly started to drive away.

"Hey!" Larry yelled. "Someone's taking our car!"

"I told you we shouldn't leave the keys in it!"

"You never said that!"

"Did too!"

"Did not!"

The sight of the patrol car moving through the parking lot quickly ended their debate. The two policemen ran out of the building. The unrelated brothers were both wearing a three hole ski mask, and they smiled at each other when they saw the Oslifers emerge from the school. The officers started to chase them, so Ted increased the car's speed.

"Those boys can use the exercise," Felix observed with a laugh.

"We'll never catch them this way," Larry Oslifer concluded.

He looked around and saw several bicycles chained to the bicycle rack.

"Go into the janitor's room and get something to cut the locks off," he told his sibling.

"Why don't you go?"

"Don't be a baby, for Christ's sake. We have to catch those guys."

"Call for backup," Tommy suggested as he begrudgingly ran into the school.

"No way. We have to catch them ourselves. If we tell the sheriff that we left the keys in the car again we'll be out of a job."

Ted saw that they had abandoned their pursuit. He turned the car around and stopped just outside the school grounds.

"We have to give those jackasses a chance to catch us," he said.

"I'm with you partner," Felix concurred.

A breathless Tommy Oslifer explained his need to Henry Pabst. The head custodian did not really understand him since the officer was reticent to give a full explanation for his request. He did provide a pair of wire cutters, however.

"These belong to the kids," Tommy reminded his brother while watching him cut the chain on one of the bikes. "We could get into trouble for taking them."

"They're at basketball practice," Larry told him. "We'll have caught the terrorists by the time it's over."

"They got a hell of a head start. They're probably miles away from here by now."

"Don't be so negative," said Larry as he cut a second bike loose. "Let's go."

The bicycles they commandeered were too small for an adult, but the officers still managed to ride them. The two men were a comical sight as they rode out of the parking lot. The officers peddled for all they were worth, believing their primary occupation (though not their only source of income) was at stake.

The Orpus' watched them emerge from the parking lot. Ted drove up behind them. The pursuers had now become the pursued.

"What the hell are they doing?!" Larry exclaimed.

"We should call for backup!" Tommy told him.

"We can handle this!" his brother insisted.

Ted harassed them for several blocks before pulling ahead of the officers. He drove just fast enough to maintain a distance of approximately two hundred feet between them. The pedestrians and other drivers observed the scene with curiosity, and amusement.

"I can't believe those asses think that Sara Simpson is a terrorist because they saw her use a GPS," Felix said with a grin as he watched the Oslifers pursue them.

"They couldn't find their asses with a GPS," Ted remarked in the same fashion.

■ ■ ■

Oscar had taken a shower after the unrelated brothers left. There was nothing to do now but wait to see if they would be successful. He started to dress after a quick shave, but then thought better of the idea. Oscar walked downstairs wearing only his boxer shorts and joined Sylvia in the living room.

"What are you doing?" Sylvia asked him.

"I'm watching t.v. with you," he responded.

"Do you think this is appropriate?" she asked while pointing to his underwear.

"There's no one else here. What's the difference?"

"Civilized people wear clothes when they're not in the bedroom."

"What's the big deal? You've seen me without clothes plenty of times."

"For which I consider myself blessed," Sylvia said sarcastically. "But what if someone knocks on the door? Or what if Woosey and Binny come through the door?"

"Her name's Windy," Oscar corrected her, and then glanced at the clock.

"Let me watch my program," Sylvia said impatiently.

"Who's that?" Oscar asked her after noticing the woman on the talk show his wife was watching.

"Autumn Reeser. She's an actress."

"Is she related to Reese Witherspoon?"

"Don't be ridiculous!" Sylvia responded in an exasperated tone.

"Well, the names sound the same. You know woman should really have hose on when they're wearing a short dress."

"Why?"

"Because it makes their legs look much more attractive."

"Autumn's legs look fine," Sylvia, who was not wearing stockings either, insisted.

"Women look better with hose on," Oscar said emphatically.

Sylvia stood up and ran up the stairs. She came down in the same fashion, with a pair of panty hose pulled over her head.

"There! Do I look better! I have hose on," she asked in a muffled voice.

Oscar was tempted to respond in the affirmative, pointing out that since her face was now covered Sylvia did appear more attractive. His instinct for self preservation prevailed, however, and instead he said, "You look like you're going to rob a bank."

"We already did that! That's why we're here!"

"You had nothing to do with it!"

"I brought the fake id to you."

"That was nothing. And you did nothing but bitch and moan about doing it!"

"That doesn't matter. I still had something to do with robbing the bank!"

"A couple of days ago you said you weren't involved at all!"

"Let me watch my show!"

Oscar removed his boxer shorts and put them on top of his head.

"Do I look better?" he asked with a grin.

"Let me watch my show!" Sylvia implored him again.

"How can you see it with the pantyhose on your head?" Oscar asked her before glancing at the clock once more.

Ted and Felix were supposed to drive by the house after stealing the patrol car so Oscar would know they had been successful. The clock read three fifteen, so the bookie ended the debate with Sylvia and went to the window. He saw the police cruiser go by and began jumping up and down with delight. This made for a very unsightly spectacle, given his current state of undress. Sylvia ignored him, focusing instead, as best she could with her limited vision, on the television.

Forgetting his nakedness, an exuberant Oscar suddenly ran out the door, wearing only his gloves and the boxer shorts on his head. He waved to the Orpus', though they were too far away at that point to see his gesture. Mary walked by with Timmy and almost fainted when she saw Oscar. The landlady let out a shriek just as the Officer Oslifers rode by.

"I'll check it out," Tommy, who was tired of peddling, told his brother.

Mary ran into house and called the police. Her cry had alerted Oscar to his nakedness. The bookie started to run towards the house, just as Tommy ran up to him and wrapped his jacket around his waist. Oscar struggled to get away. Tommy decided he needed help to subdue this naked man. The officer bent down to talk into the microphone on the jacket's shoulder, which was aligned with Oscar's crotch.

"Tommy Oslifer here," he began.

Mary returned, unable to resist the sight of her naked neighbor's imitation of Adam in Eden. She thought Larry was performing an unnatural act on Oscar. Mary did faint now, just as several policemen responded to her call.

■ ■ ■

Rick had begun to walk towards Sara's classroom when Larry came into the building. The police officer ran right by the janitor, and returned in an instant, running out the door with wire cutters in hand. After watching the two police officers ride away Rick began to walk towards the classroom. Sara Simpson and Sheriff Reinhart came around the corner, so the bank robber slipped into the boy's room. After waiting five minutes Rick opened the door slightly to see if the hallway was clear. Miles Gouveia was moving quickly towards the school door. After another short interval Rick looked again and saw no one in the corridor.

He went into Sara Simpson's room and approached the only obstacle to the success of their criminal enterprise. Rick paused for a moment to regain control of his emotions. The thief's hand shook ever so slightly as he moved his finger towards the on button.

"This is it," he softly said to Bowmarc, who was in his pants pocket.

"Hey, what's going on, Jesse," Dan Gartner said as he walked through the door.

"Oh, hi, I saw one of the cops go running out of the building, so I came in here to make sure everything was all right," Rick, to his own amazement, responded casually.

"I don't know what those clowns are up to," Dan said with a laugh. "Gouveia asked me to watch the computer until the guys on the evening shift show up."

"I can do that for you," Rick volunteered.

"There you are," Henry Pabst said as he walked into the classroom. "Are you goofing off again, Jesse?"

"Not at all boss. I saw one of the Oslifers run out of the building, so I came down here to see what was going on."

Pabst smiled at Rick, and then playfully chucked him on the cheek.

"I mean, is this guy beautiful, or what?" he said to Gartner. "The man actually thinks. Sometimes a little too much, but he always notices when something's not right. Jesse, you've made it here, my man. And just to prove that to you, I'm taking you bowling."

"Bowling?"

"Yeah, that's what I do when a new guy has proven himself. You and I are knocking off early and hitting the lanes."

"I appreciate it, but I haven't bowled in years."

"I think he's scared of you, Henry," Gartner remarked with a smile.

"No, he's beautiful," Pabst responded. "He just needs to lighten up a little. You'll still have your job, even if you bowl a twenty-five. Now I'm not taking no for an answer. The Pabst says let's hit it!"

Rick was crestfallen as he drove to the alley. The opportunity to end his stay in Morgan Town had slipped away. Now they needed another plan.

"This is one of the perks you get for being a Pabst employee," Henry said enthusiastically as they put on their bowling shoes.

"It doesn't get any better than this, boss," Rick barely managed to answer in the same manner.

"Remember to check out the faucet in the boy's bathroom near room six tomorrow," Henry told him. "It's like the energizer bunny-it never stops running."

Rick responded with a forced laugh as he thought, *it really doesn't matter. Because we're going to have to blow up the school to get rid of that damn computer!*

■ ■ ■

Sara Simpson sat in a chair facing the members of the school board, all of whom were held in high regard by the citizens of Morgan Town. The meeting was taking place in the cafeteria, the far wall of this large room consisting of many windows. The light streaming through them fell directly on Sara, giving her face a beatific quality. None of the other people noticed this, however. Principal King sat in the center of a long table. Ellen was on his right side, with eyes riveted on the young teacher who she believed was plotting her demise. The other six members had been briefed about the incidents that had instigated the meeting.

"Miss Simpson," King began. "We're here to discuss the implications of your recent conduct. We're all familiar with the details, so I won't recount them now. We would like to hear your explanation."

Sara cleared her throat.

"The first time I was taken to the police station was because I was Geocaching," she told them. "I wanted to show the students how to use a GPS. The officers had never heard of Geocaching, so they were suspicious."

"I can verify that," Sheriff Reinhart, who was also attending the meeting, interjected. "I don't think there was anything illegal about what Sara did that morning."

The young teacher, who did not notice the sheriff when she walked into the room, thought *I must be a really dangerous character if they need him here.*

"Have you ever heard of Geocaching before," Al Cleveland, a local merchant, asked him.

"No, I'm not really familiar with that term," Reinhart answered him.

"So there could be more to it than you know," Al added.

"I guess that's possible," Reinhart, who was up for re-election next year, replied.

"I dug up a box of junk," Sara said. "Nothing in it could be used for an illegal purpose. I wanted to teach the children how to find their way around."

"Now this morning, you were involved in two attacks on Ellen King. Isn't that correct?" Anna Sims, another member of the board, asked her.

Ellen's icy stare made it difficult for Sara to respond. With no one to champion her cause in the room, she felt nervous and very vulnerable. The teacher tried to placate the board in spite of that.

"I am really, really sorry, Mrs. King," she began awkwardly while absent mindedly rearranging her hair. "I didn't throw the water bottle in front of the lawnmower on purpose. I didn't even know you were in your car. And this afternoon, the bag just stuck to the Velcro on my coat. I didn't throw it at you. Those things just seem to happen to me."

"What about your terrorist friends besmirching my husband's reputation!" Ellen shot back. "They made that fake recording of him talking about an affair that never happened."

"Ellen, please," her husband said softly.

"What affair?" Anna enthusiastically inquired.

"There was no affair!" Ellen bellowed before pointing at the schoolteacher. "It was just an attempt by her, and her friends, to destroy my husband!"

The members of the school board, except for Principal King, looked at Sara as if she was evil incarnate.

"Sara, we think it best for you to take some time off," Principal King said, while using his eyes to plead with Ellen to cease her accusations. "The moral fiber of this school is as important as the books and other tools we use to nurture the young minds that come here. I can't have my teachers being arrested-it disrupts the children's education. Until these events are explained to everyone's satisfaction, you're suspended. When you're exonerated, you can apply for reinstatement."

"You're suspended without pay, of course," Al added for good measure.

Sara stood up and started to walk away in a daze. Then she turned and faced the board once more.

"I didn't have anything to do with the CD that has you

talking about Lady Ha Ha on it, Lion King," she told the principal in a robotic tone.

Tracy Hawa, who was taking the minutes of the meeting, looked at her with a very serious expression and asked, "Who's Lady Ha Ha?"

"You wouldn't know her," Sara answered in kind. "And as for the Geocaching, maybe you're not comfortable with someone who uses new technology and presents new ideas. You want us all to be like Plainz Jane, never changing from one day to the next, or from one year to another. And Elsa, whether you believe it or not, I never tried to hurt you, in any way."

"What's she talking about?" Anna wondered aloud.

"It's the strain. She's losing her marbles," Al remarked. "Turn yourself in, Miss Simpson. You'll feel better."

"I think she's talking in code," Anna suggested.

"She probably knows the name of the man who pointed the gun at me in church!" Ellen said with disdain.

"Please, dear, that was explained," Principal King reminded her. "It was a water pistol."

"Hah!" his wife responded.

"What am I supposed to do now? I can't open a business, like Marlon Blando. Teaching is all I know how to do. Everyone is running away from me."

Sara started to leave, but then spun around to address Ellen one last time.

"Elsa, if you really think someone faked the voice on that CD, then you're ready to go on your own Gullible's travels."

Sara turned again to leave, not realizing that she was so close to the door. Her face impacted it, yet there was no pain. The events of this day had made her numb. No one even smiled at her comic misfortune, not even Lady Ha Ha.

"At least the Pope and Jackie Gleason are still on my side," Sara said before walking out the door.

Rex was standing in the hall. Everyone knew everything about each other in Morgan Town., and the majority of the people did care, though no one as much as this young boy cared about his teacher. Rex had tears in his eyes as he approached Sara.

"It was my fault, Miss Simpson. I typed *Miss Simpson smells* into the computer. That's when all that stuff came on the screen. I'm sorry, I don't think you smell."

Sara got on her knees and hugged him.

"It's all right, Rex. Things will work out fine. Besides, I do smell. With my nose."

They shared a brief laugh, and then Sara told him to keep up the good work he was doing in class. She managed to smile when they said goodbye, saving her tears for the ride home. Gus Hanson approached her before she reached the door.

"This is it!" he proclaimed while holding up a piece of paper. "A Tanzanian Prince that was killed in a polo game mentioned me, and only me, in his will. I'll have five-million-dollars by the end of next week. Will you come to my party, Sara?"

"There's no place I'd rather be, Gus," said Sara sadly. "Don't forget to invite Elsa."

"Who? Are you all right?" Gus, who had suddenly noticed her woebegone expression, asked.

"What have you got there, Gus?" Sheriff Reinhart asked as he approached them.

"Oh, nothing, Sheriff. I have to go."

"Principal King asked me to escort you out of the building, Sara. He knew you were upset and wants to be sure you make it out of here safely."

"I can walk out of the school without hurting, myself," Sara responded indignantly. *At least I think I can.*

Sara walked to her car with Reinhart right behind her. She took a long look at the brick building where her heart had resided for what now seemed to be a lifetime. Then she drove away.

Reinhart suddenly noticed that the Oslifer's patrol car was gone. He peered into the suspended teacher's classroom and discovered that no one was watching the computer. Before the sheriff could go inside to remedy the situation Gouveia came to him.

"I think you should follow her," he suggested. "She might be going to see one of her associates."

"My officers have disappeared. I guess they got another call. There's no one watching the computer."

"I'll take care of that," Gouveia assured him.

The sheriff took off in hot pursuit of Sara Simpson.

The subject of his surveillance had gone home. As Sara arrived at her apartment building she suddenly decided on another destination.

I need a drink.

She drove around aimlessly for a while, considering but then rejecting various establishments along the town's main road. Then Sara saw the bowling alley. The bar inside was never crowded, especially at this time of day. She went inside.

"I'll have a Budweiser, Matt," she told the bartender.

"Coming right up, Sara. I guess the little ones drove you to drink today."

The former teacher smiled while fighting back her tears. She swigged the beer down, eliciting a surprised look from Matt.

"Really long day," she explained. "Keep em coming."

Sara took out her cell phone and called Maya. Her roommate's voicemail came on, asking Sara to leave her name and number.

"Hi Maya," Sara began. "I can't leave my name and number because I might have to use them later. My ass just got canned, so I might have to start living on the street. I'm at the bowling alley getting inebriated. It was nice sharing an apartment with you. Bye."

Rick was at lane seven, in the process of losing his bowling match with Henry. Under any circumstances this would have been the inevitable outcome, since he hadn't picked up a bowling ball in ten years. On this day it was even more likely, since he could think of nothing else but the missed opportunity to eliminate the incriminating computer program.

"Bingo!" Henry exclaimed when he threw a strike.

"You'd probably beat me at that too," Rick observed.

"Hey, I know what your problem is. You're afraid to show up your boss. Believe me, there's nothing for you to be worried about. There's no ego involved on my end. This is just two guys having a good time."

It's more like one guy having a good time, Rick thought as he threw another gutter ball.

"You wanna grab something to eat," Pabst asked him after the rout was over.

"I'd like to, but I have a previous commitment," Rick responded. "Thanks for a fun afternoon."

"My pleasure. We'll do it again sometime. Try to get some practice in before then."

"Will do, boss."

Rick was walking out of the alley when he saw Sara sitting at the bar. Preoccupied with the task of devising an alternative plan, his first impulse was to keep walking. Yet Rick's conscience would not let him leave without talking to her, though he dreaded hearing about the outcome of the meeting.

A potential suitor had taken a seat next to Sara, though his attempts at starting a conversation with her had accomplished nothing.

"I'm a Capricorn," he said to her. "What's your sign?"

"Yield," Sara said suggestively. "I just love yield signs."

"They'll let anyone in this place," Rick said jokingly as he walked up to her.

"Jesse! How the hell are you," Sara responded in a loud voice. "This is my new friend what's his name."

The man smiled weakly.

"Nice to meet you," Rick told him. Then to Sara "How did things turn out?"

"Could you excuse us, person that I just met thirty minutes ago," Sara asked the other customer at the bar.

"Can I have your phone number?"

"Don't you like your own?"

He stood up and walked away.

"You didn't have to be that tough on him," Rick pointed out.

Sara put her head down and hesitated before answering.

"I know, but people have been pretty tough on me today. And in answer to your question, well that's a long story, my used to be fellow employee. Let's sit in a booth so you can hear my tale of woe."

Sara stood up, and got her leg caught on the bar stool. She managed to maintain her balance, however.

Alcohol has the opposite effect on her. Sara gets more coordinated when she's had a few. Someone should do a scientific study on her, Rick thought

"I'll have a bud light," Rick told the bartender. He took his drink and escorted Sara to the booth.

"I thought you didn't drink, Sara," Rick said with a smile.

"It's my new hobby. Well, they did it. They canned me."

"What!" Rick said incredulously. "Those assholes!"

"I mean, I show up every day, do my job....and I care so much about those kids," Sara's voice started to break. "And they just throw me out the door, even though I did nothing wrong."

I know that feeling.

"I don't know anything about that computer, or the bank being robbed," Sara continued. "I was the one who begged them to buy new machines. I told them that by accepting used ones they'd just be getting someone else's problems. Boy, did I know what I was talking about!"

"So that's it?" Rick asked while trying to mask the guilt he was feeling.

"Well, technically it's just a suspender."

"You mean suspension."

"Right, that's what I said. But they'll never take me back. I mean being accused of attempted murder doesn't look good for an elementary school teacher. If I was a high school teacher, especially in a big city, it might be an asset. But enough about me, I hear you met the Man Solos, Ted and Felix."

"Yes I did. How did you know that?

"This is a very small town. Some people call them the non-brothers. But I've always called them the Man Solos."

"But not to their face."

"Of course not."

"That's from Star Wars, right?"

"Cor

"I'm not Amanda," Rick said with a smile. "You mean correctamundo."

"That's what I said. It's sad that they're both alone, but it's great that at least they have each other."

"You're really good at coming up with names for people."

"Yeah, well, at least I'm good at something."

"You're a wonderful teacher!" Father Joseph said emphatically as he walked up to the booth.

"But no one will ever know it now," she said sadly.

"I'll get this straightened out, Sara," the priest said confidently as he sat down. "Hello Jesse."

"Hi father. Care for a drink?"

"That sounds good. I'll have a glass of white wine."

"I'll have another beer," Sara said just before belching loudly.

"Well, I never thought I'd recommend burp control to one of my parishioners," Father Joseph said with a laugh.

Rick smiled at his remark before walking over to the bar. Sara, who did not get the reference immediately, went into hysterics several moments later.

"That's so funny," she told him. "Burp control instead of birth control. I always enjoyed your sermons, but I didn't know you were this quick. Did you ever think of becoming a stick-up comic?"

"You mean a stand-up comic."

"That's what I said."

"I don't think the bishop would approve. Don't let what happened today get you down, Sara. I'll find a way to make the school board regain their senses."

"I appreciate it, father. But it's too late. Elsa, I mean Mrs. King, will always think I was out to get her, and the Lion King.

I can't believe they think I'm a terrorist. But what I really can't believe is that Mrs. Elsa bought her husband's explanation for what he said on that CD."

"It was a miracle," Father Joseph said while smiling at her nicknames for the principal and his wife. "Look, Sara, between you and me, Ellen King tends to be a bit of a drama queen. I know, because I've dealt with her before. But don't tell Ellen I said that, or I might be defrocked."

"My lips are seals," Sara responded while nodding her head. Then she recognized her error.

"Did you hear what I said? I said my lips are seals, instead of my lips are sealed. That's funny!"

She began to bark like a seal and clap her hands together as though they were flippers. Rick was amused, but the priest became aware of the stares Sara was receiving from the rest of the people in the bowling alley.

"I think we should leave," he said. "Why don't you come back to the rectory so we can talk a little more."

"Do you have beer there?" Sara asked as she took a long drink from her glass.

"No, but I'm sure I can find something for you."

"Wine! You must be swimming in wine!" Sara exclaimed.

"Not enough to swim in, but I do shower in it occasionally."

She shrieked with laughter before asking "Can Jesse come too?"

"I wouldn't think of leaving without him."

Rick was about to say that he had to go home, but something in the priest's demeanor stopped him.

This guy suspects something.

"Sara, you've got to keep it down," Matt said politely as he came over to their booth. Then he saw Larry Oslifer walk in.

"You're late," he told him. "Where's your brother?"

"He's in the happy house with his uncle," the officer answered dejectedly as he pointed to Rick.

"The happy house?" Matt asked.

"The Happy Hill Mental Health Clinic. Someone claimed they saw him doing something…weird with his uncle."

Rick's heart almost came to a complete stop.

What did you do now, Oscar?

"What happened?" asked Matt.

"We were chasing two terrorists…"

"My only friends!" Sara exclaimed, while raising her beer in a toast.

Larry gave her a disapproving sneer before saying "They had…stolen something. Anyway, when we went past the house where this guy and his family are living, we heard Mary Popkins scream. His uncle was on the front lawn, naked as a jay bird. My brother went to deal with that situation while I continued to pursue the terrorists. Mary claims that something weird happened. So they took Tommy and his uncle to Happy Hill."

Now that's how you keep a low profile, Oscar thought Rick.

"That guy is out of control!" Sara said as she raised her glass in a toast to the bookie.

"I'll bet Tommy loses his job at the airport," Larry lamented. "They're a lot stricter about who they hire than the police department is."

Those two guys are everywhere! Rick thought.

"I'm sorry to hear about Tommy, Ofifer Oslicer." Sara said sincerely.

"That's Officer Oslifer," he responded with disdain.

"That's what I said. At our next meeting to discuss the destruction of Morgan Town, I'll ask my *pals* to set the record straight about Mary Pop Ins' accusations of weirdo behavior by the police department," Sara told him with an exaggerated wink.

Rick sat there silently, wondering how they were going to get Oscar out of the happy house. The idea of Binny's Uncle being in such a place seemed appropriate to the thief, yet it could also ruin his dream of financial independence and cost him his freedom. They were about to leave when a man and woman stepped onto the small stage next to the bar.

"Dot and Dash are here!" Sara exclaimed when two middle-aged performers appeared. "We have to stay for a couple of songs!"

"At least we have one fan in the audience," Dash said with a smile as he picked up his ukulele.

"Ladies and gentlemen, we're Morse Code," Dot added as she did the same with her flutophone.

They've got to be kidding, Rick thought with a grin.

They opened with Jim Croce's *Time in a Bottle.* Rick and the priest listened politely, even though the performance left much to be desired. Sara was moved to tears, however. She accompanied the pair, though her performance left even more to be desired.

Sara called Larry, who had assumed his post behind the bar, over to the booth after the song was finished.

"We'll have another round," she told him.

"I think we should be going," the priest suggested.

"Please, oh please, Father," Sara implored him. "I won't be noisy."

"All right."

"I want to see about my Uncle," Rick said as he began to stand up.

"Relax," Father Joseph said in an insistent tone. "Happy Hill is an excellent facility. And I'm sure you won't be able to see him until tomorrow anyway. This rounds on me."

"What will it be?" Larry asked them.

"I'll have another bud," Sara said. "And you don't have to worry about me annoying the other patrons. I'm now practicing burp control."

"A glass of white wine for me, Larry."

"A Bud Light for me," Rick told him with little enthusiasm.

They remained there for a while longer, until Sara started singing along to *The Wichita Lineman.*

"I know I need a small vacation, but it don't look like rain," she sang into her beer bottle, drowning out the increasingly irritated middle-aged duo on the stage. "Do you guys know *I Fought the Law and the Law Won?*"

Dash gave her an annoyed look, which was not surprising, since they had not finished performing *The Wichita Lineman.*

"Doesn't she play a great flutophone," Sara remarked when the song was over. "I'll bet she learned to play it at Morgan Elementary."

I'm sure it wasn't at the Juilliard School of Music, Rick thought.

A waitress walked by with a birthday cake that she was delivering to one of the bowlers. Sara took a lit candle off the cake and held it up to salute the entertainers.

"We've arrived," Dot said sarcastically to her partner.

Sara then cheered loudly in response to a strike thrown by someone on lane five, after Dot had acknowledged it by raising her plastic flutophone in the air. Morse Code then began the next song as the tall, lanky priest escorted Sara Simpson from the bar. A preoccupied Rick was close behind them.

"Why Sheriff Reinhart," Father Joseph said as they walked past him. "What brings you here?"

He had been watching Sara from a distance and replied, "I knew Sara was upset, so I was just checking up on her."

You mean spying on her thought Rick.

"He's my male escort," Sara slurred. "He made sure I got out of the school without hurting anything except my heart."

"She won't be driving, Sheriff. But it's very nice of you to worry about her safety," said the priest in a sarcastic tone.

"Just doing my job, Father," Reinhart said.

"Father Joseph will take care of me now, Sheriff Reinfart," Sara assured him. "You can be a male escort for some other girl."

Reinhart took his leave. After waiting for Sara to use the ladies' room they drove to the rectory, a modern brick structure that was located next to the quaint old church. Sara got out of the car first after they arrived.

There were renovations going on at that time, which included a new front door for the building. The old one had been propped up against a tree until it could be disposed of. Sara, in her condition, did not realize this. She saw the door and failed to recognize that it was no longer attached to the building. When Sara tried to open it, the soon to be discarded door fell on top of her.

"Are you all right?" the priest asked as he ran up to her.

"Someone stole the rectory!" Sara shouted. "Call the Ocifers Osiffers!"

Despite the unfavorable events of the day, Rick struggled to stifle his laughter. He helped remove the door from Sara and guided her into the rectory. They sat on a couch in Father Joseph's office while he made coffee.

"I'm just like the Man Solos," Sara said in a melancholy tone. "Everyone's moving away from me, even my Dad. No one around here will have anything to do with me."

"Don't give up," Rick said while trying to stifle the guilt that rose up within him. "The father is still on your side. You'll be back in the classroom before you can say Ocifers Ossiffers."

"That should be Ofifer Oslicers," Sara corrected him with a laugh.

"That's what I said." Rick told her with a smile.

"Did you ever want to just chuck it all? Did you ever just say this isn't working, I have to start over?"

"Sure." *Quite recently, in fact.* "But you like what you're doing. You'll be able to teach again."

"The man speaks wisely," the priest said as he entered the room with three cups of coffee. "I'm going to straighten this out for you, Sara. You just take it easy. Go on a vacation."

"Just like *The Wichita Lineman!*" Sara said.

"And before long, you'll be back to work," the pastor quickly added before she could begin to sing the song.

Sara fell asleep, and Father Joseph carried her to his car. Rick opened the door so he could place her inside. They drove back to her apartment. The priest placed Sara in her bed, brushing the tangled hair away from her face before departing.

"She had a tough day," Rick remarked as Father Joseph drove him back to his car. "I thought everyone was afraid of Sara's father. How could they do this to her?"

"Some people believe she's a terrorist. The instinct for self-preservation will overcome fear every time. That uncle of yours is quite a handful."

"Yeah, he has his moments. I don't know what we're going to do about him."

The priest said nothing more until they arrived at the bowling alley parking lot. After stopping the car, Father Joseph turned and looked at Rick, with a menacing glare.

I'll never let this guy hear my confession, Rick thought just before the father began to speak.

"Some people think I live in a kind of netherworld because of the vocation I've chosen. They believe that I spend all week in the clouds, just waiting for the parishioners to return from the real world to join me there on Sunday."

The pastor paused, moving his face closer to Rick's before continuing.

"I hope you're not foolish enough to believe that, Jesse. I don't know what you're doing here, or what if any part you played in creating the situation at the school, but my instincts tell me that you have something to do with it. And I'm sure your uncle, and the other people you're living with, know something about it too. But I don't care about all that. I'm only concerned about Sara. She's always been a favorite of mine. And I think the kids would be missing out on something very special if Sara wasn't allowed to teach again. So you better find someone else for them to blame. Do whatever you have to do, but make sure that Sara Simpson gets her job back. Or I'm going to come down out of the clouds and fuck you up! Good night."

You might have to stand in line for that, Father.

Rick drove back to the house, his foreboding about the

inevitable discussion with Binny, and even more so, Sylvia, increasing along the way.

"This isn't working," he repeated Sara's words after parking in front of the house. "I should just go away and start over. Of course, that was the whole idea behind robbing the bank."

He went inside. Sylvia was sitting at the kitchen table, with a stoic expression on her face.

"What happened?" Rick asked her as he sat down.

"That jackass never listens to me! I told him to put some clothes on, but he wouldn't do it. I'm well rid of Oscar."

"Why did he go outside naked?"

"He wanted to watch television in his underwear. We were watching Autumn Reeser on a talk show, who's no relation to Reese Witherspoon by the way. We had an argument about whether woman looked better with hose on. I put a pair on my head to be sarcastic, so he took off his boxer shorts and put them on his head. Then my stupid husband got so excited when those old guys drove by in the patrol car that he ran outside with nothing on. A cop saw him and tried to wrap his coat around him. That nosy neighbor Mary saw the whole thing, and thought they were acting like a couple of homos."

Rick looked at her incredulously for several moments and thought, *I'm sure this kind of thing happens to married couples all the time. If they both happen to be out of their mind, that is.*

"I always knew he was mentally ill," Sylvia continued. "I'm well rid of him!"

"I can understand why you're mad, but under the current circumstances, we've got to get Oscar out of that place. What name did he give the cops?"

"His real name! I kept giving him a look that said don't you screw this up. But he did! He gave them his real name."

"Maybe that's a good thing. His alias would have never checked out. We'll just have to think of a reason for his being here."

"Did you erase the program?" Binny asked when he joined them.

"No, I was just about to when Gartner showed up. And we've got another problem. Father Joseph is really pissed that Sara Simpson was suspended for being a terrorist. He told me that if I don't get her reinstated, he's going to cause a lot of trouble for me, and us."

"How does he know we're involved?" Binny questioned him.

"He has divine sources, I guess," Rick said with a grin while pointing above him.

"What are we going to do?" asked Binny.

"The first thing we have to do is to get Oscar out of the booby hatch. Then we'll sit down and come up with a new plan."

"Leave him there!" Sylvia exclaimed.

"You don't really mean that," Rick said in a kind tone. *Because if we do, you'll have to argue with yourself for a very long time.* "I'm going to bed. We'll visit Oscar early tomorrow. I really don't want to call in sick, because the custodian job could turn out to be my new career, if we don't pull this off. But you have to do what you have to do."

"I hate to think of him in that place," Sylvia said as a tear rolled down her cheek.

"He'll be fine," Rick assured her. "The priest told me it's a good facility."

He went into the bedroom and started watching television, hoping that it would put him to sleep.

Rick was just about to fall into his slumber when the sound of Sylvia's voice made him sit up in the bed. She was carrying on both sides of a heated conversation.

"I was watching the t.v. I didn't see him go outside," Sylvia told herself.

"You should've been watching him! You could have grabbed him!" she retorted.

"How could I grab him? He was naked. There was nothing to grab on to!" Sylvia defended herself against her own attempt to affix blame for Oscar's predicament.

"You could have grabbed his..."

"Don't be disgusting!" Sylvia objected to her own apparently vulgar suggestion.

"I was going to say his arm!"

"You were not! I know what you were thinking, believe me!"

"How do you know what I was thinking!" she fired back.

She's really arguing with herself, Rick thought incredulously.

At that moment Wispy, who was making love to Binny in the room next to Sylvia's, reached climax and screamed *"Nada Prodigalidad,* my love!"

I'm the one who's in a nut house! Rick thought as he pulled the covers over his head.

R ick arose early the next day and showered. As the warm water ran over his body he searched for a way to save their illicit scheme from ruin. All his efforts would be for naught, with only a very uncomfortable confinement to show for them, if the priest was not appeased. The only way to accomplish this, apparently, was for the thieves to surrender the bank's money so that Sara would be cleared. The idea of walking away with nothing did not appeal to him, however. He went downstairs and stepped outside.

Rick took out his cell phone and called Henry Pabst.

"Morning boss," he began. "I have to take care of a personal matter today. I won't be able to come in."

"I know all about it, Jesse. Your uncle's mind has taken a vacation from reality. Poor son of a bitch. The Pabst understands. Do whatever you have to do. Family comes first."

A permanent vacation, he mused before saying aloud "Thanks boss. I'll see you tomorrow."

He put his phone away just as Marvin Blando approached

him. He was dressed in his usual attire, a very expensive gray suit.

"Good morning," Blando said in a casual tone.

"Hi there."

"Your uncle, he's getting help?"

"Yes, although this is really just a big misunderstanding, Mr. Blando."

Marvin gave him an almost imperceptible nod. A thoughtful expression came over his face before the spurious don spoke.

"When someone in a man's family brings shame upon it, he has to lead the one who's gone *alla deriva* back into the fold. To help you do this I will send a pie from my family's business to your uncle tonight."

He must have a pizza for the pervert's promotion going on at his restaurant, Rick thought to himself.

"It's so your uncle knows he can still live among us. But I need something from you, too." He paused to make a sweeping gesture with his arms before continuing. "This is where my wife looks out our bedroom window every morning and our children play with their toys."

I saw that movie, too Rick thought before saying: "But you don't have children."

"If we had children, they would play here," Blando responded in an impatient tone. "I can't have naked people in this neighborhood. You say it's a misunderstanding, I can accept that, once. But I want no more of that. Capiche, compagno?"

"You don't have to worry, Mr. Blando. And the pizza isn't necessary, though I do appreciate the offer."

"You don't want my friendship?"

Here's where I get rubbed out. Though I bet this guy carries a cap pistol, so just like him, the wounds won't be real. Then aloud he said, "I most certainly do."

"Then accept this gift for your uncle."

Marvin put his sunglasses on and walked back to his home.

"What did he want?" Binny asked as he joined Rick.

"He's sending over a pizza."

"For breakfast?"

"For dinner. It's to bolster Oscar's spirits," Rick told him. "I guess he doesn't care about you and me. Let's make some coffee and come up with another plan."

The two of them drove to the Happy Hill Mental Health Clinic with Sylvia after breakfast. They waited there in a comfortably furnished visiting room for the patient to arrive.

"I just hope they didn't give him any shock treatments," Sylvia said nervously.

"It's not that kind of a facility," Binny assured her. "They don't treat the seriously ill people here."

Then they took him to the wrong place, Rick thought.

Oscar finally arrived with a large intern by his side. He looked relaxed, as though Happy Hill had been on his itinerary all along.

Nothing bothers him, Rick thought to himself. *He's the type of person that gets away with things. And since I'm his partner, maybe I will too.*

The intern stepped outside, remaining by the door and occasionally glancing through the window in it to monitor Oscar.

"Did you get to the computer?" the bookie asked Rick anxiously.

"It's good to see you too," Sylvia said sarcastically.

"No," Rick told him. "I was just about to when Gartner showed up. Gouveia saw the Oslifers chasing the Orpus', so he asked him to keep an eye on Simpson's classroom."

A perplexed Sylvia asked him, "Who are they?" The only name she was familiar with was Carman.

"I don't know Ri...eh Jesse," Oscar began in a disappointed tone. Then he said softly, "We might just have to blow up the school. When no one's in it, of course."

I'm starting to think like Oscar. I should have myself checked out while I'm here.

"Hello!" Sylvia almost screamed. "Your wife is here."

"Keep it down," Rick implored her.

"I know you're here," Oscar said pleasantly as he put his arm around her. "I just had to get caught up with business."

"Have they given you any drugs?" Sylvia asked him.

"No. The doctor said that he just wanted to observe me. So I said sure, you can observe me watching the ballgame. By the way, I cleaned up on the Royals-Angels game. Then this morning he asked me if I had any dreams last night. And I did. I had a weird dream about being on a beach in Barbados with a bald baboon. We were dancing. I don't know how my mind came up with something like that."

"It's because you're really mentally ill," Sylvia told him. "You must be to have a dream like that! And you told the doctor about it! You'll be in here for the rest of your life!"

"Now Harry, he got some heavy drugs this morning," Oscar said while ignoring his wife.

"Who's Harry?" Rick asked him.

"A guy I was talking with at breakfast. Harry likes sausage patties, but they served link instead. He tried to stuff one of them up the chef's nose. You'd think they'd ask people what they want to eat, for Christ's sake. It's like the one intern said: *the hill at Happy Hill might be happy, but not all the people here are.*"

"Why would anyone react that way to a sausage? It makes no sense. If you don't like it, you don't eat it." Sylvia said.

"You have to understand the people here. They're a little uptight, babe."

"Why did you call me babe?"

"I always call you babe."

"But when you call me that during a discussion, it comes across as a little condescending."

"Well excuse me. I guess it must be because of my mental condition."

"You don't have a mental condition."

"I have a mental condition. Everyone has one. Mine happens to be very good, even though these people think it's questionable."

"It sounds like the people here really know what they're doing."

I agree, thought Rick, who had declined to claim authorship of Oscar's dream but did note that dancing with a baboon was no longer the farthest thing from the bookie's mind. Then aloud he told them, "Look guys, we should keep this conversation very low key. If you two start talking loudly that guy in the white uniform will be in here really fast. He'll think the patient is about to lose it. And we want to get Oscar out of here right away. If the doctor thinks he's unstable, that won't happen."

"I'm sorry, Ri... eh Jesse," Oscar said apologetically. "And may I say that I'm truly sorry about getting arrested. I just forgot that I was naked."

Happens to me all the time.

"I screwed up. I made an ass of myself. I loused up. I'm a bonehead. I fu..."

"I get the idea," Rick cut him off.

"But I'll be out of here by this afternoon. So you don't have to worry."

"The doctor told you that?" Rick asked hopefully.

"No, but a friend of mine is going to take care of it. He'll tell us, and the doctor, what really happened."

"What do you mean?" Rick questioned him.

"It's like when you hear about something really bad happening on the news, and you say to yourself, boy, someone must have really screwed up. The person who's responsible for that is finished. Then a while later the official version of the incident comes out, and it turns out that person didn't screw up at all. You just didn't hear the right story. My friend will come up with the right story for me."

"That's good," Rick responded skeptically. "But we've got another problem. Sara Simpson got suspended, because the school board thinks she's involved with the people who took the bank's money."

"Is she?" Oscar asked.

"We're the people who took the money," Binny pointed out. "You'd know if she was in on it."

"Are you sure they didn't give you drugs?" Sylvia asked sarcastically.

"I just meant…"

"It really doesn't matter," Rick interrupted him again. "Father Joseph has told me that if she isn't cleared very quickly, he will fuck me up."

"A priest said that?" Sylvia exclaimed.

"That's nothing," Oscar told her. "Where I grew up those guys could have given lessons in gutter language."

"We grew up in the same place," Sylvia pointed out. "And I don't rem…"

"Anyway, if he puts the bank people onto us, we could be in deep shit," Rick interjected.

That silenced both Oscar and Sylvia.

"So what do we do?" Oscar finally asked.

"It turns out the bank just wants to get the money back," Binny told them. "The security guy, Gouveia, is afraid to tell the directors that I was able to hack into their system after he convinced them to spend a ton of money to protect it."

"So if we give the money back, there'll probably be no questions asked," Rick added. "Of course, that would make us all a lot poorer. And we'd have to get the casino people and the others we paid off to give back their money, or we'll be short."

Oscar smiled and said, "That ain't gonna happen. Maybe we can get the bank to settle for less."

"I doubt it," Rick said while shaking his head. "But fortunately Binny and I have come up with another alternative."

"We have another plan," said Binny in a confident tone.

"First we have to get my husband out of here," Sylvia said. "This place gives me the creeps."

"It's not so bad, as long as they don't give link sausage to someone that wanted the patty kind," Oscar told them.

"The food is all that bothers you about this place!" an

exasperated Sylvia exclaimed. "You're out of your cotton-picking mind!"

"What does that mean?" Oscar asked her.

"You know what it means!" Sylvia responded.

"My mind picks cotton? How? Do I use telegraphy to pick the cotton?"

"What the hell is telegraphy?" Sylvia asked him.

"I think you mean telepathy," Binny said.

"Whatever. Your aunt isn't making any sense. After living with her for all these years it's no wonder that I wound up here."

A well-dressed man with dark glasses came into the room before Sylvia could offer her retort.

"My man!" he said enthusiastically to Oscar.

"Terry! Thanks for getting here so quickly. This is my friend Jesse. This is my lawyer, Terry Manson."

Perry Mason, Rick thought as he shook his hand.

"And you know my wife."

"Boo bola!" the slender individual addressed her with a smile.

"You always know how to make a woman feel elegant, Terry," she replied in the same fashion.

"And this is Ralph."

"How are you, young man?"

"So what are the odds of me getting out of here today?" Oscar asked him.

"I'd say much better than the ones you gave me on Kansas City versus Oakland," Terry said confidently. "This is all a big misunderstanding. Now how many times have I told you not to wear that flesh tone bathing suit in public?"

"What flesh tone bathing suit?" Oscar questioned him.

"The one you were wearing when this incident occurred. The lady who saw you, her name is Mary I believe, simply *thought* you were naked."

"And the cop?" asked Oscar.

"Same thing. He just didn't realize that you were wearing a swimsuit."

"I think you can get Mary to believe anything," Rick interjected before taking a quick look behind him to see if the landlady had suddenly appeared. "But the cop probably noticed some things that you could only see if he was naked. I don't think you'll change his mind."

"That would be true, if not for the fact that Officer Oslifer has a vested interest in seeing this matter cleared up quickly. He was in the process of trying to recover something that had been stolen. If his superior were to find out about the theft, it would make him very unhappy, and possibly cost the officer his job."

"This guy is amazing!" Oscar proclaimed. "You've been here for how long?"

"Since yesterday evening."

"And you already have it all down."

"But what if they want to see the swimsuit?" Sylvia asked.

"I'll think of something," Terry assured them. "I'm going over to the police station to speak with the sheriff, and Tommy Oslifer. I'll be back here in an hour."

"Those guys never had to deal with someone like Terry before!" Oscar said enthusiastically.

"That's for sure. I'm the only black man within five hundred miles of this town."

"I'll talk to Mary," Rick told them. "I think she'll listen to me."

"Any help you can give would be appreciated," said the barrister as he walked out the door.

Terry drove over to the police station. Sheriff Reinhart escorted him into his office in a wary fashion. Dealing with a lawyer from New York City was a new experience for the small-town lawman.

"Can I get you a cup of coffee," he asked him.

"No thanks. I've already drank my limit for today. What I would like to do is to speak with Officer Tommy Oslifer, if he's available."

"He just got back from the...I'll get him for you."

Reinhart returned with a contrite and embarrassed patrolman by his side. His stay at Happy Hill had broken his spirit. The sight of this city slicker did little to improve it.

"Officer, I understand that you accused my client, Oscar Anastas, of being naked on the front lawn of the house that he's renting with several other members of his family."

"The whole family was naked?" the sheriff asked incredulously.

"Just the uncle," Tommy told him. "The guy was naked as a jay bird."

"How did you ascertain that he was naked?" Terry asked him.

"I looked at him," Tommy replied in a tone that indicated he thought the question was absurd.

"That's the problem," Terry said while nodding his head.

"That's a problem?" Reinhart sought clarification.

"There's nothing wrong with my eyes!" Officer Oslifer said emphatically.

"But anyone's eyes, no matter how good they are, can play tricks on them Would it surprise you to know that he was actually wearing a flesh tone bathing suit?"

"It sure would. Especially since I saw his eh.... private parts. He didn't have anything on."

"What were you doing when you came upon my client? Would you mind if I borrowed something to write on, Sheriff? His answer could be important in building the case for Mr. Anastas' lawsuit."

"Lawsuit? What lawsuit?" Reinhart asked.

"I believe this was a false arrest. Now could you answer the question, officer?"

"We were chasing a...speeder," Tommy said haltingly.

"Oh, I see."

Terry managed to communicate his knowledge about the real target of the Officer's Oslifers pursuit with a skeptical glance at Tommy. His back was facing Reinhart at the time, so he was not aware of this nonverbal communication.

"Could it be that with the excitement of the chase, and then having to abandon it in order to come to the aid of a hysterical woman, that you simply thought my client was naked as a... what was it, a jay bird?"

Tommy hesitated. He would not admit that his police car had been stolen again. Yet it galled him to lie in front of his boss.

"Well, I guess he could have had something on," he finally muttered sheepishly.

"What!" the sheriff exclaimed. "You said he was butt naked. And so did Mary! What the hell is this?"

"I'm sorry, Sheriff, but now that I think about it, I'm not so sure."

"Look, Mr. Manson, if we made a mistake, I'll be the first to apologize. And the officer will be second!"

"That's not necessary, sheriff. If you could just have my client released from Happy Hill, and the indecent exposure charge dropped, I'm sure he'll be willing to forget the whole thing."

"I can do that. I would like to see this bathing suit, though."

"Unfortunately, my client's wife was so upset by the incident she burned it. Now it's my turn to apologize."

"How convenient," Reinhart said sarcastically. "It's also a shame, though. You could have used it for the lawsuit."

"True, but that won't be necessary now, will it, sheriff?"

"I suppose not. Good day Mr. Manson."

"Good day to you sir. And to you, Officer Oslifer."

■ ■ ■

Rick stood on the porch of Mary's house. The front door was open, leaving only the screen door, which now contained a glass window in anticipation of winter, to discourage intruders. Rick was tempted to walk inside without knocking, sneaking up on the landlady as she had done to him on so many occasions. He was just about to give into that urge when Mary appeared behind him, and almost succeeded in stopping his heart.

"Hi Jesse. How's your uncle?"

"That's what I came to talk to you about," Rick replied after catching his breath. "Can we go inside?"

"Sure. Would you like some tea?"

"That sounds good."

Mary boiled the water and then placed two cups of tea on the table, along with a plate of cookies.

"I'm sorry I had to call the police," she told him after taking a sip from her cup. "But I mean the man can't walk around the neighborhood that way. It's indecent!"

"I know it looked that way to you, but believe me, looks can be deceiving. My uncle was wearing a flesh tone swimsuit. He wasn't really naked."

Mary looked at him incredulously.

"You know, it's been a long time since I've seen a man's…a man naked," she responded. "But I haven't forgotten what one looks like. And the officer…talked to it. He said *Oslifer's here.*"

Mary's facial expression conveyed both fascination and disgust.

"Talked to what?" asked Rick.

Mary, who was too shy to elaborate, said "Look, I like you Jesse, but your uncle needs help."

I can't argue with you there. Then aloud "I know it's hard to believe, but he really didn't do anything wrong. And I promise to keep an eye on him. I'll make sure that this doesn't happen again."

Mary looked at him with a smile and then said "I guess a person who rents a house to someone without the owner's permission can't be too judgmental. You will keep an eye on the man, right."

"Absolutely."

"I heard him tell the police that his name was Oscar Anastas."

"That's right."

"But he told me his name was Steve LaSalle."

"No, that was my Uncle Steve. He visited us last week."

"Now I'm sure that the man the police arrested was Steve LaSalle."

"Remember the day that you snuck.... I mean came into the house and said Oscar looked different." *Not as different as he looked the last time you saw him, of course.* "But you couldn't figure out why."

"Yes, I remember that."

"It was because you were confusing Uncle Oscar and Uncle Steve. You met both of them."

"If you say so," Mary told him while still pondering his explanation. Then she smiled and said: "Oh, what the heck. I confuse things all the time. I'm sure you're right. You will be out of the house by Sunday, right?"

"Guaranteed."

"I'll call the sheriff, and say I was mistaken."

"Thanks for the tea, Mary."

"Don't leave without saying goodbye, Jesse."

` "I wouldn't dream of it," Rick assured her. *Because if I did you'd just pop up behind one day to get your goodbye, probably at the most inconvenient time.*

■   ■   ■

Rick emerged from his rented abode that afternoon and got into the car with Binny. The two of them drove up to the Morgan Estate. The now almost barren trees on the hillside were a perfect compliment to this overcast gray day. Binny was impressed by the house, and his imagination allowed him to envision a day when Wispy would live with him in a manor like the Morgan's.

"Do you think they're home?" Binny asked as they got out of the car.

"From what I hear they're hiding from the rest of the people in Morgan Town. So they should be home."

Rick rang the bell, then gave his name and reason for being there to the servant. After twenty minutes a distraught Edgar Morgan appeared.

"You'll have to forgive me, but I don't remember you," he said. "We're in the middle of a family crisis, as I'm sure you've heard."

"We're sorry to hear about your daughter's problems. I work at the school. I was at Sara's apartment the other night when you visited her. You asked me to fix a toilet in your home."

At the mention of the word *Sara* Edgar recoiled, as if his daughter's name had become synonymous with the devil himself.

"I know its lousy timing, but I have the time to fix it today," Rick told him. "This is my cousin Ralph. He's an expert on these types of problems."

"Yes, sir, I sure am. I must have fixed a thousand toilets," Binny assured him. "My autobiography is going to be called *The Shitter Is My Life.*"

Edgar gave him a quizzical glance before responding.

"It won't be noisy, will it? My wife has a severe headache."

"We won't make a sound-with the exception of the flushing, of course," Rick assured him.

"All right."

They followed him inside. Laverne Morgan came out of the den holding a cold compress on her forehead.

"Who are these people, Edgar?"

"This is Jesse and Ralph. They're going to fix the toilet bowl on the second floor."

"I'm sorry to bother you, Mrs. Morgan," Rick apologized. "But this was the only day we could do it. And may I say that though I've only known her for a short time, I'm sure Sara is innocent."

"We are desperately hoping that you're right," Laverne said with a weak smile. "I can't believe our little girl would try to murder someone."

"Sara was a hairy little ape when she was born," Edgar said bitterly. "She must be capable of anything!"

"I've never seen her baby pictures," Rick said.

"It's a condition called Lanugo, which many premature

babies have. Sara was such a beautiful baby, once she got over that unsightly condition," the frail Laverne said in a melancholy tone. Then she nearly shouted "Oh, another compress Martin, please hurry. Neither my head, nor my heart, can take another minute of this!"

The butler came running in response to her command with the desired article.

What great parents Rick thought sarcastically. Then he said aloud "We'll get right to work. Which bathroom is it?"

"The third one on the left. Right across from my office," Edgar responded after a stricken Laverne went back to the den.

Binny and Rick went upstairs. They asked Edgar to join them after flushing the malfunctioning bowl several times.

"I think the problem is being caused by the angle of the armature. It's holding the float too high," Binny said with authority in his voice. "It's a subtle thing, but one that can cause the toilet to keep running even though it looks like everything is fine."

"So what do we do?" Rick asked him.

"There's a website that has the recommended armature angle for any given toilet," Binny said. "You see, the geographic location of the bowl comes into play. For instance, if you live in an area with high humidity, the float angle should be more acute. I'll go home and see if I can find the web site on my computer."

"Why go home? Use the one in my office," Edgar suggested.

"All right," Binny agreed.

"I have to try and persuade my wife to eat some dinner," Edgar told them. "Poor thing, she's too distraught to even look at food. But life goes on, I suppose."

Edgar made a dramatic exit, bowing his head in shame for the actions of his offspring. Binny went into the office and spent three hours on the computer. He emerged with a smile on his face.

"We'll all set," he told Rick, who had been waiting anxiously for him to finish.

"You covered our tracks?"

"Yes, my liege. I erased my copy of Morgan Widgets accounts payable software from the spare hard drive on their computer. After I requested the money for the invoices I created from the Defense Department, of course."

Rick reached into the toilet bowl tank and bent the arm that held the float. After several flushes he was convinced that the problem was solved. They went downstairs and informed Edgar.

"It's fixed," he told him.

"Thank you, gentlemen," Edgar said while handing him a five-dollar bill. "At times like these it's very distracting to hear a toilet bowl running all night."

"We're happy to help. I hope Mrs. Morgan feels better," Rick said before leaving.

"He's got a gazillion dollars, but he only gives us five," Binny said with a laugh as they drove away.

"Yeah, I guess that's how you wind up with a gazillion dollars," Rick observed. "Or at least one of the ways."

They smiled at each other.

■　■　■

That evening found Sara Simpson lying in bed, watching a movie that she had lost interest in five minutes after it began. Like her mother, the former schoolteacher had a cold compress on her forehead. The alcohol Sara had consumed the night before was exacting a heavy price for the hours of bliss it had provided.

"How are you feeling?" Maya, who had just returned from doing the laundry, asked as she entered the room.

"Everything's a blur. I just remember snippets of conversations. Do you believe that Father Joseph was talking to me about birth control?"

"What! I think you're imagining that. The next time you drink a lot, go into the refrigerator…"

"I don't think I'd fit," Sara said with a weak smile.

"As I was about to say, get something carbonated to drink.

You'll feel much better the next morning. And you'll avoid having a hideous hangover."

"How was Dad today?"

"How should I know? He stayed home. But you don't have to worry about his loyalty to you, as long as you're my friend. He tells everyone that I'm his very own personal stimulus package. I'll make sure he gets you out of this."

"I guess with a father like Edgar, one needs to have friends like you."

The doorbell rang and Maya answered it.

"It's Jesse," she told Sara after returning to the bedroom.

"Oh, no! I made such an ass of myself last night. How am I supposed to face him?"

"Well, if you ruined any chance you had with him, how about putting in a good word for me."

Sara rolled her eyes and stumbled out to the living room while still holding the cold compress on her forehead.

"How are you feeling?" Rick asked her as he noted how much she resembled her mother, in no small part because of the compress on her forehead.

"Better than I deserve," Sara said with a weak smile.

"Just in case anyone is interested, I'm feeling fine, too," Maya said as she joined them.

"You remember my roommate," Sara said.

"Yes."

"I hear they arrested someone you live with for public nudity," Maya said with a grin. "What kind of people do you hang out with?"

"People who like to let it all hang out," Rick replied flippantly.

"Obviously. Well, I have to run down to the store," said Maya, who sensed that he wanted to talk with Sara alone. "Can I get anyone anything?"

"Ten more bottles of aspirin," Sara responded as she collapsed into a chair.

"I'll just take some of hers," Rick told her with a smile.

"See you later, kids," Maya said as she left.

"Look, I'm really sorry about the other night Jesse. I don't usually drink that much. It was just a really shitty day."

"No apology necessary. How would you like your job back?"

"What do you mean?"

"Well, I happen to know something about the money that was stolen from the bank. I also know that Gouveia, the Bank V.P. whom I believe you've met, would be willing to forget everything that's happened, if the bank gets the money back. Then all this talk about terrorists would fade away."

"But my problem is with the school board, especially Elsa and the Lion King. They won't change their minds because the bank is willing to forget about it."

"What you need is a good lawyer. Someone who can convince those people that you did nothing wrong. And I've got one for you. His name is Terry Manson."

They looked at each other and smiled.

"Perry Mason!" they exclaimed together.

"So you're telling me that you were in on this all along!" Sara's voice suddenly became stern as her alcohol impaired mind belatedly comprehended the implication of his words. "You could have stopped all the terrorist talk yesterday! But you let me go through all this bullshit!"

"I never thought it would go this far," Rick said somberly, and sincerely. "I like you Sara. And I want to make it right."

"And Rex! That kid's been through hell. Which is exactly where you should go!" she exclaimed before pressing on the compress and saying "Ouch, that hurt."

Sara stood up and walked over to the window without the headache aid. Morgan Town had never seemed smaller to her than at that moment. *Everyone knows everything about everyone. And in my case they even know things that aren't true,* she thought sadly. Then Sara turned and said "Of course you were involved in the robbery. But this town makes people dumb, me included. That's why I didn't see it."

Sara sat down before continuing.

"Before my own personal Armageddon day nothing was more

important to me than teaching at Morgan Town Elementary. But now I want more. I received an email from an old friend of mine recently. He teaches at a place where his efforts are appreciated. And there's no pretentious talk about how morally superior teachers have to be. The people there simply appreciate a job well done. That's where I want to be. I want to hear someone say *Sara, you're really good at your job. We need you, and more importantly, your students need you.* I don't want to deal with the Mrs. Landers' and Mrs. Childs' of the world anymore."

She looked at Rick with disdain

"I should tell you to go to hell!" exclaimed Sara once again. She then quickly put the cold compress on her forehead.

"You already did," Rick pointed out. "And I deserve it," he added contritely.

"I just want one thing from you," she said in a decidedly more civil tone. "Get them to admit that I never tried to murder anyone, or created a CD to embarrass the Lion King, or ever had anything to do with robbing a bank. Then I can get out of here."

"That's three things, but who's counting," Rick said in a failed attempt to elicit a smile from Sara. "Perry...I mean Terry will speak to you soon. I hope you don't mind, but I've already given him your address and phone number."

Rick started to walk to the door. He turned and spoke to her once more before leaving.

"I really am sorry, Sara. I didn't think anyone would get hurt. Just sit tight, and this will all work out for you in the end."

Sara watched him leave with a skeptical expression on her tired face.

Rick went back to the house. Oscar was catching up with his clients on the phone. Binny was at the movies with Wispy. Sylvia had prepared a lasagna dinner, which Oscar was too busy to partake in. She shared it with Rick instead.

"So isn't it ironic. After all we've been through, the bank is getting its money back," Sylvia said thoughtfully.

"That's the new plan," Rick agreed. "That will get Sara off the hook. And since there's to be no questions asked, we can finally leave Morgan Town, if everything goes right."

Sylvia smiled at him as she began to eat her dinner.

That's a big if, of course, right pal, Rick silently said to Bowmarc.

■   ■   ■

Bobby Cranston sat at his desk in the Grand View Bank that morning. The first hour had been an excruciating slow one for the new accounts officer, with only one person inquiring about the services this establishment offered. He was doodling on a memo paid when a very slight woman, appearing to be in her seventies or eighties, approached his desk.

"Young fella, I hope I'm not interrupting anything important."

"Not at all ma'am. I'm just thinking about the meeting I attended this morning. Please sit down."

The woman gave him a knowing smile as she took a seat.

"I know daydreaming when I see it, young man. But there's nothing wrong with that, you know. Companies should encourage their employees to let their minds wander. You never know what bright idea might come from it."

"What can I do for you today, Ms...?"

"Hamilton. Harriet Hamilton."

"I'm Bobby Cranston, Ms. Hamilton."

"You can call me Beverly."

"Is that your middle name?"

"No, but I always liked that name better than my own."

The old woman cackled at her own attempt at humor, while Bobby smiled.

"So, what can I do for you today?"

"My granddaughters, Unis and Ophelia, are very special to me. I want to open an account for them, so that they'll have enough money to start their lives off proper when they reach eighteen."

"A college education is so important these days. We have several investment options that would suit your needs."

"College! Bah! I want them to travel, see the world. That's the only way to get a real education. I don't want my lovelies to get trapped behind a desk for the rest of their lives."

Bobby suddenly felt depressed but did not reveal that to the perspective customer.

"This is our best annuity," he said enthusiastically while handing her a brochure.

"What's that under your desk?"

"What?"

"Under your desk. There's something there."

He bent down and saw a paper clip lying on the carpet. Bobby picked it up and showed it to her.

"Young man, I hope this establishment handles its depositor's money better than it does its office supplies. We cannot waste anything in this day and age. Now I'm still interested in doing business with you, because you have a very trustworthy face. I'll take this brochure to my accountant and make a decision after we discuss it."

"I'll be here, Beverly," he said with a grin.

There was a twinkle in the eyes of the old woman as she returned his smile. Harriet appeared unusually spry for her age as she walked out of the bank, at least in Bobby's estimation.

"God bless her," he said aloud. "I hope I'm doing as well when I'm that old."

Bobby noticed a zip drive on his desk a while later. He inserted into his computer and opened it.

CHAPTER

12

Rick called in sick again the next morning, receiving the same sympathetic reaction from his boss as the day before. This was to be the pivotal day for their criminal enterprise. The thieves would either be on their way to a life that only those who possessed millions of dollars would ever know, or they would begin an existence known only to the shady characters that were running from the law. Rick paced back and forth in the kitchen.

"I need to relax. Maybe I can find some mindless dribble to watch on t.v. I wonder if the Corinthians are on."

Rick flipped though the channels for a while before going out on the porch to drink his coffee. Rex Thompson approached him. For a moment Rick smiled, the sight of the red-haired young boy reminding him of himself at that age. The visitor's words, however, only added to his angst.

"Hi Jesse," the woebegone youngster said to him. "I just can't learn nothing without Miss Simpson."

"I know it's hard," Rick told Rex as his conscience assailed him. "But Miss Simpson wouldn't want you to fall behind just because she isn't there. You'll find as you grow older that the people we like, and even love, sometimes disappear suddenly. You have to move on, while keeping them in your heart."

The expression on Rex's face turned from sadness to one of panic in an instant. He suddenly envisioned his parents, sister and friends suddenly vanishing from his life. His felt as though his feet were standing on quicksand.

It's a good thing I'm not impersonating a counselor. I'd never get away with it, Rick silently admonished himself. Then he lied aloud, "Miss Simpson might be back, Rex. This is just a big misunderstanding."

"Really?" he asked hopefully.

"No question about it. These things have a way of working themselves out."

"Okay. I know you wouldn't lie to me. I've got to get to school."

"How did you know where I live?"

"Mr. Pabst told me. See ya later."

I must remember to thank his eminence for that.

Binny joined him on the porch.

"We can do it!" he exclaimed.

Rick just smiled, the relief he felt too overwhelming to express in words.

■ ■ ■

On that same morning Sara Simpson put on a smart black dress and stared at herself in the mirror. She was meeting with the school board, and if her lawyer was successful, Sara would be leaving Morgan Town. The young woman suddenly felt very sad. The faces of the students Miss Simpson had taught and nurtured over the last three years appeared in the reflective glass, each one reminding her of a memorable moment when she had been able to stimulate their developing minds.

I should be preparing Monday's lesson, she thought while

wiping away a tear. Then Sara regained her composure. *I can't get sentimental. At least not until this is over.*

The doorbell rang and she went to answer it. Terry Manson greeted her with a smile.

"You'll knock'em dead in that outfit, Sara," he said with a confidence inspiring grin. "Just remember, you're Greta Garbo, you're the silent mystery woman. I'll do all the talking. Put these on."

Terry handed her a pair of dark sunglasses. After following the barrister's instructions Sara was transformed from a gregarious schoolteacher into a woman of intrigue. She also became a person who had difficulty seeing the world around her.

They drove to the Holiday Inn on the outskirts of town. The bank had rented a meeting room there at Manson's request. Sara got out of the car and said, "I'll knock them off their feet."

She then tripped over the curb, landing in a spread-eagle position on the sidewalk.

"Are you all right?" Terry asked her.

"Yes," Sara responded meekly.

"You can take off those glasses if it's too hard to see."

"No, this is just me being me. It has nothing to do with the glasses."

Sara stood up and lifted the eyewear to examine the damage from the fall. There was a large hole in her black hose. Sara's exposed knee had also been cut. A thin trickle of blood ran down her leg.

"You can go to the ladies' room and take care of that before we go into the meeting," Terry told her.

"No, I don't think so. This looks right to me."

They walked into the conference room, with the lawyer keeping his arm around her to eliminate the possibility of further mishaps. Miles Gouveia sat at the head of a large conference table. On his left were seated Dan Gartner and Gary Knowles. On his right were Lionel King, his wife and Sheriff Tim Reinhart. They all noticed Sara's wounded knee.

Terry and his client sat at the other end of the long table. There was an awkward moment of silence before Miles spoke.

"Miss Simpson, the rea..."

"I'd prefer that you address your comments and questions to me," Terry interrupted him.

"We're not allowed to speak to Miss Simpson?" King asked him in a sharp tone.

"My client has been through an ordeal," he responded. "I think it best that her lawyer does all the talking at this juncture."

"Can we at least verify that she is Miss Simpson?" Gouveia asked sarcastically.

"In point of fact, this is Miss Sara Morgan," Terry told him.

Sara managed to suppress the smirk that was struggling to emerge on her stoic face.

"All right," Gouveia acquiesced. "Mr. Manson, the reason we called this meeting is to verify the offer you made to me yesterday. As I remember, you stated that the money that was stolen from..."

"I never used the word stolen," Terry interrupted him once more. "I said the money that was missing from your bank had been located."

"Missing?" Gouveia said. "I think we both know that it was taken illegally."

"You'd be wrong to think that," the barrister corrected him. "Neither I, nor my client, have any knowledge of how the money in question was misplaced by your bank."

"Misplaced?!" Gouveia exclaimed.

"We only know that it was found," Manson said calmly.

Gartner looked at him and grinned. Terry Manson continued.

"The people who accidentally stumbled upon the funds in question became aware of the vindictive prosecution of..."

"She tried to destroy my husband!" Ellen King erupted.

"No one's been prosecuted," Gouveia pointed out.

"Then at least falsely accused!" Terry responded in a booming voice. He continued in a more moderate tone "These people, whose identity is unknown to us, became aware of my clients...situation. And in order to set the record straight, and allow Sara to get on with her life, they have agreed to send the money to you. That is assuming this matter will be put to rest."

There were several moments of silence, as each of the participants pondered his offer. Ellen was the first to speak.

"I think that Miss Simpson, or whatever her real name is, should issue a statement saying the CD played in her classroom was a fake."

Sara glared at Elsa. Though the dark glasses made it impossible for the principal's wife to see her eyes, she did feel the disdain emanating from them. That was enough to silence her.

"My concern is with the FBI agent," Terry spoke next. "How do we know that he'll refrain from pursuing this matter after the funds are transferred?"

"I'm not here in an official capacity," Gartner responded.

"But you are here, and you are an FBI agent," Terry pointed out. "Just because you're off duty doesn't mean you'll forget about what transpires here today."

"I can assure you that the bank will not bring this matter to the attention of the FBI," Gouveia told him. "And if we don't file a complaint, they can't get involved."

"I have a way to ensure that the matter is not pursued," Terry countered. "Since the money is being returned by people who just happened to find it, a reward would be completely appropriate. I'd say four-hundred-thousand-dollars would be the right amount, considering the amount of money that's involved."

"You want us to reward the people who took the money! Give them four-hundred-thousand- dollars! You've got to be joking!" Gouveia nearly screamed.

"As I said before, no one is admitting to taking anything," Terry explained. "And if the bank issues a reward, there will be no question that the people at Elmendorf Bank understood the nature of this transaction. Do I make myself clear?"

"I need a moment!" Miles Gouveia told him before storming out of the room. Dan Gartner was right behind him.

"The balls of these scum bags!" the red-faced Bank V.P. bellowed in the hall.

"If you get the rest of the money back, it might be worth it," Gartner suggested.

"Are you serious? As an officer of the law you'd go along with that?"

"No, but I'm not here as an officer of the law. I'm here because I'm your friend. You should get this behind you right now, because if this isn't resolved soon, you'll not only have to tell your superiors that the new security system didn't work, but you'll also have to explain why you neglected to tell them about the missing money for more than a week."

"But I can't let her get away with this!"

"Sara Simpson?! She didn't have anything to do with the robbery, and neither did the little boy. You know that! Getting her of the hook is another reason to make the deal. I told you that someone would get hurt if you blamed the theft on terrorists. Sara Simpson hasn't done anything wrong. You owe this to her."

Gouveia thought for a moment before responding.

"I think the bank spent four-hundred-thousand-dollars on the Lake Tahoe get away last year," he said. "So I guess I can come up with it, especially since the President of the bank won't be too eager to explain the missing money to the board of directors either."

They went inside.

"We can do that," he told Manson.

"Good. That amount will be deducted from the funds that will be transferred to your bank. My last concern is the most important one. All this nonsense about my client being a terrorist, or having committed attempted murder, will be expunged from the record."

Ellen was about to speak, but Lionel quickly turned to her and shook his head.

"There will be no charges," Sheriff Reinhart told him. "I never really believed it anyway, Sara."

She offered no response, verbal or otherwise, to his comment.

"Your suspension is lifted," Principal King said with a smile, despite his wife's outraged expression.

"Then we're through here," Terry told them.

"When will we see the money!?" Gouveia asked.

"It will be returned by the end of the day."

"How will we get it," Gary Knowles asked him.

"You'll find it in an account opened under the name COA," Terry responded. "Good day, everyone."

The barrister and his client started to walk out the door. Then Sara stopped and turned to address the principal.

"I don't want the job anymore. I'm through with this town. I'm going to teach at a school where my efforts will be appreciated. Tell Lady Ha Ha I said goodbye."

"Who is Lady Ha Ha?" the Lion King asked without receiving a reply.

"Verify that we have the money," Gouveia told Knowles. "Then we can get the hell out of here."

"Should I take the computer with me?" he asked.

"No," Gouveia responded. "We're done with this. It never happened, and it's your job to make sure it never happens again!"

■　■　■

"What does COA stand for?" Sara asked as they drove away.

"Cover Our Asses," Terry replied with a grin.

They arrived at the thieves' rented, though not by the owner, house.

"Tell me something good!" Oscar said with anticipation when Terry walked through the door.

"It went off without a hitch," he told him. "This little lady makes a great Garbo."

"It's all about the glasses," Sara, who was holding them in her hand, said with a smile.

"We're almost there," Binny said.

"Did they agree," Rick asked as he walked into the room.

"You're all set," Terry informed him. "I thought Gouveia was going to have a conniption when I mentioned the reward. But he agreed to it. Gartner convinced him."

Binny went to the internet cafe to wire the money.

"So that takes care of your fee, my friend," Oscar said as he shook his hand.

"We're square, my man. Nice to have met you all. Can I give you a ride home?" he asked his client.

"I'll do that," Rick told him. "Could you wait for me for just a minute, Sara? I've got to talk with Oscar and Binny."

"I'll be here," she responded.

Terry left while Rick and the Anastas' went into the backyard. Binny returned shortly after and joined them.

"The wires are done!" he breathlessly informed them.

"Both of them?" Rick asked him.

"Yes. One to Elmendorf Bank and the other to Terry."

"So he's taken care of," Rick began. "Now what about Ted and Felix?"

"You won't believe this," Oscar responded. "But they just want enough money to open an Indian restaurant."

"Do they know anything about Indian food?" Sylvia questioned him.

"It doesn't matter. They're just bored. Those guys need something to do. They're going to call it the Boredelhi. Isn't that clever. They combined the words bored, which is why they're opening it, and Delhi, which is a city in India."

"That's crazy!" Sylvia exclaimed.

"Hey, I know crazy," her husband pointed out. "Do you remember where I was yesterday? Their idea isn't crazy."

"You need to go back to Happy Hill for further evaluation if you..."

"Sara's waiting for me," Rick interrupted her. "She's the one I really need to talk about. Considering what the woman's been through, and the way that we paid off the bank, I think she deserves a big piece of the pie."

"Did she ask for anything?" Oscar questioned him.

"No, but I haven't explained things to her yet. After she finds out what we did, it might occur to her that some compensation is in order."

"Some, yes. But a big piece of the pie? Is that really necessary?" Sylvia wondered.

"I'm going to explain everything to her. And with what she's going to know, I think we'd do well to make her happy," Rick told them.

"Why tell her?" Oscar questioned him.

"Because if Edgar comes under suspicion, then Sara might be implicated as well. I don't want her to get in any trouble over this. If she knows what we did, she'll be able to defend herself."

"I think you have a point," Binny nodded.

"So a full share for Sara," Rick said while looking at the Anastas'.

The two of them hesitated, and then acquiesced. They both understand the necessity of keeping the former Morgan Elementary School teacher happy.

"What about Wispy?" Rick asked them.

"What's mine is hers," Binny said in a romantic tone.

"And we're all really happy for you," Rick said sincerely. "But those things can change over time. And she did help us pull this off."

"Hey, if we can stay together...." Oscar began.

"What's that supposed to mean!" Sylvia objected.

"I'm pressed for time here," Rick pointed out again "I think we should give her a full share, too."

Oscar and Sylvia again hesitated, but finally agreed.

"I'll talk to her about it," Binny said. "But I don't know if she'll want it."

"Insist," Rick said with a smile.

"What about moi?" Sylvia asked them.

"Who's moi?" Oscar questioned her.

"Me! I should get a share?"

"Why?" asked Oscar.

"I've been in on this all along. I bought the fake id..."

"Don't start that again. And you've already got a share. What's mine is yours, babe."

"There's that condescending *babe* talk again when we're discussing business," Sylvia objected.

"You're killing me!" Oscar told her.

"She's right, Oscar. Sylvia's been in on the thing since the beginning. And we'll still get over six million each. Let's give her a share," said Rick, in a far less enthusiastic tone. He would say anything to end the conversation and get away from the Anastas'.

"I wonder if Carman is going to want a share," Sylvia said to Oscar after the others left.

"Don't bring the subject up," her husband told her. "If we have to let anyone else in on it, I'll barely get enough to pay the tolls on the ride home."

Rick drove Sara to the park. The weekday crowd was sparse, which made him feel secure. He brought the car to a stop in an empty section of the parking lot and turned off the engine.

"Sara, I'm going to be honest with you," he began.

"That would be a first," she said sarcastically.

"We really didn't give the money we stole back to the bank."

"So you lied to me again," Sara responded. "You have no intention of helping me. I guess I'm not a very good judge of character or I would have realized that. If the bank doesn't have its money back, then everything that Terry worked out at the meeting is meaningless, and I've still got a problem."

"No, the bank has been paid back. It's just that the money they received isn't the money we took from the bank. It's from the Defense Department."

"What!"

"We used your father's company to do it. You see, Binny, he's a friend of mine..."

"Binny? Is that his real name or did you make it up?"

"That's his real name. He created a program that copied the Grand View Bank's software onto a different part of their computer, a partitioned section of their hard drive. That enabled him to do some transactions without the bank being aware of it. He also accessed Morgan's Widgets computer and did the same thing. Then Binny requested a payment from the Defense Department for a bunch of invoices. They remitted the money. It went to the Grand View Bank, but the transaction was routed to the copied software. From there it was sent to Gouveia's bank. Binny erased the software copy after he was finished, so there's no trace of the transaction."

Sara looked at him with her mouth open for a moment before speaking.

"Don't you think the Defense Department will miss the money?"

"I've heard that they're pretty loose when it comes to financial matters. And since the transaction was also erased from Morgan Widget's computer, your father's company probably won't be held accountable for it."

"Probably?"

"I think it's unlikely that the Defense Department will be able to get the money back from Morgan Widgets, since there'll be no evidence that the company ever received it."

"But if they do, they might think that I was involved, since I've just been accused of being involved in another robbery!" Sara pointed out with despair. She gave no consideration to the possible consequences her father might face.

"That's true, but we won't let you take the fall."

"How do I know that?"

"We didn't let you go down for the first robbery, right. And we're also giving you an equal share of our proceeds from the second robbery. How does six-million-dollars strike you?"

"Who are you? My Nigerian Prince?"

"My real name is Rick Gaines. I lost my job a while back for a completely bullshit reason."

"I can relate to that."

"A friend of mine came to me with this plan to get rich fast. I went for it. And I've never felt so vital in all my life."

"So I could wind up being accused of doing something I had

nothing to do with. Again. Only this time, I'll have millions of dollars to show for it."

"That's one way of looking at it."

"Of course, Edgar and Laverne will absolutely freak if the Defense Department accuses the company of doing anything illegal. And then if I'm suspected of being involved they'll really be ready for Happy Hill. But in that case, I'll find my way back here and straighten it out. Eventually."

"We could really have a lot of fun, Sara," Rick said with a smile.

"We could, I suppose, if I ever stop being mad at you," Sara answered in the same fashion. "But really, I'm not interested in a life of opulence. I just want to teach the kids, no matter where they're from, and see the light of recognition in their eyes when they learn something new. I might even use my money to build a new school for them. Home, Jesse, I should say Rick. I've got a plane to catch. I'm flying to New York City tomorrow, and then on to Thailand."

"What a coincidence. I'm flying to New York City tomorrow, too. What time is your flight?"

"Two o'clock."

"We're on the same plane. I'm going to the Cayman Islands from New York City. And you're coming, too. You'll be taking a little detour before you go to Thailand."

"Why?"

"Because that's where our money is. It's in a bank that's about as sophisticated as one you'd find in Mayberry."

"Where?"

"I guess you didn't catch those reruns. Let's just say a bank that you'd expect to find in a Stone Age village somewhere in the middle of the jungle."

"I get it. Why do you have it there?"

"It's not traceable. They'll give you a password so you can access your funds from anywhere in the world."

"That sounds pretty sophisticated."

"Well, they've had a little help with that, from a real bank.

And they've invested my money in U.S. Treasury Bonds, which makes me just like the big banks in this country. I got a bunch of money from the government for free and then charged interest when I loaned the money back to the government. "

"How ironic. But I'm moving my money to the Cook Islands."

"Where?"

"You sound just like me. They're in the Pacific Ocean. It's the new Switzerland, in terms of hiding money. I came across them when I was preparing a geography lesson for my class. That's the great thing about my profession. When you teach, you learn. I feel just like a pirate."

"I know where you're coming from."

They left the park and went down the main thoroughfare. Father Joseph was riding his bicycle alongside the road. He flagged them down.

"There you are young lady. I hear that you've been fully exonerated."

"Yes I have," she said with her sincerest smile.

Sara managed to maintain a pleasant demeanor despite a conscience that was now inflamed by her encounter with the priest.

"I also hear that you're no longer teaching at Morgan Elementary. That's very disappointing."

"I've decided to teach abroad, Father. I'm going to a place where my skills are desperately needed."

"Our loss is the world's gain," he responded. "You wouldn't want to tell me where you're going?"

"After everything that's happened, I need some privacy, if you know what I mean. But I will keep in touch with you via email."

"Fair enough. You'll be missed," he said sadly. Then the priest looked at Rick. "And you, sir. I assume you'll still be at the school."

"No, I'm going back to Schenectady. The woman I left behind misses me. And I miss her. So I'm going to pack it in too."

"Can't say I've had that experience, but I understand. You'll be missed as well," he said in a less sincere tone.

He gave Sara a hug and pedaled away. She watched him leave with an affectionate smile.

"I still have a sense of right and wrong," Sara said thoughtfully. "I guess the guilt is just the price one pays for breaking the rules."

"You'll learn to live with that. Trust me," Rick assured her.

They drove to Sara's apartment, where Maya was waiting for her.

"How was the meeting?" she anxiously asked her roommate

"It's all taken care of. I'm going to New York City with you. I'm getting out of Munchkin Town. What did Dad say when you quit?"

"He was in shock. But I told him I had received an offer I couldn't refuse."

"Sounds like you've been talking to Marlon Blando," Rick commented.

Maya smiled at him before saying "Edgar said he'd miss my efficiency. And something else as well, I'm sure."

"I don't want to hear it," Sara told her. "I'm going to Thailand."

"The infamous Haji will be pleased, but I'm going to miss you, my friend," Maya said as they embraced.

"I'm going to the Cayman Islands first. Do you want to come? It's my treat. I've come into some money."

"I can't wait to hear about that," Maya said enthusiastically. "You can tell me about it on the beach."

"I'll come by at ten o'clock tomorrow morning to take you to the airport," Rick told them.

"We'll be here," Sara assured him. "Don't be late."

The Morgan Elementary School was deserted the next morning when Rick and Binny arrived there. The janitor used to his keys to open the door, and the two men casually walked to Sara's old classroom. They went inside.

Binny solemnly said "This is it."

"Turn on the machine."

"Good idea."

Binny pressed the *on* button and then anxiously waited with Rick for the computer to boot up.

"My liege," Binny said after the machine was ready. "You can have the honor of completing our caper."

"You're faster, and I want to get out of here. So just do it."

The hacker typed in several commands. The responses that appeared on the screen confirmed that Binny's software had been erased.

"We're home free," the techie said in dramatic fashion.

Rick took Bowmarc from inside his pocket and put it in the boy's desk. A note attached to it read: *Rex, He's all yours, pal. Jesse.* He also left the water pistol there.

"That's nice of you," Binny told him.

His partner was now thinking about Sara. *I hope she's happy in Thailand,* a self-reproaching Rick Gaines thought while looking around the room. Then he said aloud "Let's get out of here!"

They moved quickly down the hall, with the urgency that only the guilty feel.

"What did I tell you," a booming voice said from behind them. "You're Pabst material. Working on a Saturday without being asked to. What a guy!"

Rick turned around slowly while gradually mastering his frantic psyche.

"Hi boss," he said, in a voice that barely sounded like his own. "What are you doing here?"

"I left my cooler in my locker on Friday. I'll need it to carry my lunch on Monday."

Couldn't you have just skipped lunch? Missing a few meals could only help you Rick thought.

"What are you working on?" Pabst asked him.

"Well, I was going to leave you a note. But then my cousin Ralph pointed out that I should at least tell you over the phone. So I was just about to call you."

"Nice to meet you, Ralph,"

Binny smiled weakly at the head custodian.

"Tell me what over the phone?" Pabst asked.

"Well, my girlfriend in Schenectady really misses me. I just can't bear the thought of her being unhappy. So I've decided to pack it in. I was going to leave my keys with the ubiquitous ones, since I happen to know they work at the airport on Saturdays."

"Who?"

"The Oslifers."

"Oh, I thought they were Swedish. I also thought you had a thing for Sara Simpson, since you always seemed to be working in or around her classroom, but I guess not. Well my man, the Pabst hates to lose you. I understand, though. The heart is all that matters in this world. You can have all the fast cars and money there is to have, but they won't matter without your woman. Is your Uncle coming with you?"

"I wouldn't think of going anywhere without Uncle Steve," Rick replied with all the sincerity he could muster as he handed him the keys.

The Pabst embraced him. Binny and Rick then left the building, moving at an even faster pace than before.

"You're truly Captain Cool, my liege!" Binny said after they were in the car. "You deserve an Oscar!"

"I'll skip the award-just show me the money!"

They drove back to the house.

"We did it!" Binny exclaimed as he got out of the car.

"I'm going to get higher than Sylvia's hair!" Rick shouted.

He went to remove Bowmarc from his pants pocket to let the action figure join their celebration, then remembered that he was no longer there.

"Bowmarc is gone," he said. "I guess it's really over."

"You look like you lost your best friend," Binny observed.

"He was with me every step of the way," Rick said in an almost somber tone. "Bowmarc was my confidant, and a good luck charm. He used his powers to make our endeavor a success."

"Actually, he's a crusader for good," Binny pointed out.

"Bowmarc losses his powers if he does anything wrong. I don't think he could help us succeed in robbing a bank."

"People change and do things they never thought they'd do. Goodbye, my friend," Rick said thoughtfully.

"You can buy plenty of them now," Binny pointed out.

"It won't be the same," Rick responded.

Wispy walked in and Binny ran up to her exclaiming "It's over!"

"That's great!" she responded in the same fashion.

Rick walked over to her and they hugged while he said, "You did a great job in the bank."

"It was my pleasure. You know how the Defense Department *wastes* money. It was my duty to take it away from them. But I guess I'm just as bad. I've been wasting my talent. I should be an actress. But here's the real star."

Wispy hugged Binny.

"Nothing to it," he said after their long embrace ended. "Turning a p.c. into a bank is child's play."

"Are we done?" Oscar asked as he walked into the room with Sylvia.

"We're in the clear," Rick said with a grin. "I'll be right back. I have to pick up Sara and Maya."

The two women were packed and ready to leave when he arrived at their apartment.

"We have one stop to make before leaving for the airport," Sara informed him. "I want you to follow us over to my parent's house so I can leave my car there. I'll ask them to sell it for me."

Sara looked at Rick, who was now contemplating what it would be like to encounter the Morgans again after having used Edgar's company to rob the Defense Department. Sara had a smirk on her face as she whispered to him: "Afraid to return to the scene of the crime? How ballsy a pirate are you?"

"Hey, I just put one over on the Pope," he said confidently. "I'll follow you."

The exquisite mansion was framed against a clear blue November sky when they arrived there. Rick followed Sara and

Maya inside, reminding himself to be very careful about what he said to the billionaire.

"Hi Mom, hi Dad," Sara said as they walked into the den.

"Well, If it isn't the prodigal daughter," Edgar remarked. "I hear you've worked things out with the authorities."

"I'm so glad, Sara," Laverne said in a dramatic tone.

"Now you can get on with the business of rehabilitating your reputation," said Edgar.

"You remember Jesse. And I *know* you remember Maya," Sara said, aiming the last at her father.

"Yes, my office will never be quite as...efficient without her," Edgar lamented.

You don't know the half of it Maya thought to herself with a sense of satisfaction while smiling pleasantly. *I'm the only one who knows where everything is and what to do with it. Good luck, boss.*

"The toilet is running remarkably well," Laverne told Jesse. "During the...crisis I was able to get some sleep because you eliminated the noise it made. I'm forever grateful."

"There are some other things around this old barn that could use your expertise," Edgar told him.

"I'd love to help you out," Rick responded with feigned regret. "But I'm going back to Schenectady. I had a girlfriend there, and she misses me, so I'm going home."

"Really, Jesse," Sara asked with a sincere expression on her face. "What was her name again?"

"Um, Karen. It's Karen, Sara."

"That's what you should do, young lady," Edgar told Sara.

"Get a girlfriend?"

"No, you should find a young man to settle down with. There are plenty of fine bucks in this town. It will help restore your reputation. Teaching at the elementary school hardly constitutes a life. And just thinking about you in that place is multiplying the number of gray hairs on my head exponentially."

"Well, Dad, I won't be teaching at the elementary school anymore."

"Wonderful! You're coming to work in the family business."

"The hell with that!" Sara retorted.

"You said hell to your father!" Edgar objected.

"You've heard me say hell before."

"I have not."

"Have too," Sara responded while fighting the urge to laugh.

"Sara, please, your language," her mother interceded.

"Anyway, I'm not working for Morgan's Widgets. I'm going to teach abroad."

"What does that mean?" Edgar asked.

"I've accepted a teaching position in another country. I won't have to worry about my reputation in Morgan Town anymore."

"What!" Laverne almost swooned. "Martin!" she called to the butler. "Prepare another compress! And bring my medication!"

"Don't panic, Mother. I'll come back to see you."

"Why on earth do you want to teach a bunch of foreigners in a foreign place?" a bewildered Edgar asked her. "You realize that most of those countries are full of illegal drugs!"

"As opposed to this country, Dad?" Sara replied sarcastically. "Besides, foreigners are people, too. They should have the opportunity to learn, just the like the children here do."

"There are plenty of children in Morgan Town that need to be taught. You're needed here," Edgar, who apparently had suddenly recognized the merit in being a teacher, pointed out.

She hesitated for a moment. There were so many students that had touched her heart, in one fashion or another, during Sara's tenure at the school. Despite the strong emotions that welled up inside her, she managed to compose herself and continue.

"But the jackasses here won't let me do my job." The people I'll be working for now will appreciate my skills a lot more than anyone at Morgan Elementary ever did. Which isn't saying much, when you think about it. But it's enough for me."

"Stop using that language when you're talking to me, young lady," Edgar chastised her.

"Those words are just not necessary, Sara dear," her mother

said in a weak voice. "At least not when you're speaking to your father."

"What should I call them? Doodey heads, like the kids do."

"Look at the state your mother is in! Is this the thanks we get for all we've done for you!?" Edgar exclaimed. "If you leave Morgan Town you'll make everyone think you're guilty!"

"I need a change, Dad. And as for what other people think, the hell with them! I didn't do anything wrong!" Then to herself: *At least not yet.*

"There's that word again," her mother almost moaned.

"I'm sorry to spring it on you like this, but I have a plane to catch. I'll be in touch. Sell my car, if you can. Here's the paperwork you'll need. The keys are on the front seat."

Sara handed the documents to her father. She then gave each of her parents a hug and a kiss before leaving. Sara withheld the scathing recriminations that leapt to her mind while doing so. Their daughter did not want to leave on a bitter note, despite her still smoldering resentment at their lack of support during her ordeal.

Sara stared in silence through the car window at the estate as they drove away, wondering what kind of relationship she'd have with her parents after this day. Rick and Maya said nothing at first, in deference to her contemplative mood. Then Rick finally spoke sometime after a lone tear appeared on Sara's cheek.

"Have you ever used words like *ballsy* in front of your parents? I know you've used hell and jackass," he said with a grin.

"No, I usually save that for the really depraved people I know," she answered in kind.

"I could tell you a lot of colorful words she's used in front of me," Maya said with a laugh.

"You could, but no one has asked you to, Maya dear," Sara said with mock annoyance.

Rick parked the car in the driveway of the rented house. The three of them went inside. Oscar and Sylvia were upstairs packing, their conversation assaulting Rick's ears as soon as he walked through the door.

"Why don't you get rid of your red shirt?" Sylvia asked her husband in a disapproving tone as he put it in his suitcase.

"I've had it for years. It's like an old friend."

"But I haven't seen you wear your old friend since Reagan was president!"

"There are a lot of friends I haven't bothered with in a long time. But I'm not throwing them out!"

Boy, am I going to miss the sound of their voices, Rick thought sarcastically.

Wispy and her beau came downstairs.

"Binny and Wispy, this is Sara and Maya," Rick introduced them.

"Nice to meet you," they responded in unison. Then Binny said to Rick, "We've decided to drive cross country."

"There's so much to see," Wispy added excitedly. "We're going to the Coral Castle in Florida. It was built by one man using these giant blocks of coral. No one can figure out how he did it. And the best comes next September. There's a roadkill cooking festival in West Virginia."

Everyone else in the room, including Binny, cringed at the thought of eating dead animals that had been found alongside the road.

"I know it sounds terrible," Wispy acknowledged. "But we can't let anything go to waste."

"Bon appetit," Rick told her while avoiding the temptation to roll his eyes.

"And scientists are talking about sending a couple to Mars," Wispy told them. "The ship would use the waste produced by the astronauts to line the walls of the spacecraft to protect them from radiation. Talk about wasting nothing. They're not even going to waste the waste! Imagine me and my hunk floating among the stars!"

"Bon voyage," Rick said with a smile.

"Keep in touch, my liege," Binny said to him.

"Will do, partner," Rick shook his hand.

"Thanks for the traveling money, Rick," Wispy said as she kissed him.

"You earned it."

"Enjoy the trip, you two," Sylvia said to Binny and Wispy, as she walked into the kitchen with Oscar.

"I will, Aunt Sylvia. Tell my mom that we'll see her soon."

"Should I tell her to expect an announcement?" she asked them. "You and Wussy make a beautiful couple."

"What's the matter with you? They're not going to tell you before they tell their parents," Oscar chastised her.

"Why not? I can keep a secret."

"Are you shitt...," Oscar began to respond but was cut off by his nephew.

"We've got to be going. We'll see you over the holidays."

"You're a genius!" Oscar said as he hugged him.

"It takes one to know one, Uncle Oscar."

Sylvia embraced them both as she said to Binny, "You take care of Wiley."

"Do you think your Aunt will ever learn my name," Wispy asked Binny as they walked to the car.

"It's not likely, mon amour," he responded.

"You're so European." She kissed him.

"Why don't we all sit down and have a quick drink before we leave for the airport," Rick suggested.

"Why not," Sara agreed.

"Sounds good to me," Maya also acquiesced.

He poured a glass of wine for Maya and Sara, and then took a beer from the refrigerator for himself. The Anastas' declined.

"Let's get going. I want to miss the traffic," Sylvia told her husband.

"We can't leave before twelve o'clock," Oscar told her, with a self-satisfied expression on his face.

"Why not?"

"Trust me. It will be worth your while. And by the way, you were right."

"I think I'm going to faint," his wife said while holding on to the kitchen counter for support. "What was I right about?"

"I can't sell the car."

"Of course not," she said.

"I'm going to donate it to charity instead. I saw an ad for some outfit that will come and pick it up. It'll be a nice thing to do. And I was going to buy a new one anyway."

"You can't donate the car," Sylvia protested. "We leased it; we don't own it."

"The leasing company will figure out a way to make it work. I mean it's a charity; they're not going to take the car back from them."

I wonder if the scientists would consider doing everyone on earth a big favor by putting Oscar and Sylvia on the shit ship to Mars, Rick thought before saying "This is Sara and Maya."

"Nice to meet you," they said while smiling at the Anastas'.

"Likewise, I'm sure," Sylvia responded for the both of them.

"I'll put our suitcases in the car," Rick said after finishing his beer. "Then I want to say goodbye to Mary."

He walked out the door with the luggage and nearly fell over Mary Pop Ins, who was standing on the porch.

"Are you ready to go?" she asked him.

"We're just about to leave. Here are the keys. It's been a pleasure."

"Under the circumstances, I should give you the rent money back."

"Keep it. Buy a toy for Timmy."

"Then at least let me help you take the suitcases to the car."

"That sounds good to me."

The two of them put the luggage in the trunk as Marlon Blando waved to them.

"This will be our little secret, won't it?" Mary asked when they were finished.

"You don't know how into secrecy I am," Rick responded with a smile. "But do you think Blando would say something to Gutner about the strangers that were living in his house?"

"They don't speak to each other."

And Blando said they were friends Rick thought to himself before saying aloud "Then you got away with it."

After a brief hug, Mary started to walk away. Then she came back and whispered in his ear.

"I'm glad you got away with it, too, Rick."

Mary went home to Timmy.

I guess I should be concerned about what she knows, Rick thought to himself. *But I don't think Mary wants anymore than she has now. Her life is on Street Street.*

The five of them got in the car. Rick sat in the back with Maya and Sara.

"It's twelve o'clock. What's going to happen?" Sylvia asked her husband.

Oscar just smiled, and then drove to the end of the block.

A dump truck came down the street and backed into Marvin Blando's driveway. The driver pulled a lever, and a truckload of manure was deposited on the restaurant owner's asphalt, courtesy of Oscar. Blando's usually stoic demeanor was usurped by the uncontrollable rage that resulted from the sight, and pungent smell, of the bookie's going away present.

"Son of a bitch!" the recipient of Oscar's farewell gift exclaimed.

The truck driver asked him to sign for the delivery, and Marlon Blando responded by chasing him around the yard with a rake.

"Where did the guy in the three-piece suit get a rake?" Maya asked as she laughed at the comical scene.

"That's not the point," Rick could barely say through his own laughter.

"This is how I'll remember Morgan Town," said Sara with a grin.

Oscar wore a self-satisfied expression as he drove away. This was in spite of his wife saying, "You really do belong in the nut house!"

They arrived at the airport forty minutes later, with the

expression on the bookie's face still the same. Rick removed their luggage from the trunk as Sara and Maya said goodbye.

"Have a good trip," they smiled at the Anastas'.

"Same to you," Sylvia responded. "I apologize about the manure. My husband is mentally unbalanced."

"I thought it was funny," Sara told Oscar.

"It was my pleasure." He then turned to Rick and said warmly, "Well, I guess this is it. Let's get together for the holidays, Ricky."

"I'd love to, but I don't know where I'm going to be. Take care of yourselves."

"We'll be in Paris," Sylvia said.

"Who wants to go to Paris?" Oscar objected.

"It's a beautiful city, with the lights on the Eiffel Tower and other things."

"The damn thing isn't even finished," Oscar retorted. "It's just a skeleton."

"Don't forget the traffic, Oscar," Rick reminded him.

The three of them embraced.

"Have a good one, everybody," Oscar and his wife shouted as they drove away

So begins my new life, Rick mused. *Goodbye, Karen. I'll miss you baby. There is no easy money. And losing you is the hardest part.*

They went inside the terminal. After checking their bags, the three of them walked towards the departure gate.

"Do you think I'll be able to find something to do in the Caymans?" Maya asked Rick in her husky voice while displaying a seductive smile.

"No doubt about it," he smiled back

"I might have to shop for a dress. I have a feeling that Sara will have a major announcement in the near future. Haji is anxiously waiting for her in Thailand."

"The infamous Haji?" Rick asked her.

"That's the guy," Maya confirmed. "She's meeting him there. I'll need something to wear at their wedding."

"Well, nothings for certain in this world, roomy. I'm a rich woman now. And money changes everything."

As Sara said that she tripped over another traveler's suitcase. Maya looked down at her former roommate, who was now sprawled on the terminal floor, and smiled.

Rick helped her up and said with a broad grin "not everything, Sara."

Printed in the United States
By Bookmasters